Jacqueline Wilson

Illustrated by Nick Sharratt

WE ARE THE BEAKER GIRLS

CORGI BOOKS

CORGI BOOKS

UK | USA | Canada | Ireland | Australia
India | New Zealand | South Africa

Corgi Books is part of the Penguin Random House group of companies
whose addresses can be found at global.penguinrandomhouse.com.

www.penguin.co.uk
www.puffin.co.uk
www.ladybird.co.uk

First hardback edition published 2019
First paperback edition published 2020

001

Text design by Becky Chilcott
Printed and bound in Great Britain by Clays Ltd, Elcograf S.p.A.

A CIP catalogue record for this book is available from the British Library

ISBN: 978–0–552–57790–8

All correspondence to:
Corgi Books
Penguin Random House Children's
One Embassy Gardens, 8 Viaduct Gardens,
London SW11 7BW

MIX
Paper from
responsible sources
FSC® C018179

Penguin Random House is committed to a
sustainable future for our business, our readers
and our planet. This book is made from Forest
Stewardship Council® certified paper.

To Kenny, Olivia, Farrah Leigh,
Shannon, Samantha, Carlos,
Ashley and Sandi

'**THREE CONES PLEASE**, all with chocolate flakes. One with chocolate sauce too, one with strawberry and one with sprinkles.'

The ice-cream man smiled at me. 'All for you, Jess?'

'Yes, yum yum yum.'

It was our little joke. Of course I wasn't going to eat them all. There was one for my mum, one for Flo and one for me. We treat ourselves whenever we make a big sale in our shop. Well, it's really Flo's shop, but we moved in a month ago and my mum has been in charge of the stock, and we've had ice cream

seven times! And today we'd made an absolutely HUGE sale.

It had been a quiet morning. Flo was sitting on her old chintz sofa, balancing a bowl of water on her lap and gently cleaning a china crinoline lady with an old toothbrush. Mum was on her knees at the back sticking scraps onto a wooden stool to make it look pretty. I was curled up on a faded velvet chair with my dog, Alfie, snoozing on a cushion at my feet.

I was meant to be doing some horrible sums in my notebook. Mary is worried that I've missed so much school. She was my teacher when we lived on the Duke Estate in London. I still sometimes forget and call her Miss Oliver. I like her, but I wish she wouldn't keep sending me homework. I especially wish she wouldn't set me problems. My problem is, I can't *do* the problems. I was doodling instead, drawing lots of little cartoon Alfies.

I drew him fast asleep, wide awake, running crazily, jumping for a ball, lying on his back to be tickled. I even drew him having a wee. I love Alfie soooo much. Almost as much as my mum. Do you know my mum Tracy Beaker? Everyone knew her when we lived in Marlborough Tower. Heaps of people already know her here in Cooksea. She's that kind of person.

Early on Sunday mornings when we go to car boot sales, the folk there have a laugh with her, and Bill, who runs the bacon-roll van, chats her up. He doesn't call her Tracy, he calls her Curly because she's got these mad black curls 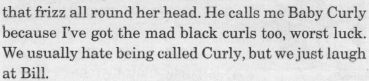 that frizz all round her head. He calls me Baby Curly because I've got the mad black curls too, worst luck. We usually hate being called Curly, but we just laugh at Bill.

Bill's always laughing and joking, and cheers everyone up when it's raining. He's got a dog called Gladys – a big white Staffie with a pink diamanté collar and a pink lead which he tethers to his van. She looks a bit fierce but she's the sweetest dog ever. Alfie adores her. He adores Bill too, because he gives him scraps of bacon.

Bill asked Mum if she had a boyfriend. Mum just laughed. She says she's given up on men. I'm very, very, very glad she's given up on her old boyfriend, Sean Godfrey, because I never really liked him. But I like Bill. And Gladys. And bacon rolls. Maybe she'll change her mind about men.

Anyway, it was very quiet in the antiques shop this morning – just two old ladies passing  the time, poking around the stock, oohing and aahing in the corner Mum calls Memory Lane. She's arranged four Teletubbies on top of an old television set, and some long-eared bunnies listening to a Roberts radio. There's an old Dansette record player and a pile of vinyl LPs with a Barbie and a Ken doll jiving beside it. She's stuffed an old cradle with Tiny Tears and Cabbage Patch babies, and several baby piggy banks.

One of the old ladies bought a jigsaw of a country cottage for a pound, but that was it, all morning. And then at lunchtime this rather arty-looking lady came wandering into the shop, bangles jingling as she sorted through all the vintage dresses on the rail. Then she stopped and stared.

She was looking at this little desk Mum had found at the boot fair one Sunday. It had been very bashed, with half the drawer handles missing and the leather top stained. It had looked like total junk to me, but Mum whispered that it was early Victorian. The man selling it wanted £125 and said he couldn't do it for less, but Mum eventually talked him into letting her have it for ninety. I still thought it was way too much, but Flo had given a nod when she saw it.

'Well done, Tracy,' she'd said, grinning. 'My goodness, girl, you've only been in the trade five minutes but you've got an eye for a bargain already.'

'Two eyes,' said Mum, winking each in turn.

They'd spent hours treating it with wood stain and polishing it up and fitting it with handles. Mum added a tatty quill pen and some manuscript paper she'd brushed with tea so that it looked like parchment. She'd  written on several of the pages, copying out the first paragraphs of Victorian novels she'd found on the shelves in our Book Nook.

Mum had made a special big label for the desk – it dangled from a piece of string. She's getting famous for her messages on all our stock.

Did Charlotte Brontë sit demurely at this desk in her cold vicarage to write her passionate book Jane Eyre? Or perhaps Charles Dickens came home from a wintry walk through a graveyard and began Great Expectations sprawled over it? You can start your very own masterpiece for the modest sum of £600!

'Six hundred pounds!' Flo had gasped, squinting at the label. 'That's a bit steep, Tracy! The punters will never pay that.'

'Wait and see,' Mum had said.

So we waited – and saw this jingly lady stare at the desk, read the label, stroke the wood, pick up the pen and paper, wander around the shop biting her lip, return to the desk, and then take a deep breath.

'What's the best discount you can do for the desk?' she asked.

'Our lovely little early Victorian desk?' said Flo. 'Ooooh! We'll be sad to see it go. It's a bargain, dear. Do you know what these lovely pieces of furniture go for in London antique shops? I've seen some advertised for over a thousand. I really don't think we can reduce ours any more.'

'Oh dear, I don't think I dare pay so much,' said the arty lady, but she started opening the little drawers one by one. Mum had put a tiny trinket in each – an old stamp, a marble, a coin, a little glass bottle. They weren't worth anything, but the arty lady gave small squeaks of excitement at every discovery. 'It's so lovely!' She sighed, but turned and looked as if she was about to walk out of the shop.

'Maybe we could knock off fifty quid, Flo, just

to make sure the desk goes to the right home . . .' said Mum.

Flo sucked in her breath and shook her head.

'But see how much the lady likes it.'

'I've always wanted a desk like this,' the lady admitted.

'I think you're a writer, aren't you?'

'Well, I'd like to be. I just can't seem to get started.'

'Think how inspirational this desk could be,' said Mum. 'Tell you what – you can have the quill pen and the parchment for nothing, just to put you in the right mood to start writing.'

'It's still an awful lot of money,' the lady said, sighing – but unable to take her eyes off the desk.

'All right. Five hundred and fifty – though it means we're practically giving it away,' said Flo.

'I'll have it!' said the lady, fumbling in her bag for her credit card. 'You're right, it *is* a bargain.'

'Do you live in Cooksea? Just outside? Then I'll deliver it for free in the van,' said Mum.

It was Flo's van but she hadn't driven it for so long that it had needed all sorts of repairs. She didn't have enough cash to fix it and neither did we – so Mum sold her pink Cadillac to pay for it. She'd loved

 that pink Cadillac, and so had I, but it couldn't be helped. Besides, the

ex-boyfriend, Sean Godfrey, had bought it for her and we didn't want anything to do with him any more.

The lady went away happy and will hopefully write her own masterpiece one day. And Mum and Flo and I were even happier because we'd made so much money – a total profit of £460! I'm hopeless at problems but my mental arithmetic is getting much better!

So Mum let me go to buy ice cream to celebrate, telling me to be very careful crossing the road to the esplanade. The van is a little further down on the seafront, near the beach huts. It's only five minutes from The Dumping Ground. That's the name of our shop. It's also Mum's old nickname for the children's home where she lived when she was my age. But then Cam became her foster mum. Cam's like my foster gran. I've got a real gran, Carly, but I don't like her anywhere near as much. Mary – who was my teacher, Miss Oliver – is a sort of gran too, as she's Cam's partner. And Flo is a kind of gran as well because we live with her and run the shop. Which means I've got four grans! But only one mum of course – my mum Tracy Beaker.

So I paid for our treat and took

8

the three cones, the ones with sauce in one hand and the one covered in rainbow sprinkles in the other. The ice-cream man knows that one's for me. He always gives me extra sprinkles, with a cherry on the top!

'Careful now, poppet,' he said.

'I'm always careful,' I said, and set off up the esplanade.

I was tempted to have just one lick of my rainbow sprinkles but decided not to risk it. I walked quickly but carefully, arms held out in front of me. The sun was out and I knew I had to hurry or the ice creams would start to melt. I breathed in deeply, still unable to believe I lived in such a lovely place. The sea sparkled in the sunlight, the beach huts shone bright red and blue and yellow, and the seagulls wheeled above me, screeching away.

I looked up warily, not wanting one to poop on me or my precious ice creams. And then suddenly someone snatched my ice cream and ran off with it!

'Hey!' I yelled indignantly. 'My ice cream! Bring it back!'

Of course the someone did nothing of the sort. It was a big bulky boy in a baseball cap, grubby T-shirt and faded jeans. The white soles of his trainers were a grimy

grey, but that didn't stop them flashing as he made off down the esplanade, the ice cream like a trophy in his hand. He dodged between two of the beach huts, and by the time I'd thudded after him he'd vanished.

I could have wept. It wasn't just the fact that he'd stolen my ice cream, with its generous topping of rainbow sprinkles and a cherry on the top. He probably wasn't even going to eat it. He'd just taken it for a laugh. That was what was so humiliating. People talked about snatching an ice cream from a baby. I wasn't a *baby*. I was ten and a half. I hated to be seen as small and weak and helpless.

I had been bullied a bit at my old school. There was this big boy called Tyrone, who pushed and shoved me and once knocked me over so my knees bled. My mum found out, and that was ever so embarrassing because she yelled at Tyrone and his mates and then went storming into my school and *yelled at my teacher, Miss Oliver*! I didn't know where to put myself, Mum yelling her head off while Miss Oliver stayed so calm and controlled.

It all came right in the end, because Mum and Miss Oliver – Mary – made up, and now she's almost like Mum's foster aunty (weird!). And, even weirder, one day quite by accident I knocked Tyrone over and we both ended up in the sick room at school and we

made friends too. I actually miss
him now, though Mum says he can
come and stay soon. And my friends
Ava and Alice. Though probably not
all together, because Ava and Alice are very polite
and well mannered, and Tyrone is the exact opposite.

I get why Tyrone and his mates bullied me. My
hair looks a bit mad and I wear glasses and I'm very
small for my age. I was also generally near the top of
my class – well, top actually, though that sounds like
boasting. So they called me Curlynob and Four Eyes
and Geeky Beaky, and followed me about making
fun of me.

I hated it, obviously. I hated being the sort of girl
who gets bullied. I hated Mum knowing. I especially
hated it when she charged about defending me – it

 was so humiliating. When we moved to
Cooksea I decided I wasn't going to be that
pathetic girl any more. I was going to be
strong and feisty and bold, just like Mum
when she was little. No one would ever have
dared bully Tracy Beaker.

I couldn't make myself bigger. I tried to
tame my hair with gel, but that just made
it look greasy – and it was a total disaster
when the hairdresser straightened it. I
tried taking my glasses off, but I couldn't

see where I was going and had to hold my book right up to my nose to follow the story. Still, I wasn't going to school until term started again in September so no one knew I was a geek, which was a relief.

I tried to *act* different, even if I couldn't look it. I practised walking with a bit of a swagger, head up, striding out. I practised wisecracks in my head in case anyone said anything rude to me. But no one in Cooksea was really rude. It was a lovely warm summer and everyone seemed happy to be here and went around with smiles on their faces.

I got extra smiles when I took Alfie for a walk along the esplanade. All the old people sitting on the benches wanted to chat to us, and the little kids playing on the beach wanted to pat him. There were several small gangs riding their bikes or skateboards, but they were friendly too, and didn't mind when Alfie barked at them.

I was so happy to be here, in my new home, where everyone seemed to like me. And now this big lout in a baseball cap had spoiled it all. There were heaps of kids much smaller than me holding ice creams. So why had he picked on *me*?

The two remaining ice creams were starting to drip a little. I couldn't hang about feeling sorry for myself. I had to get back to The Dumping Ground sharpish. I held one ice cream in each hand and then set off at a brisk pace. I was clutching the cones so tightly they were at cracking point.

I got home in double-quick time. The shop used to smell really musty, but Mum had spent a whole weekend dusting and scrubbing, and airing the old clothes on a rail in the sunshine. Now it simply smelled fresh – of paint and beeswax polish and the flowers in the old vases that were too cracked to sell, along with Flo's scent and Mum's coconut shampoo and Alfie's warm smell of happy dog.

Flo started ding-a-linging like an ice-cream van when she saw me, and then shook her head. 'Watcha, darling! Gordon Bennett, can't you count?' she said, putting on her funny cockney accent. Long ago she'd played a comical cleaning lady in a television sitcom. 'Better get back to them maths lessons! Two ice creams into three don't go!'

'Jess?' said Mum, looking up from her stool. 'What's up? What happened?'

I took a deep breath. 'Nothing's up. Nothing happened. I just got a bit greedy, that's all. I started licking mine on the way home, and then I got carried away and couldn't stop. It was soooo delicious.' I licked my lips for emphasis.

They laughed at me, believing every word. I knew it was wrong to fib, but I couldn't stand the thought of the fuss they'd make. Flo would be 'poor darling this, poor darling that', and she'd insist on giving me her chocolatey ice cream instead. And Mum would get all fierce and angry and go storming out of the shop, scouring the streets of Cooksea for big boys in baseball caps. I didn't want them to react like that. I just wanted to forget it had ever happened.

It wasn't easy to forget with my mouth so dry and hot and empty and longing for soft, sweet, cold ice cream. We only had a quick scratch lunch too – a tuna-and-tomato sandwich each, with ginger beer for Mum and me, and a small can of real beer for Flo (she says it stops her getting indigestion). But at least in the evening we had a really big celebratory meal, and no one could snatch it away because it was safely on a plate in the dining-room part of the Spade and Bucket pub.

I love the Spade and Bucket. Outside, it's got little buckets of geraniums along each windowsill, with umbrella stands full of children's spades on either side of the front door. It's lovely inside too, painted in bright seaside colours, and the walls of the ladies' loo are covered with funny old postcards, most of them rude. I like to sit there, laughing at all the silly jokes.

We went there on my very first visit to Cooksea –

which was also Mum's birthday. We didn't have much money for a birthday meal but we shared a spaghetti bolognese and it was totally delicious. We ended up having birthday cake too, because this man called Peter Ingham was having a birthday party. You'll never guess what: my mum and this Peter were at the children's home together when they were young! Peter said they'd been great friends. Mum later told me that they hadn't really – Peter had been a bit of a wimp, and she'd always called him Weedy Peter.

He didn't seem weedy to me. Well, not very. He's a head teacher now but he didn't look a bit fierce, like Mrs Michaels at my old school. He looked friendly. He wore a very bright jazzy shirt but he seemed a quiet, gentle sort of person. The exact opposite of Sean Godfrey.

We'd been back to the Spade and Bucket a couple of times for a quick lunchtime snack of cheesy chips – just Mum and me, while Flo was having a lie-down. Of course we wanted Flo with us this time, though it would be a bit of a problem getting her there. Flo is a very big lady and her legs are weak because she had a stroke.

Mum thinks she should have a wheelchair.

'I should cocoa!' said Flo, acting the cockney again.

'Seriously, Flo. It would make such a difference. I could wheel you everywhere,' Mum told her.

'Seriously, Tracy – no! I'm not going to be shoved about slumped in a wheelchair like a helpless old lady,' said Flo.

Mum managed not to say that she *is* a helpless old lady. 'You could come to all the junk fairs and car boot sales with us,' she pointed out instead. 'You'd love to join in the banter with the other dealers.'

'Do I really want to get up before dawn and freeze to death? No thanks very much,' said Flo firmly. 'Besides, you're only a skinny little thing. Look at those puny arms! I bet you couldn't even budge me, let alone wheel me round a muddy field. If I can't go out on my own two feet, I won't go out at all.'

'Couldn't you have one of those push-along frame things, Flo?' I asked. 'You know, it's got wheels and you just have to edge it forward.'

'No, ta very much,' she said. 'I'd look a right banana. What if someone recognized me?'

Flo had appeared in some films and then as the cleaning lady in an old sitcom called *Life with the Lilliputs*. Mum and I watched an episode on YouTube. It wasn't actually very funny, though Flo was marvellous of course. She was half the size then. I doubt if anyone would recognize her now, but it would have been cruel to say so.

'You two girls go out and have a meal at the Spade and Bucket. I'll be fine here,' Flo insisted now.

'You're coming with us,' said Mum. 'I'll drive you there in the van.'

'Don't talk daft. You'll never get me in it!'

She had a point. Mum and I tried heaving her up onto the seat at the front but it was much too high. We shoved, and Flo let go of her walking sticks and tried her best to pull herself up, but her arms had no strength left.

'It's useless, darlings,' she gasped, red in the face with effort.

'I know!' said Mum. 'We'll pop you in the back!'

The van has big doors at the back, and there's a ramp so you can wheel heavy furniture up. We couldn't wheel Flo because she might have wobbled off, but we helped her stagger the five paces up the ramp. Alfie followed behind, nudging her gently as if she was a giant sheep.

'Hurray!' said Mum.

'But I'll never keep my balance when you drive off, and I can't sit on the floor – you won't be able to heave me up again,' said Flo.

It was my turn to say 'I know!' I got the keys and ran back into the shop and found an old Lloyd Loom chair, light enough for me to carry

17

but big and sturdy enough for Flo to sit on. 'Here you are, Flo. Your special seat!' I said.

'You Beaker girls!' said Flo. She looked a bit teary behind her glasses. 'You don't give up, do you? Bless you, darlings!'

It only took two minutes to drive down to the Spade and Bucket, going very slowly so that Flo wouldn't get too shaken about in the back. Mum stopped the van right outside the pub door and we helped Flo down the ramp again, while Alfie did his best to encourage her, nearly tripping her up in the process.

There were quite a few people having a drink outside and they couldn't help staring.

Flo stuck out her chin. 'Make way for the royal procession,' she said, using her posh, fruity voice now, then warbled the beginning of the National Anthem.

They all started chuckling and Flo played to the crowd, leaning on just one stick so she could give them a royal wave.

'Careful, Your Majesty!' Mum hissed.

Somehow we got her safely down, and then I helped her into the pub while Mum went to park the van. It turned out that Flo knew Lizzie, who ran the pub. They threw their arms round each other, and Flo nearly went crashing to the floor. Her legs were wobblier than ever after the journey, but I hung onto her, and eventually we made our way to a table at the back. Lizzie even brought Flo her own big comfy chair with a cushion because the ordinary wooden ones were rather spindly.

By this time Mum had come back, and Lizzie insisted on giving us drinks on the house. Flo had a large gin and tonic, Mum had a glass of wine, I had a St Clement's (orange juice and lemonade and delicious!) and Alfie had a bowl of water which he slurped appreciatively. Apparently Flo used to be a regular, popping down nearly every night for a drink or two after work. 'Or three or four,' she said, laughing.

Lizzie had been an actress too – she'd even had a bit part in *Life with the Lilliputs*, Flo's sitcom. They nattered on – and on and on – about the show and the cast and the director, while Mum and I looked at the menu and got a bit bored.

'I was an actress too once upon a time,' Mum said suddenly.

'Really?' said Lizzie.

'*Really?*' said Flo, who was getting used to Mum and her stories.

'Yes, I had the lead part in a Christmas show once.

19

A Dickens adaptation. Very jolly. I got good reviews, didn't I, Jess?'

'Brilliant,' I said, deadpan. Mum had played Scrooge in *A Christmas Carol* – she'd shown me the cutting from the local paper, saying *'little Tracy Beaker was brilliant'*. Little Tracy Beaker was only my age at the time, and it was just a school play, but Flo and Lizzie weren't to know that.

'And Mum was in an hour-long television show,' I told them.

She'd been even younger then – it was a documentary about children in the care system. Mum said she was the star of that too, and I bet she was.

Lizzie was all round-eyed, but Flo gave Mum's knee a tap under the table.

'Shall we order our grub then, dearies?' she said. 'I'm in the mood for one of your steak-and-ale pies, Lizzie.'

Mum chose a special burger and chips, and I decided to have sausage and mash because I knew who'd like to share my sausages. We all ate heartily and then decided to have a pudding too, even though we were quite full up.

 Flo had treacle tart and custard, Mum had banoffee pie, and I had a banana split. It was good to have some ice cream after I'd lost out on my cone. Alfie didn't have any pudding because he'd gone to sleep under the table, already very full indeed.

Lizzie had to serve the other customers, but she joined us again when Flo and Mum were having cappuccinos. I like a spoonful of the froth on the top, but I hate the actual coffee underneath.

'Do you remember when Jess and I came to have supper one evening a few weeks ago – there was that big birthday party . . . ?' Mum said, making little twirls in her coffee with her spoon.

'Course I remember! The birthday boy was an old pal of yours, wasn't he?' said Lizzie.

'Sort of,' said Mum. 'Is he a regular here, then?'

'He's a teacher, isn't he? They come here whenever they're celebrating,' said Lizzie. 'They can get quite raucous.'

'I wouldn't call Peter Ingham raucous!'

'So who's this Peter chappie then?' Flo asked. 'An old boyfriend of yours, Tracy?'

'Hardly!' said Mum. 'Just someone I knew as a kid, in the children's home.'

'Shall I say you were looking for him next time he comes in?' Lizzie asked.

'No! Yes. Well, maybe. I thought he might come looking for me actually, just to see the shop. Flo's called it The Dumping Ground, and that's the name we gave to the children's home.'

'Sounds like you *are* a bit sweet on him, Tracy,' said Flo.

'Rubbish!' said Mum.

I looked at her hard. She'd gone very pink. Perhaps it was just because it was hot in the pub and she'd had a lot to eat. Perhaps.

WE SETTLED FLO into her bed downstairs, behind the shop, with her usual flask of tea and a packet of digestive biscuits in case she got hungry in the night (unlikely, after such whacking great portions of steak pie and treacle tart). She also had a hot-water bottle, even though it was the middle of summer, to stop her feet getting cold and crampy. Her book lay beside her reading lamp just in case she couldn't sleep. It was the biggest book in the shop, *Gone with the Wind*.

'That's my motto in the night,' Flo giggled. 'Good job no one shares my bed any more.'

She also had her radio on, turned down low.

'But you can't hear it properly,' I said.

'It's still a comfort. It makes me think someone's there,' she explained.

'Well, you always have someone here now,' said Mum. 'Jess and me, right up above you. If you need anything in the night you just have to give a shout.'

'You're lovely girls, you two,' said Flo, and her voice went husky. 'Don't know what I'd do without you now.'

'We don't know what we'd do without *you*,' said Mum.

'You're not going to suddenly up sticks and leave, are you?'

'Absolutely not. You're stuck with us. Now go to sleep. Night, Flo.'

'Night, darling. Night night, Jess, sweetheart,' said Flo.

'Night night,' I said, giving her a kiss. Her cheek always felt soft and powdery and she smelled of very musky perfume. She hoarded old bottles of scent and used them liberally, even though some of them were years old. I always had to hold my breath when I leaned over her, but I suppose there were much worse things she could have smelled of.

Mum took Alfie outside for his last wee. She

wouldn't let me go out by myself after dark. I got ready for bed. We hadn't had time to do the upstairs rooms up properly because we'd been so busy sorting out the shop, and the little one was still stuffed with junk, so I was sharing with Mum. The ceiling had cracks and a damp patch, and the floral wallpaper was torn in places. Still, we were used to cracks and damp and peeling paper after our flat in Marlborough Tower, and the bedroom had all our favourite things in it, making it feel like home.

Mum had hung our picture of a mother and daughter having a cuddle above our bed, and I'd arranged our china dogs all along the windowsill. My old toy dog, Woofer, was lying on the  pillow, his head flopping. I knew he was droopy because he'd lost some of his stuffing, but it made him look sad. I couldn't help worrying

that he minded being left on the bed while I played with Alfie.

I picked him up now, gave him a stroke and took him over to have a chat with the china dogs. I made each of them greet him in turn, giving little sniffs and barks. I know some people would think me a great daft baby playing such silly games, but it's fun, so who cares?

I peered through the window, Woofer tucked under my arm. I saw the pizza place and the Indian restaurant and the fish-and-chip shop on the corner. If Mum was too tired to cook we had lots of alternatives. I saw Mum now, turning down our road, Alfie trotting along beside her, pausing at every lamppost. When she walked under the light I saw that she was talking on her phone. She was holding it tight against her ear, looking very absorbed. When she got to our shop, The Dumping Ground, she didn't come in immediately. She stood there, still talking, for a good five minutes, while Alfie skittered about impatiently.

My heart started thudding. Who was she talking to? Why didn't she want me to hear her? It wasn't Sean Godfrey, was it? He'd tried to get in touch with Mum several times since they broke up. We hadn't told him we were leaving Marlborough Tower, but he'd tracked Tyrone down and asked him where we were living now.

Tyrone thought the world of Sean Godfrey.

According to him, Mum was off her head to walk out. Maybe he imagined he was doing her a favour, telling Sean Godfrey we'd gone to live by the seaside. Luckily he didn't remember *which* seaside, so we felt pretty safe. Tyrone texted me to check he'd done the right thing. I texted back in capitals:

NO YOU'VE DONE THE WRONG
WRONG WRONG THING!!!

I expected Mum to be furious but she thought I'd been a little hard on Tyrone. 'He can't help being a bit thick,' she said.

'*Mum!* We've agreed. We're not telling anyone where we are, apart from our special friends,' I said.

'Yes, I know. But Tyrone would think Sean and I *were* special friends, seeing as we lived together and actually got engaged.'

'We didn't live with him *long*. And OK, you got engaged, but it wasn't as if you were *married*. And Sean Godfrey is the number-one person we *don't* want tracking us down!' I said. 'It seems to me *you're* the one who's being thick, Mum!'

'Hey! Less of that cheek, Baby Beaker! And there's no need to act like Sean is some scary serial killer. Maybe he's just . . . missing us,' she said.

I hated the way she said it. As if *she* was missing

him. We were so happy here in Cooksea. We had Flo and the shop and the sea, we had Alfie, we had each other. What more did Mum want? All right, we didn't have Sean Godfrey's huge great house and his huge great swimming pool and his huge great car.

We didn't want them. And anyway they weren't on offer any more. We were pretty sure that Mum's worst ever enemy, Justine Littlewood, had already moved in.

Mum was *still* on the phone now, nodding and muttering and listening intently. Alfie was starting to get fed up. He ran around her, tying her up with his lead, and then, when she still didn't take any notice of him, he started barking at her impatiently. You didn't need to be an expert in dog language to interpret what he was saying: *Hurry up! I'm bored! I want to go indoors! I want my bedtime chew! I want my bed! I want Jess!*

I opened the bedroom window and leaned right out. 'Mum!'

She looked up, startled. 'Don't lean out like that!' she hissed. 'It's not safe!'

'Well, come back in! Alfie's upset!' I called.

At the sound of my voice Alfie's barks got even louder. Mum sighed, said a quick goodbye to whoever it was, and opened the shop door. Alfie came charging up the stairs, shoving the bedroom door open, and then leaped into my arms as if we'd been parted for weeks.

'For goodness' sake!' Mum said crossly, following him. 'What were you doing, hanging out the window like that! I'm sure you've woken Flo – and half the street into the bargain.'

'Well, you were such ages.' I took a deep breath. 'Who phoned you?'

'No one,' said Mum, starting to get undressed.

'Mum! I *saw* you!'

'What are you doing snooping on me? For heaven's sake, Jess, I can do what I want,' she said, putting on her pyjamas.

'Yes, but you shouldn't tell fibs, especially not to me.'

Mum went off to the bathroom. I tried to calm Alfie down and get him settled in his dog bed. I wanted someone to calm me down too. I hated it when Mum and I quarrelled.

She came back into the bedroom, wiping toothpaste stains off her mouth. 'I wasn't fibbing,' she said. 'No one phoned *me. I* phoned *them*.'

'So who did you phone then?'

Mum sighed. 'Look, I don't have to tell you. I'm the mother, not the kid. I check up on you, not the other way round.'

'It was Sean Godfrey, wasn't it?' I said, ready to burst into tears.

Mum stared at me. 'No, it wasn't!' she said.

I knew Mum well enough to see that she was telling the truth. I felt limp with relief. 'So who was it then?' I asked as we got into bed.

'If you must know, I was just having a quick catch-up with Cam,' said Mum, and switched off the light.

Cam! I was the one who used to phone Cam when we were living with Sean Godfrey. I still wanted to phone her now, but Mum said we should give her a bit of space and not keep pestering her now that Mary was round her place most of the time.

'How come you get to phone Cam and I can't?' I asked.

'Because I wanted to have a little chat, OK?'

'What about? Me?'

'Yes, you. And me. And whether we've done the right thing coming here. I just wish she was here so we could have a hug, that's all,' said Mum. 'I miss her.'

'Oh, I miss her too, Mum! Here, *I'll* give you a hug!'

We had a great big hug, and it was lovely being friends again. Then we settled down to sleep, curled up together. I felt for Woofer because I still liked to snuffle into his soft fur in the night. I felt the pillow. I felt under the pillow. I felt under the blankets. I leaned out and felt the floor.

'What are you doing, Jess?' Mum murmured.

'I can't find Woofer!'

'Oh, for pity's sake!' She snapped on the light. We both looked. And looked some more.

'He's not here!' I said.

'Well, he's hardly taken himself off for a walk down to the beach,' said Mum. 'Think where you had him last.'

'It was just now, when I was at the window,' I said. Then, 'Oh no!'

I jumped out of bed, ran to the window and peered out. I could just make out a pale crumpled heap on the pavement.

'Woofer!' I wailed. 'Oh, Mum, he must have fallen out when I opened the window.'

'There! I told you not to lean out like that,' she said. 'What are you doing?'

I was scuttling around trying to find my jeans and T-shirt. 'I've got to go and rescue him!'

'He'll be all right till morning. No one in their right mind would want to take him. He looks very scruffy and old,' said Mum, but she'd already swung her legs out of bed. 'OK, get back into bed, Jess. I'm not having you blundering about in the dark. You know how raucous some of the lads get when they come out the pub and head off for a curry. *I'll* go and get him.'

'What if they're raucous with you?' I asked.

'I'd like to see any of them try it on with me,' said Mum, practising one of her kick-boxing moves to demonstrate how she'd deal with them. 'Now, *don't* open the window again to watch, or *you'll* end up on the pavement.'

I lay obediently in bed. I heard Mum unbolt the shop door and open it. All she had to do was dash out, grab Woofer and come back. It should have taken ten seconds tops. I waited, counting. I got to a minute, and I still hadn't heard the door shut downstairs.

Couldn't Mum find Woofer in the dark? Had

someone already taken him? I thought of the big boy in the baseball cap and how quickly he'd snatched my ice cream. He could be off with him in a trice – and then he'd chuck him in a wheelie bin or even throw him in the sea. Maybe he was with a group of other silly louts who'd use him as a football just for a laugh. I wasn't a baby any more. I knew perfectly well that Woofer wasn't real. There was no brain inside his balding head, no nerves in his floppy arms and legs, no heart inside his small chest.

Yet I could picture him crying in the bottom of a dark bin, bobbing desperately in the choppy sea, or flying through the air, ears flapping wildly.

I shot out of bed and ran to the window. I couldn't see him! I couldn't see Mum either – but I could hear the buzz of her voice. She must have been standing in the shop doorway – and I could just about make out the shape of someone standing close to her, talking too.

Sean Godfrey *had* tracked us down! I opened the window just a crack to hear better. It was a man's voice – but not Sean's. This was a gentler voice, cheery, and somehow vaguely familiar. Then I heard a little bark. Alfie heard it too and lifted his head, woofing back in a friendly fashion as if he knew who it was.

I was so tempted to open the window further and lean out so I could see properly, but I didn't quite dare. Then I heard Mum say goodbye, and the shop door opened and closed again, and her light steps were coming up the stairs. I shut the window quickly and jumped back into bed.

'Mum? Did you find him?'

'Shh! And you shh too, Alfie. Go to sleep, both of you!' Mum said. 'I've got Woofer safe, Jess.'

'Can I have him?'

'No, I'd better pop him in the washing machine tomorrow. He might be all germy from the pavement.'

'I don't mind,' I said. 'Alfie sometimes lies on the pavement but I still cuddle him.'

'Woofer's being washed and that's final,' said Mum, getting back into bed. 'It's nippy out there, even though it's summer. Come here and give me a cuddle to warm me up.'

'Who were you talking to? He didn't sound raucous,' I said.

'Bill couldn't be raucous if he tried,' said Mum.

'Bill the bacon-roll man? Oh, so it was Gladys barking outside! Was he going for a curry?'

'Just collecting a takeaway on his way home from taking Gladys for a walk,' said Mum. 'He hadn't bothered with supper earlier.'

'Why didn't he make himself a yummy bacon roll?'

'I expect he gets a bit fed up with rolls, selling them every day.'

'Doesn't he have a Mrs Bill to make him a proper supper?'

'*I* don't know. I don't think so.'

'I think Bill sounds a bit lonely,' I said.

'He's got Gladys for company.'

'Yes, and she's lovely, but she's hardly going to put her apron on, stand on her hind legs on a chair, make Bill spaghetti bolognese and then watch a box set with him, is she?' I said, giggling as I pictured it.

'Shh! Settle down now and go to sleep,' said Mum.

'But I'm wide awake now. Poor Bill. You should have invited him in for a coffee, Mum,' I suggested.

'In my pyjamas? Oh my God, I've been chatting to him for ten minutes *in my pyjamas*!'

'But they cover you up just as much as a tracksuit.'

'Even so! I shall feel such a fool when I next see him,' said Mum. 'I hope he won't tell all his mates.'

'He isn't that sort of guy,' I told her.

'Oh yeah, Miss Jess Beaker the world authority on men?' said Mum.

'Well, I knew Sean Godfrey couldn't be trusted,'

I said, and then immediately regretted it. 'Oh, Mum, I'm sorry.'

'It's OK,' she said, but she turned over and curled up tight.

'You don't . . . miss him, do you?' I asked in a tiny voice.

'Not at all,' she said, but she didn't sound very sure.

We stopped chatting then, though I don't think either of us got to sleep for ages. I tried to console myself by thinking that at least we'd never have to see Sean Godfrey again. Mum would soon forget all about him.

However, it turned out we *were* going to see him the very next week. Sean Godfrey really *did* phone Mum. We were all in the shop, Flo and Mum and Alfie and me, singing along to this funny old Elvis song Mum was playing on the Dansette record player. Alfie  truly was singing too, yowling happily, which was very appropriate because the song was all about a 'hound dog'.

Mum's mobile rang and she took it out of her jeans pocket, still dancing. She checked the caller number, looked puzzled, and answered a little warily.

'Hi, who's this?' she asked. Then her face screwed up as he answered. 'Oh, very clever. So you've got another new phone. Well, you can buy all the phones in the Apple Store, I'm still not talking. Bye.'

But then he was saying something else and Mum was still listening.

'Mum! Switch him off!' I said, and I went up and tried to grab the phone out of her hand. 'I'll do it!'

She stepped backwards, waving me away. 'No, wait a minute, Jess,' she said.

I had to wait. I sat down on the sofa beside Flo. She took up all the space, but I have a very small bottom so I could just about perch.

She reached out and held my hand. 'It's him, isn't it? The footballer chappie, your mum's ex?' she whispered.

I nodded.

Flo's hand tightened on mine. Elvis and his hound dog blared from the Dansette, bizarrely jolly. We sat watching Mum. She turned her back on both of us, concentrating on what Sean Godfrey was saying.

'Do you think she'll go back to him?' Flo whispered. She sounded as worried as me. We'd made such a difference to her life, and she said the shop was doing really well. She'd be devastated if we walked out on her now. She wouldn't be able to manage on her own.

I wouldn't be able to manage, full stop. I loved my new life. I didn't miss anything about living with Sean Godfrey. I didn't even care about not having the swimming pool, not when I had the whole sea to wade into any time I fancied.

Alfie didn't know what was going on. He'd never understood mobile phones and didn't get it when people suddenly became absorbed and talked to someone who wasn't there – but he sensed that Flo and I were worried. He trotted over and jumped up onto my lap, licking me lovingly. I realized I had tears rolling down my cheeks.

Mum suddenly turned round and held out the phone.

'No! I don't want to talk to Sean Godfrey!' I gabbled.

'It's not him,' she said.

'Of course it is!' I was shocked that Mum would tell such a stupid fib.

But when she forced the phone to my ear I realized she was telling the truth.

'Hi, Jess. It's me. Tyrone. Your mate,' said the voice.

'Oh goodness! I thought you were Sean Godfrey!' I said.

'Yeah, well, he's here, and he was talking to your mum, but now he's put me on the phone. I wanted to talk to you.'

'Yes?' I said.

'Yes,' he said, but he didn't say anything else.

I waited several seconds. I could hear him breathing. 'Are you OK, Tyrone?' I asked.

'No, I'm not,' he said. 'I thought you was going to invite me over to your new place.'

'Yes, well, you must come,' I said awkwardly. I felt bad. Our friend Marina and her girls Ava and Alice had visited us a couple of Saturdays ago. I'd been so looking forward to seeing Alice – she'd been my best friend once – but she'd spent the whole time chatting about her new school friend, Natasha. Natasha was even visiting their house in France during the summer holidays. Mum and I had never been invited, though we'd have jumped at the chance.

Ava was just the same, showing off her brand-new hairstyle and her brand-new jacket and her brand-new boots. She had a brand-new phone too, and kept messaging her friends on it, even when we were talking.

Marina was ultra polite and kept saying everything was marvellous, and she made a great fuss of Flo and said privately to Mum and me that she thought she was a total darling – but it was obvious she didn't really think that at all. She insisted that the shop was amazing, but from the way she looked around you could tell she thought it was a load of old junk, even with Mum's brilliant displays.

Mum had made a special cake and they all said it was delicious, and it *was*, and then we left Flo in charge of the shop while we took them for a walk round Cooksea. It was a drab, drizzly sort of day, and somehow our lovely seaside seemed drab too, the pier falling to bits and the amusement arcade tacky and some of the shops boarded up.

'Well, I think we'd better be making tracks now. Don't want to get caught up in the rush hour! It's been absolutely lovely,' said Marina. 'Promise we'll stay in touch.'

She wasn't acting like she wanted to stay in touch at all. I didn't want to stay in touch with her either, or Ava, or even Alice. They belonged in our old life.

I suppose I'd wanted Tyrone to stay in our old life too. But now here he was, breathing in my ear, wondering why I hadn't invited him down.

'You should come and visit, Tyrone,' I said lamely.

'Yeah, but how?'

'Well, could you get the train?'

'I don't know where to go. I've never actually been on a train before. My mum won't take me. And catch her coughing up the fare even if she had it,' said Tyrone. 'But Sean Godfrey says he'll bring me. In the Porsche! Please say yes, Jess.'

'No! We don't want Sean Godfrey back in our lives,' I said loudly, hoping he could hear me. 'We're doing just fine without him.'

'Please,' said Tyrone, and his voice cracked. He was the toughest boy at Duke Primary but it sounded almost as if he was crying.

It was awful. I felt so sorry for him. He had a horrid mean mum and never had any fun – at home or anywhere else. The only person who showed an interest in him now was actually Sean Godfrey. But we never wanted to see *him* again. Never ever ever.

MUM GAVE IN. I couldn't believe it.

'You're mad, Mum! I bet Sean Godfrey put Tyrone up to it! Look, we could have found someone else to bring him down. Cam and Mary would give him a lift next time they come to see us.'

'Yes, well, I didn't think of it. And I didn't give Sean our address. I've said we'll meet them at the ice-cream van on the esplanade. Sean can clear off and do his own thing while Tyrone comes to our place,' said Mum.

'That's just plain daft! He'll follow us!' I said.

'Well, what if he does? For goodness' sake, Jess, we can't hide from him for ever.'

'Yes we can.'

'You're such an unforgiving little kid. People think it's cool to stay friends with your ex nowadays.'

'That's plain stupid! Are you going to be friends with Justine Littlewood too?'

That shut her up. Justine Littlewood has always been Mum's worst enemy, from the days when they both lived in the children's home. She came slithering back into our lives when she heard that Mum had Sean Godfrey for her boyfriend. I was the one who found all her lovey-dovey messages on his phone. Mum wasn't putting up with that. She wasn't going to be two-timed by anyone, especially not Justine. We walked out. She didn't love him any more. So what was she playing at now, saying that he could bring Tyrone here? Mum didn't even *like* Tyrone because he'd once bullied me.

Mum turned her back on me and put another old record on the Dansette. Elvis sang a song about a guy who always remembered his old sweetheart. Mum stopped the record abruptly, probably scratching it, and marched out of the shop.

'Mum?' I called.

'I'd let her have a little walk by herself, Jess,' said Flo. 'She needs to get her head straight.'

'You're telling me. She's so silly. How can she do this, Flo?'

'Oh well. We can all be a little bit batty at times. Your mum's clearly still got a soft spot for this footballer chap. Is he good looking? Does he have lovely eyes like Georgie Best? *He* was the football pin-up in my day. I'd have made a fool of myself over him if I'd ever had the opportunity!'

'Did you ever make a fool of yourself over anyone else, Flo?' I asked.

'Course I did! I was forever falling in love, and always with the wrong sort of guy who let me down. And there was my old pal Arty in the background all the time, but I just took him for granted, treating him like a comfy old slipper. Then, when I was on my beam ends, he took me in and left me the shop in his will, bless him!' Flo looked up and waved wistfully, as if Arty was on the ceiling, peering down at her.

If Mum had to have any kind of boyfriend, I wished he could be a comfy old slipper. I thought about Bill, the bacon-roll guy. He'd be perfect. We could all live happily with Flo. Alfie already adored Gladys. I just had to get Mum to fall for Bill.

Meanwhile I had to stop her falling back in love with Sean Godfrey. On Saturday she spent a suspiciously long time getting ready. She didn't wear her red dress or anything obvious, but she spent ages trying on her three different pairs of jeans to see which was the most flattering. She tried nearly all her tops too, before fishing her stripy one out of the laundry basket.

'Mum!'

'It's not really grubby. And it's my favourite top,' she said defensively.

I wondered if Sean Godfrey had ever told her it was *his* favourite top.

She wore her sparkly red canvas boots, with matching red lipstick, even though she hardly ever bothered with make-up nowadays.

She'd told Sean Godfrey to be at the ice-cream van on the front around eleven. We were waiting there by quarter to, just in case. Mum kept peering this way and that, looking out for him and Tyrone. I peered too, wondering if the boy in the baseball cap was lurking nearby. I very much hoped he'd just been a day tripper – then I'd never see him again. My mouth watered as I stood beside the van. I longed for a cone with rainbow sprinkles.

The ice-cream man saw me staring. He gestured at the cones and the ice-cream machine, his head on one side.

'Mum, can I have an ice cream?' I asked.

'I suppose. And then we'll buy one for Tyrone when he gets here,' she said.

'Great!' I said, and ordered my sprinkly ice cream. 'And are you having your strawberry-sauce special, Mum?'

'No, I feel a bit sick,' she said. 'Like I'm going down with something.'

She was very pale, and her red lipstick looked much too bright. She was shivering, though it was warm with just a light breeze. Perhaps she was *love*sick.

'Are you looking forward to seeing Sean Godfrey?' I asked sternly.

'No! I'm beginning to think I was a fool to go along with this mad idea. Oh, Jess, you don't think he'll bring Justine too, do you?' Mum asked, giving me the money for my ice cream.

I paid and started licking slowly and appreciatively, holding the ice cream very close to my chest. 'Well, if he does, we don't even have to speak to them,' I said. 'We'll just march off with Tyrone, OK?'

'OK. Yes, good plan.'

'And act like you couldn't care less that they're a couple now,' I advised.

'Well, I *don't* care,' said Mum, tossing her hair. 'It's just this all seems a bit weird. I'm only doing it for you, Jess. Are you looking forward to seeing Tyrone?'

I shrugged, careful not to tilt my ice cream. 'Sort of. Though he might be a bit different now. You know, like Ava and Alice were different when they visited us.'

'Maybe *we're* the ones who are different now, Jess,' said Mum.

A little crowd of children from the campsite came rushing towards the ice-cream van. Most of them were wearing baseball caps. I stood to one side, guarding my ice cream, holding it so close that it started dribbling down my T-shirt.

'Jess! You're getting all mucky! Hold your ice cream properly. You're acting like someone's going to snatch it,' said Mum.

'Someone might,' I said darkly.

We walked along the promenade towards the beach huts. There were a couple of big lads walking along, eating fish and chips out of cardboard boxes.

'Is that their breakfast or their lunch?' I wondered.

'Goodness knows,' said Mum, wrinkling her nose. 'The smell! I really *do* feel sick now.'

The lads ate with relish and then chucked their boxes in the bin and went to queue for ice cream.

'Dear God!' said Mum. 'Those boys must have stomachs the size of suitcases.'

A boy in a baseball cap suddenly dashed out from behind the beach huts and, quick as a flash, delved into the rubbish bin for the two boxes. It was hard to tell – most boys in baseball caps look pretty similar – but I reckoned it was the ice-cream snatcher.

I started gulping my cone as quickly as I could.

'Look at that boy!' said Mum. 'What's he doing, rummaging in the bin like that?'

We watched him open one box. There wasn't much fish left, but he crammed the nasty grey skin into his mouth, along with a few leftover chips. Then he started on the next box, running his fingers round the edges for little crispy bits of batter.

'How disgusting!' I said.

'Yes, but he actually looks desperate,' said Mum, frowning. 'Like he's really, really hungry.'

'Well, you said boys have stomachs like suitcases,' I said, swallowing the last of my ice cream and chomping up the cone.

'No, this boy looks like he's starving.'

'No he doesn't. He's quite chunky.'

'Well, he's not going to stay chunky eating rubbish

out of bins,' said Mum. 'Do you think I should give him some money to go and get his own fish and chips?'

'No! I don't like the look of him,' I said fiercely.

Maybe he heard me. He stopped eating, looked up and pulled a hideous face at me. Then he ran off behind the beach huts again.

'See!' I said.

'Well, I'm not going chasing after him, but if we see him again I'll have a little chat. He might be a runaway, fending for himself,' said Mum.

She said it with such feeling that I stared at her. 'Did *you* ever run away when you were a kid, Mum?'

'Yep,' she said. 'Quite a lot.'

'You stayed out all night?'

'Well, sometimes I only got as far as the flipping bus stop before someone from the Dumping Ground came and carted me back. But I did do a runner once or twice when I was older. When I was living with Cam.'

'You ran away from *Cam*?' I said, looking at Mum as if she was mad. 'But she's the loveliest, kindest person in the whole world.'

'I know. But I was all mixed up and angry then. Whenever we had a row I pushed off, just to show her. And then, when I was fifteen or so, I had this awful boyfriend and we ran off together. But he was horrible and I soon went running back to Cam.'

'Oh, Mum!' I gave her a quick hug, feeling so sad for her. But I couldn't resist saying under my breath, 'You always pick awful boyfriends.'

'Tracy! Hey, Tracy!' Right on cue, Sean Godfrey came swaggering down the promenade, Tyrone beside him.

Mum peered. There was no sign of Justine Littlewood. The campsite kids were all gawking at Sean Godfrey in his tight white T-shirt and tight jeans. So were the teenagers sitting on the wall and the families on the beach and the old folk in their deckchairs. They began to point, muttering his name. Two girls came running up, holding their phones, asking for selfies. Sean flashed his bright white teeth and started posing.

It was even worse than I'd remembered. I looked at Mum. She looked at me and then rolled her eyes comically.

'I'd forgotten about the constant attention,' she murmured. 'And doesn't he just love it!'

'Let's grab Tyrone and leave him to it,' I said.

'Good plan,' said Mum, walking towards him.

Alfie suddenly gave several high-pitched excited barks as he spotted Sean Godfrey in the middle of the crowd. Sean had never made much of a fuss of him. He'd been furious when Alfie chewed a chair leg or did the tiniest little puddle. Once he'd even shut Alfie in the kitchen just because I'd been feeding him little morsels of steak from my plate. He'd never done more than pat him absent-mindedly – yet now Alfie was clearly desperate to see him.

'Sorry, guys, I'm here to see my girl,' said Sean Godfrey to the gathered crowd. He smiled for one more photo and then rushed up to us, holding his arms out to Mum.

She backed out of an embrace. 'Hi, Sean. *Ex*-girl,' she said.

Alfie jumped up into Sean Godfrey's arms instead, licking him enthusiastically, trembling with joy.

'Well, at least someone's pleased to see me,' said Sean Godfrey, making a fuss of Alfie while the crowd clucked and chuckled.

'Hey, Alfie, remember me?' Tyrone said, patting him too.

Alfie gave him a brief lick and then concentrated on Sean Godfrey, wagging his tail so hard it looked like he would whirl up through the air any second.

'Alfie! Down boy!' I said. 'Down, I say!'

Alfie stayed *up*, loving Sean Godfrey to death. I turned my back on them.

'Hi, Tyrone,' I said, hoping he'd be pleased to see me as he'd made such a fuss about coming here.

'Hi, Jess! We came in the Porsche and it simply flew! Everyone was staring!' Tyrone's face shone with happiness. He looked so different with his face smoothed out and smiling. He wore a football strip – Sean's old team – and sensible shorts down past his knees. He had new trainers as well, navy with brilliant white soles.

'You're looking great,' I said. liking his new gear.

I waited for him to say I was too. I'd got very tanned from all the sea air and I hoped I might have grown just a tiny bit.

'Yeah, *don't* I look great!' Tyrone said proudly. 'It's all the new clobber Sean's bought me. And get my six-pack!' He sucked in his breath and patted his tummy. 'We do really fierce workouts down the football club, but I can cope, easy-peasy. Sean says I'm one of the best. I am, aren't I, Sean?'

'Yep, you're one of the best all right, Tiger,' he agreed, giving him a nod and a wink over Alfie's head.

'Tiger's my new nickname,' Tyrone explained unnecessarily.

I looked at Mum. She looked at me. It was my turn to roll my eyes.

'So how are you two girls?' Sean Godfrey asked, putting Alfie down at last.

'We're just fine,' said Mum.

'We love it here,' I said.

'That's good. I'm really pleased,' said Sean Godfrey. 'Though of course I'd much sooner you were back with me. I don't suppose there's any chance you've changed your mind, Tracy?'

'It might get a bit crowded, sharing with Justine,' said Mum.

'Justine's history,' he told her. 'I was never, ever serious about her, you know that.'

'Well, it doesn't really matter now,' said Mum breezily. 'You can have any girlfriends you fancy, it's nothing to do with me. Anyway. Come on, Tyrone. We'll have him back here around five. Is that OK, Sean?'

'Can't I come too?' he asked.

'No, we had a deal,' said Mum. 'Don't start!'

'OK, OK.' He raised his hands in mock surrender. 'I'll be here at five. If you change your mind you know my new number now.'

'I think I deleted it,' said Mum
airily. 'But I won't need it. Bye then.
Come on, Jess. Come on, Tyrone.'

But Tyrone's face crumpled. 'Why
can't Sean come too?' he asked.

'Because Mum and Sean aren't together any
more, you know that,' I said.

'Yeah, but Sean still wants to be friends,' said
Tyrone. 'He said we could all go for a ride in his car
and then have fish and chips, all four of us.'

'Five, counting Alfie!' said Sean Godfrey, bending
down and giving Alfie's ears a rub. Alfie generally
hates anyone doing that and snarls, but this time he
went limp with pleasure. I was shocked to see how
thoroughly he was betraying me.

'We're not having fish and chips. I know you have
meals from the chippy nearly every day of your life,
Tyrone. You're having a proper home-cooked meal,'
said Mum.

'I don't think I like home cooking much, so Sean
can have mine. Then there'll still be enough to go
round – one, two, three, four,' said Tyrone, pointing at
each of us.

I could see he was simply trying to help his hero,
but Mum took it personally.

'Look, I've spent hours preparing a proper meal for
you this morning, you ungrateful little whatsit,' she

said. 'One more word out of you and you can push off with Sean, and you two guys can fend for yourselves.'

Mum wasn't exactly telling the truth. She *had* wanted to give Tyrone a proper meal – back on the Duke Estate he only ever ate takeaways from the chippy and the chicken shop and the kebab place. But she knew he wouldn't want anything too fancy or elaborate, so she'd decided on sausage and mash and onion gravy. She'd prepared the gravy and I'd peeled the potatoes, while Flo had hulled some strawberries for pudding. The preparation had taken minutes, not hours.

'It's not four people anyway,' I said. 'It's five.'

Sean Godfrey stared. 'Five? So who else is coming?' he asked suspiciously.

'Well, you're not invited, so it's none of your business,' I said.

'Jess! Don't talk to Sean like that!' said Mum.

I stared at her, wounded. I'd only been sticking up for her.

'Who's your other guest, Tracy?' Sean Godfrey asked. 'Have you taken up with someone else already?'

Mum put her hands on her hips and stuck her chin in the air.

'So what if I have?' she said. 'Like Jess said, it's none of your business.'

He was glaring. It looked like he'd start shouting at Mum any minute. I put my hands on my hips too. I wasn't going to have him yelling at my mum, no matter what. Tyrone was staring at Mum, staring at Sean Godfrey, his head swivelling as if he was watching a tennis match. The crowd was staring too. Even the ice-cream man was leaning right out of the van window to see what was going on.

Sean Godfrey took a deep breath. His lips moved as if he was counting silently. 'You're right, ladies. It *is* none of my business. And I'm not a bit surprised you've got a new guy in your life, Tracy, a fantastic sparky girl like you. I hope he realizes how lucky he is.'

I think he was just playing to the crowd, pretending to be Mr Nicey-Nicey to get their approval. I hoped Mum would see this too and walk away. But she didn't. She looked at Sean Godfrey in a silly soft way, as if she was an ice cream melting in the sun.

'Thanks, Sean,' she said. 'Though actually Jess meant Flo, my business partner.'

'A business partner? So you've got your own business? Already?' This time he sounded genuine. 'What is it?'

'I'm in the antiques trade now,' said Mum proudly.

'Mum!' There were only two other antique-type shops in Cooksea. It would be easy enough to find out which one was ours. But then Mum blew it anyway. 'Oh, come on then. I'll show you,' she said.

And that was that. I couldn't believe she'd rolled over like that. What was the *matter* with her? She was suddenly smiling up at Sean Godfrey like a member of his fan club. He was smiling back at her. Alfie was fawning round his feet. Tyrone was grinning from ear to ear. I was the only one glaring as we made our way up the road.

'There it is, Sean,' Mum said proudly as we turned the corner. 'See the shop over the road?'

'*The Dumping Ground*,' he read out. 'Isn't that what you used to call the children's home? So this business partner of yours let you change the name?'

'She'd called it that already! Isn't it an amazing coincidence? It was as if it was meant to be,' said Mum.

'Like the day you breezed into my gym and asked for kick-boxing lessons,' he muttered.

If I heard him I'm sure Mum did too, but she didn't

react. There was a man looking intently in one of the shop windows.

'We're doing really well too,' said Mum. 'Look, there's an eager customer if ever I saw one. Something's taken his fancy.'

Then the man moved slightly, so that the sunlight shone full on him. He was fair and slender, wearing a patterned shirt and jeans. I suddenly realized who it was.

'Hey, Mum, isn't it Peter, the one who shared his birthday cake with you?' I said.

'Yes, it is!' said Mum. She quickened her pace. 'Hey, Peter,' she called.

He turned, saw her and waved, his face lighting up.

Sean Godfrey looked at me. 'Who's this Peter chap then?' he asked. 'Your mum looks pretty pleased to see him!'

'Well, she is!' I said. 'He's an old friend from way back, when they were both children.'

'That's me, silly!' he said.

'No, she knew Peter before, when they were in the children's home. He's a head teacher now,' I said, hoping to impress him.

'Never!' Sean Godfrey pulled a face. 'He's a friend of Tracy's? She can't stand teachers.'

'Well, she thinks the world of Peter and he thinks the world of her,' I said, exaggerating for all I was worth.

He sniffed incredulously. Tyrone sniffed too. 'You can tell *he* doesn't work out,' he said.

'So what?' I said, irritated.

Peter was chatting eagerly to Mum and she was nodding, her head on one side. Sean Godfrey hurried closer. So did I.

'Well, I'm really glad you came to see the shop at last,' said Mum.

'Who's this then, Tracy?' said Sean Godfrey, as if he actually owned her.

'This is Peter, Sean – an old friend,' said Mum. 'Peter, this is Sean. He's – well, I suppose he's an old friend too.'

'How do you do, mate?' said Sean Godfrey, holding out his hand. I knew his handshake would be crushing.

'Oh! Hello!' said Peter. He suddenly seemed half Sean Godfrey's size. 'Well, I'd better be going. Good to see you, Tracy.'

'Don't go, Peter! Come in and have a coffee,' said Mum.

'Perhaps another time,' he said,

and scurried off, giving Tyrone and me a quick nod.

'That's a shame,' said Mum, looking disappointed. 'I wanted to show off my shop.'

'Show it off to me, Trace,' said Sean Godfrey. 'Hey, I like the window displays!'

In one of the windows Mum had sprinkled sand everywhere and then laid a tartan picnic blanket on top. She'd set out a blue jug and lemonade glasses and a plate with little iced cakes, pink and white and yellow. There were several battered teddies wearing sunhats and swimming costumes gathered round. In the other window there was a toy dog on wheels wearing a sombrero. The little doll's tea set had a

pink or yellow or blue Smartie on each plate, with our collection of china dogs and my blue bunny staring at them hungrily. The white Pekinese and the tiny Chihuahua each had a paper parasol, the kind you get in fancy cocktails.

'You've always had a way of arranging all your little knick-knacks,' said Sean Godfrey. 'It looks great, Tracy.'

When we'd moved in with him he was always moaning about our ornaments, making us keep most of them in a cupboard: he couldn't stand silly little bits and pieces cluttering the place. Tyrone didn't look as if he thought much of them either.

'Are they *your* toys, Jess?' he asked, wrinkling his nose.

'As if!' I said. 'They're stock. I don't play with toys.'

I was glad Woofer was upstairs in the bedroom, unable to hear.

'Come in and meet Flo,' said Mum, opening the shop door. The bell gave a little ring.

'Seconds out!' said Sean Godfrey. He was even more irritating than I remembered.

Tyrone cackled with laughter. 'Me and Sean do boxing together now,' he said. 'I'm getting good at it so you'd better watch out, Jess. If you disrespect me I could bloody your nose, easy-peasy.'

'I seem to remember that *I* bloodied *your* nose once,' I said haughtily.

'Don't you go all stuck up on me, Jess Beaker,' said Tyrone, giving me a little push.

'Well, don't you go throwing your weight around,' I said, giving him a dig with my elbow. My arms are like sticks, but luckily my elbows are very sharp.

'Uh-oh! Lovers' tiff already!' said Flo, lounging on her sofa and laughing at us. 'Hello, big boy. I'm Flo and you must be Tyrone. And, hey, even bigger boy! You're the famous footballer! Sean Godfrey, I do believe! Tracy's told me all about you.'

'I'll bet she has,' he said, leaning over to shake her hand. 'Pleased to meet you, Flo.'

'Ooh, that's a bone crusher of a handshake! Good job I've left off my diamond rings – they'd be embedded in my fingers by now! So what are you doing here, then? I thought you were just bringing his lordship and then pushing off elsewhere?'

'Yeah, well, that was the plan. But I talked Tracy round,' said Sean Godfrey, sitting on a velvet pouffe beside Flo.

'I bet you did,' she said.

'Hey, I know you, don't I?' he said. 'You used to be on telly, didn't you? It was some comedy thing, right?'

'You've told him, haven't you, Tracy!' said Flo.

'I didn't breathe a word, Flo,' said Mum. 'I'll put the kettle on.'

'I used to watch it when I was a kid. You were the funny cleaning lady. You cracked me up every week. What was it you used to say – "Allo, dearies," and then something about mucky bits,' said Sean Godfrey. 'Priceless!'

'*Allo, dearies, let me slosh a bit of disinfectant in all your murky corners!*' said Flo, putting on the right voice.

'That's it!' he said, roaring with laughter.

Tyrone and I exchanged glances. It wasn't even funny. I felt ultra-gloomy. Flo was clearly enchanted by Sean Godfrey too.

Tyrone wandered around the shop in a bit of a daze. 'Is this where you live now? Is this your living room?' he asked.

'It's a shop. This is all our stock. We sell it,' I said. Honestly, Tyrone could be so thick sometimes.

'You sell all this old junk?' He looked at the price tag on a faded patchwork quilt. 'Seventy-five quid? You could get a brand-new duvet for twenty-five in Argos!'

'Yes, well, this is all hand-worked. And it's maybe a hundred years old. It makes it an antique,' I explained.

'It still wouldn't keep you very warm,' said Tyrone.

'Are you denigrating my lovely Victorian quilt, youngster?' said Flo, leaning forward so that all her necklaces jingled.

'You'll have to excuse the boy, Flo, he doesn't know any better,' said Sean Godfrey, though he'd never got the point of antiques either. The newer and shinier the better, like his house and his cars.

Yet when Mum came back into the shop carrying the coffees in willow-pattern china, he went on about how lovely it was, drinking out of a proper cup – much better than slurping out of a mug. He was trying to impress so much that it made me want to spit.

Mum had brought in some hazelnut cookies (my favourite), the whole packet arranged in a circle on a plate. She ate one – so did Sean Godfrey and Flo and I. Well, I ate most of mine but gave Alfie a couple of tiny chunks, though he's not supposed to eat biscuits. That meant there were four left – and Tyrone ate them all!

'You must be feeling peckish!' said Mum. She had a slight edge to her voice, but Tyrone didn't notice.

'They're good,' he said, patting his tummy. 'I like your home cooking, Tracy.'

'That's not the meal, Tyrone,' I said. 'That's just elevenses. Well, half past elevenses today. And they're not home cooked, we got them from Morrison's. We'll have the meal at lunchtime.'

I was a bit worried about what we were going to do *until* lunchtime. And the rest of the afternoon, come to that. Tyrone was my friend but I'd never really hung out with him. He was just in my class at school. We hadn't even seen each other much on the Duke Estate. I'd lived in Marlborough Tower and he'd lived in Devonshire, and the kids from each tower didn't really mix much. In fact, you were taking your life in your hands if you went strolling around Devonshire.

There were at least two gangs, one with the really big lads and one for the younger ones, like at school. Tyrone was boss of the primary school lot, and they could be really mean if they felt like it – but the older ones were truly scary and carried knives. You ran if they came anywhere near you. That's what I loved about Cooksea. No one was out to get you. The worst that could happen was a boy in a baseball cap snatching your ice cream.

No, the worst that could happen was Sean Godfrey swaggering back into our lives. He was listening to one of Flo's stories, laughing in all the right places, egging her on. She'd taken a real shine to him and was

65

patting his hand fondly as if they'd known each other for years.

Even worse, Mum was looking as if she was glad to see him. She was acting in a very aloof manner, barely joining in the conversation, sitting right at the other side of the shop, but she was watching Sean Godfrey all the time, as if he was hypnotizing her.

I HATED THE whole visit. Tyrone got a bit fidgety too, wandering around the shop and picking up stuff, having several near accidents with china figures. Sean Godfrey shook his head and told him to chill. Tyrone sat down again, but he kept cracking his knuckles and tapping his feet.

'Why don't you two kids take the dog for a walk?' Sean Godfrey suggested.

'You come too, Sean,' said Tyrone.

'Yes, you come,' I said. Mum stared at me in surprise as I'd never invited Sean Godfrey to do anything with me before. I just wanted to get him away from Mum, out of the shop, out of the town, out of our lives.

He seemed surprised too. He shook his head. 'No, kids, I've got to keep these two lovely ladies company,' he said.

So Tyrone and I were packed off together. For the first time in his life Alfie was reluctant to come for a walk with me. He kept looking round, making it plain as day that he wanted Sean Godfrey to come with us, though he cheered up a bit when we got to the seafront.

'Shall we have an ice cream?' said Tyrone.

'You've just eaten four cookies!' I said.

'Yeah, but ice cream slips down, doesn't it?' He dug into his pockets. 'Only I haven't got any cash on me. Could you lend us some, Jess? I'll get Sean to pay you back.'

'No, greedy-guts!' I said.

'Well, let's go and have a paddle then,' Tyrone suggested.

We scrunched across the pebbles, Alfie racing ahead.

'He's a cracking dog,' said Tyrone. He sighed. 'I still miss Staffie.'

He'd had a rescue dog himself but had had to take him back to Battersea.

'Maybe you'll get another dog one day,' I said, though I knew dogs weren't allowed on the Duke Estate.

'Maybe your mum will get back with Sean and then he'll let me come and live at his house too, and then I could have a dog, and we'd all be like a family,' said Tyrone huskily. He'd gone very red in the face.

'Oh, Tyrone!' I could see how deeply he longed for this. 'I wish it could all work out like that,' I added, because I didn't want to hurt his feelings. 'It's just not possible though.'

'It *is*,' said Tyrone. 'Sean *likes* me. He even said he'd really like a son. And people get adopted, don't they? Your mum was adopted.'

'Yes, but the point is, my mum is never, ever getting back with Sean Godfrey.'

'She might. I think she still likes him,' said Tyrone, sitting down on the pebbles and taking off his trainers. 'She can't take her eyes off him.'

I hated that he'd noticed it too.

'Rubbish,' I said firmly, kicking off my own shoes. 'Come on then, let's paddle.'

Alfie dashed into the sea joyfully, up to his tummy in a flash. I was much more cautious, only getting my toes wet and then jumping back.

'You wuss!' said Tyrone, running past me – but he screamed as the water splashed his feet. 'It's flipping freezing!'

'What did you think it would be like, bathwater?' I said.

'Well, I wasn't to know, was I?'

'What?' I said, and then shut my mouth quickly before I could say any more. 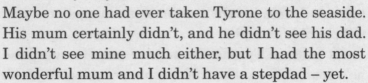 Maybe no one had ever taken Tyrone to the seaside. His mum certainly didn't, and he didn't see his dad. I didn't see mine much either, but I had the most wonderful mum and I didn't have a stepdad – yet.

I didn't want one at all – I wanted it to be just Mum and me – but if I had to, I wanted him to be gentle and cheery like Bacon Roll Bill. I one hundred per cent *didn't* want him to be Sean Godfrey.

I sighed, feeling that life was playing a trick on me. I dreaded the very situation Tyrone wanted with all his heart. I felt so sorry for him I reached out and held his hand.

'What you doing?' he said, going pink, though didn't take his hand away. 'You going all lovey-dovey on me?' He didn't sound as if he minded.

I went hot with horror, in spite of the icy water nibbling at my toes. I liked Tyrone, sort of, but I never, ever, ever wanted to get romantic with him.

'I just lost my balance,' I said, and took my hand away. I knew I couldn't say I felt sorry for him. He had his pride. And I couldn't let him think I fancied him, because then he'd go all soppy. He might even try to kiss me, and the very thought made me shudder.

'You're shivering,' said Tyrone. 'This paddling isn't all it's cracked up to be. Let's carry on walking, eh?'

It was a hard job convincing Alfie that this was a good idea. He was intent on teaching himself to swim, going deeper and deeper into the water. I waded in after him, calling till I was hoarse, and at long last he got tired of teasing me and bounded back up the pebbles, absolutely soaking.

'Look at the state of you, you daft dog!' I said, struggling back after him.

Alfie shook himself vigorously, making a rainstorm.

'Thanks, pal!' said Tyrone, flapping his wet football shirt and spattered shorts.

I was even wetter, my shorts dripping down my legs.

'Will your mum create?' Tyrone asked.

'Probably not,' I said, stuffing my wet feet into my trainers. 'Come on, let's run and maybe my shorts will dry in the sunshine.'

We bounded along the promenade, past the beach huts. Several of them had their doors open, with

71

families sitting on deckchairs drinking tea out of thermos flasks. There was one boy peering intently at his mobile and stabbing at the screen, his baseball cap pulled down over his eyes – but he was too small to be the ice-cream snatcher.

I peered into all the beach huts, hoping to see him. He'd take one look at Tyrone and decide not to pick on me ever again. But I couldn't see him anywhere, even though we went right to the end of the promenade. We climbed up the chalk path to the top of the cliffs. Tyrone was desperate to show me how fit he was now, though I could run nearly as fast. Alfie could beat both of us.

When we were at the top I put him back on his lead, just in case. I felt as if I should put Tyrone on a lead too because he kept going near the edge.

'Come back, you idiot!' I shouted.

'I'm not scared,' said Tyrone, dancing a little jig. Then he slipped in his shiny new trainers and fell backwards. His bottom landed right at the very edge of the cliff.

'Tyrone!' I yelled.

'Whoops!' he said, still clown-ing, and then glanced round and saw the sea far, far below.

He said a very rude word and clutched at the grass with both hands.

'Wriggle forward on your bum!' I shouted.

'I can't! I'll muck up my new shorts!' he said.

'Don't be crazy. *Wriggle!*'

I wanted to try to pull him to safety but he was twice my size, twice my weight. If he tried to cling to me we'd both topple over the cliff. I could barely hang onto Alfie, who was straining at his lead, trying to reach Tyrone too.

'You've *got* to wriggle, Tyrone!' I yelled, starting to cry.

'I don't know why *you're* blubbing. It's me that's teetering on the edge,' he said, but he had a go at wriggling. He did his best, grunting with effort, like a great baby trying to slide along the carpet.

'That's it! Wriggle more!'

He jerked himself forward, his shorts scraping on the grass and chalk and stones, but he kept on going until he was more than a metre from the edge.

'Now try standing up, very slowly, and then run to me!'

He stood and then he ran. I clutched him tight, while Alfie licked his bare legs. Tyrone hung onto me for a few moments, breathing shakily. I think he was trying not to cry too. I could feel him trembling.

'You idiot!' I said.

He sniffed and pushed me away. 'I was just mucking about to scare you,' he said. 'I wasn't in any danger. Your face was a picture when I pretended to fall!'

We both knew he was talking rubbish, but I let him bluster and fib so he could save face. He was desperately upset when he craned round and saw the grass stains on his shorts. They were a bit torn too.

'Oh no, look! That stain will never come out! And they're all ripped!' he wailed.

'It's only two tiny tears,' I said. 'My mum can sew them up for you.'

'I don't want them patched! They were brand new. Designer! Sean bought them for me specially.'

'Well, I expect he'll buy you some more. He's got lots of money. He won't mind. He was always trying to buy me new stuff when we lived at his place, but I wasn't having it.'

'Why?' said Tyrone, looking astonished. 'You're nuts, Jess. And so's your mum. Everyone on the estate thinks so.'

'I don't care,' I said. 'We're much happier here, Mum and me.'

'Living with a weird old lady in a tatty junk shop?' said Tyrone.

I felt like pushing him back over the cliff. We argued all the way round the town. I wanted to show off my lovely new home but Tyrone refused to be impressed.

'It doesn't have a proper sandy beach, it's just them pebbles and they hurt your feet. And there aren't any good sports shops and the clothes shops are rubbish. There isn't even a McDonald's!' he said.

'Who cares?' I said, though Mum and I missed McDonald's quite a lot. 'You wait till you try my mum's sausage and mash!'

Tyrone ate three large sausages smothered in onion gravy and a huge portion of mashed potatoes. He said, 'Thanks very much, Tracy, that was delicious.' But then he had the cheek to whisper to me, 'Just not quite as good as McDonald's.'

I kicked him hard under the table. Sean Godfrey acted like Mum was a MasterChef and kissed his fingertips in that silly way. I felt like kicking him too, though he'd actually been very kind to Tyrone about his ruined shorts.

'Don't worry about it, Tiger,' he said when Tyrone showed him, shame-faced. 'I was always ripping my gear when I was a lad. I know you didn't mean to. We'll get you another pair, OK?'

'A size bigger, after all he's eaten today,' I muttered.

After our huge lunch Flo lay on her sofa, patting her big tummy appreciatively. 'My, there's nothing beats a good sausage,' she said happily.

'Are you OK to mind the shop for a little while, Flo?' Sean Godfrey asked. 'I'd love to take a proper look round Cooksea – it seems such a lovely spot. You'll show me, won't you, Tracy? Perhaps we could take the car and drive along the seafront?'

We? Just the two of them together???

I waited for Tyrone to object, but he was sharing a leftover sausage with Alfie and not concentrating properly.

'Oh, yes please!' I said quickly. 'I'd love to go for a drive. Can I sit up front with you, Sean?'

They all stared at me. I saw a flicker of irritation in Sean Godfrey's eyes, but he smiled and said, 'Yeah, of course you can, Jess.'

'That's *my* place!' said Tyrone indignantly. 'I sit in the front beside you, don't I, Sean?'

'Well, kids are actually meant to sit in the back. So how about letting Tracy sit in the front, eh?' he said smoothly.

Mum was looking at me with narrowed eyes, but she didn't say anything. We left Flo to guard the shop and trooped off to find Sean Godfrey's car. He'd parked it up the other end of the promenade.

There was a little circle of people around it, patting the shiny red bonnet reverently or posing for photos, pretending to be the owner. Everyone squealed when Sean Godfrey walked up, car keys in his hand; he was recognized straight away. One woman even recognized *Mum*.

'You're Tracy, aren't you! I read all about your big romance in *Glossip* magazine! Childhood sweethearts, eh? I was devastated when you broke up. But here you are together again!'

'No, we're not together,' Mum said awkwardly. 'Well, obviously we are, but we're just good friends now. Aren't we, Sean?'

'Very good friends,' he said.

'On a little family outing, are you?' The woman nodded at me. 'I know you're Tracy's daughter. The spitting image of her too! And don't tell me – are you Sean's son?' she asked, peering at Tyrone.

He went pink with pride, especially when Sean Godfrey put his arm round him.

'He's one of my mini-footballers but he's *like* a son,' he said.

Tyrone glowed positively puce. I couldn't stick Sean Godfrey, and I knew he was mostly acting nicey-nicey for his little fan club, but I felt pleased all the same. It meant so much to Tyrone when he made a fuss of him. Sean Godfrey was so annoyingly slippery. I thoroughly despised him when he was acting like an idiot, but then he'd do something kind and I'd almost start liking him.

Mum was looking at him now as if she really, *really* still liked him – and the annoying woman asked if she could take a photo of them together.

'You look so lovely, you two. Like you were made for each other. Are you *sure* you're not getting back together?'

'Not going to happen,' said Mum, shaking her head, though she was smiling.

'Watch this space,' said Sean Godfrey, sounding as if he was correcting her.

Those three words echoed in my head as we drove all the way round Cooksea. I sat behind Sean Godfrey, looking daggers at the back of his head. It was a

particularly big head
too, with a ridiculous
hairstyle. I couldn't
understand all these
crazy women who fancied him. I especially couldn't
understand my mum.

'Can we drive past Seacliff Fields please?' I asked.
'Tell him the way, Mum.'

'Why do you want to go to the fields, Jess?' she
asked, turning round and wrinkling her nose at me.

'I want to show Sean where we go to the boot sales
on Sunday mornings,' I said. 'Where we see Bill.'

'Bill?' asked Sean Godfrey.

'He's the guy who has the bacon-roll van,' said
Mum. 'You've no idea how good they taste at crack of
dawn on a chilly morning.'

'Oh, I see. Bacon Roll Bill!' said Sean Godfrey, like
he was making a joke.

'Yes, he's our friend. Mum's friend,' I persisted.
'Isn't he, Mum?'

'Yes, he is,' she said evenly. 'But he won't be there
just now. The car boot sales are only on Sundays. It'll
just be empty fields.'

'Yes, but it's still lovely, and we can take Alfie for
a run there,' I said.

'If that's what you'd like to do, Jess,' said Sean
Godfrey. 'We're up for a run too, aren't we, Tyrone?'

'You bet, Sean,' he said.

The fields looked very different without all the cars parked for the boot fair. There were families picnicking, couples sunbathing, and some boys having a kickabout with an old football.

'Aha!' said Sean Godfrey, parking the Porsche.

The boys spotted the flash car first. Then they saw him getting out. He might have retired from the game but he was still a football legend, even among little boys who'd probably never seen him play professionally. They shouted his name and clustered around him, their game forgotten. Tyrone grinned proudly.

'Can we join in for a few minutes?' Sean Godfrey suggested.

They all squealed excitedly, and in seconds he was in the centre of the field, dribbling the ball, kicking it up in the air and catching it with his foot, dodging nimbly while they all charged around him. Tyrone played as well. He looked surprisingly good as he did some of the tricks Sean Godfrey had taught him. The boys treated him with awe, and he swaggered about like a mini-Sean.

'Well, this was a good idea,' Mum said sarcastically, flopping down on the grass.

'This is what it would be like if you hooked up with him again,' I said. 'Him showing off and you having to hang about watching.'

'But I'm not hooking up with him – how many more times?'

'*He* wants to hook up with *you*. It's obvious.'

'Do you think so?'

'Absolutely!'

'Good. That'll teach him what happens when you play around,' said Mum. 'And even if we *did* get together again, which isn't going to happen, I'm not the sort of woman who hangs about watching, thanks very much. I join in the action – see?'

She ran up to the boys, intercepted the ball and ran off with it. Sean Godfrey roared with laughter and tried to tackle her, but she managed to dodge round him. Well, perhaps he didn't try very hard. Anyway, she still had the ball and she could outrun the rest of the boys, though Tyrone came sprinting up. Just before he reached her, Mum kicked the ball hard and it went high in the air, flying all the way to the end of the field.

'Goal! Tracy Beaker wins the match, fair and square!' she yelled, punching the air.

'Hurray!' Sean Godfrey shouted, and he picked her up and thumped her on the back. I know he was only mucking about like footballers do after a goal – but I hated it.

'I'm bored! Let's go home,' I said.

When we got back we had a cup of tea.

'And we've got cakes too, still warm from the oven,' Flo said proudly.

She'd heaved herself up from her sofa and, in between serving customers, made rock buns. She hadn't made cakes for years, and her wrists were too weak to stir the mixture properly, so they were a bit lumpy. We were still full of lunch, but Mum and I shared one, Sean Godfrey politely ate a whole one, and Tyrone managed to wolf down two, which pleased Flo enormously. She put the rest in a bag for Tyrone to take home.

I couldn't wait for Sean Godfrey to clear off, but I was also dreading it. I was sure he'd try to kiss Mum goodbye. My full tummy turned over at the thought. When we lived at his house, I'd hated it when they got lovey-dovey. He *did* try too, but luckily Mum quickly turned her head so he was only kissing her cheek.

Tyrone kissed *me*! I was so surprised I didn't duck in time and he got me right on the lips! It was only the quickest kiss ever, but even so!

'You cheeky little whatsit, Tiger,' said Sean Godfrey, laughing.

'You can stop that right this minute, kiddo! Jess is just a little girl,' said Mum, but she wasn't really cross.

When at last they left, the shop was suddenly very quiet and very peaceful. I breathed out slowly and deeply, and then rubbed my lips with the back of my hand.

'I'm so glad they've gone,' I said.

'What, you're glad to see the back of your sweetheart?' said Flo, teasing me. Then she looked at Mum. 'What about you, Tracy? Sean Godfrey is quite a charmer, eh? He was doing his best to get round me. If I was fifty years younger I dare say I'd have fallen for him, hook, line and sinker. No wonder he turned your head. So, are you relieved he's gone?' She said it light-heartedly, but she looked anxious.

Mum sat down beside her and held her plump hand. 'Yes, I am,' she said. 'Sean can be great fun at times, and I used to be mad about him once – but it's truly all over now. I could never trust him again. He's a dreadful control freak too. You always have to do things Sean's way. I'm not cut out to be a sweet little wifey. I want my *own* way.'

'So you definitely don't want to go back to him?' Flo persisted.

'Absolutely not! We're here for good. We have a partnership now. You, me and Jess.'

Mum reached out for me and pulled me onto her lap, as if I was still a little kid. I didn't really mind.

'You can stop worrying, Jess. We're here to stay. Promise,' she said.

MUM NEVER BREAKS her promises. Well, hardly
ever. I did try to stop worrying – but it wasn't
easy. The next day a fancy delivery van drew up
outside the shop. Sean Godfrey had sent three
bunches of flowers: an enormous bouquet of red roses
for Mum, a slightly smaller one of white roses for Flo,
and a baby bouquet of pink roses for me. They each
had cards.

Mine said:

To Jess —
I miss you,
sweetheart.
Love from
Sean

It was rubbish. Of course he didn't miss *me*. I crumpled up the card and threw it in the bin.

Flo's card said:

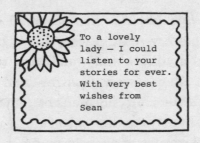

To a lovely
lady — I could
listen to your
stories for ever.
With very best
wishes from
Sean

'Oh my!' she said, and popped her card in her handbag.

I don't know what Mum's card said. She read it and then shoved it straight in her jeans pocket.

'What does your card say, Mum?' I asked.

'Oh, just a load of nonsense,' she said.

While she was in the bathroom getting ready for

bed that night, I felt in her jeans pocket. The card wasn't there any more.

I watched her like a hawk after that. I often hung around outside the bathroom, straining to hear the tiny mouse-tap of her texting. Once she came barging out without warning and knocked me flying.

'What were you *doing*, Jess?' she asked, picking me up.

'I was just waiting to have a wee,' I said.

'Leaning against the door?'

'Well, I was desperate. Still am,' I gabbled, and charged into the bathroom.

I watched her when she took Alfie out at night to see if she was on the phone. I also looked out for Bill, hoping he fancied another curry. Or maybe even fancied my mum and was trying to bump into her again.

A few nights later I saw Mum coming down the road with her head on one side, murmuring into her phone. I was sitting up in bed, arms folded, when she came in with Alfie.

'Sorry I've been such ages. Alfie hung around a lot, sniffing every lamppost. Snuggle down now, Jess,' said Mum.

My heart was thumping hard. I decided to ask her outright.

'Were you on the phone to Sean Godfrey just now?'
I demanded.

Mum pulled her jumper over her head. All her curls bounced as they bobbed back into view again. In the soft glow of my new rabbit night light I couldn't see her face properly, but I was pretty certain she was blushing.

'Oh, I just had a quick word with Cam, checking how she's doing,' Mum said airily, getting into her pyjamas.

I didn't believe her. While her back was turned, I grabbed *my* phone and hid it in my pyjama pocket. Then I got out of bed.

'What are you doing?'

'I need a wee,' I said.

'Maybe I should take you to the doctor's. You're weeing an awful lot recently. You're worse than Alfie,' said Mum.

I dashed to the bathroom, ran the taps to make a noise, and then dialled Cam's number.

'Hi, Jess,' she said. 'Is anything wrong, poppet? Has your mum come back from taking Alfie out?'

'Yes. So, were you talking to her just now?' I asked urgently. 'Don't tell fibs, please.'

'Yes, I was,' said Cam. 'And I don't tell fibs. Especially not to you.'

'Oh,' I said.

'What's up, love?'

'Nothing. What was Mum saying?'

'Oh, this and that,' said Cam. 'We were just having a catch-up.'

'Can *we* have a catch-up some time soon, Cam?'

'Well, that was one of the things your mum and I were talking about. Mary and I thought we'd drive down next Sunday. OK?'

'Yes, lovely.'

'That's great then. Jess? Are you worrying about anything?' Cam asked.

'Not really,' I said. I'm not like Cam. I do sometimes tell fibs, though I'm not very good at it.

'Is it Sean?' she asked.

'Yes!' I said. 'How did you know? What did Mum say?'

'Well, she told me he'd been to visit. With Tyrone.'

'Did she sound pleased about it?'

'I'm not sure.'

'She says she doesn't trust him any more and that she'll never go back to him – but I think she still loves him,' I said in a tiny voice.

'And you still don't like him at all?'

'I can't *stand* him,' I said fiercely. 'You don't like him either, do you, Cam?'

'Not much. Not at all, actually. I'm with you on that one, Jess,' she said.

'But do you think Mum still loves him?'

Cam was quiet for a moment. 'I'm not sure your mum even knows the answer to that,' she said eventually. 'Now, I'd better ring off, Jess. I can hear one of the girls prowling around downstairs. I'd better go and see if she's OK. Night night, darling.'

When I went back into our room, it was Mum's turn to sit up in bed, arms folded. 'You were a long time,' she said.

'Well, I had to go,' I said.

'Were you on the phone?'

'No!'

'Jess, I can see the shape of the phone in your pyjama pocket! Who were you phoning?'

'Cam.'

'For goodness' sake!'

'Well, *you* phoned her.'

'I think we'd both better stop phoning her so much. She's got her current foster girls to deal with. And now she's got her number one foster girl and the number one foster girl's daughter to contend with! She must be sick of us Beaker girls,' said Mum.

'Cam's never sick of us. I'm so glad she's coming next weekend!' I said.

On Sunday Mum and I got up very early so we could fit

in the boot sale first and hopefully find a few bargains. We set the alarm for six and rushed off in the van without bothering with breakfast. We didn't need any – we could have a bacon roll when we got there.

'Hi, Tracy, hi, Jess, hi, Alfie,' said Bill. Gladys gave Mum and me a happy lick, and Alfie a loving sniff.

Mum and Bill had a little chat while Bill made our bacon rolls. It wasn't really *about* anything – just the weather and how hard it was getting up so early. Mum said she had to set the alarm on her mobile *and* her Mickey Mouse clock. Bill said he'd probably sleep through his own alarm but Gladys always started barking when it went off, and he had to get up sharpish to take her out, otherwise he'd have a puddle on the floor.

I was pleased to see them being so friendly with each other, nattering away. It was clear that Bill really liked Mum. She laughed at all his silly jokes, her eyes sparkling, her curls bobbing about. I wasn't daft – I could see that Bill wasn't anywhere near as flash as Sean Godfrey. His faded sweatshirt was shabby, the cuffs fraying – but then he'd be a fool to wear good clothes frying bacon all morning.

I edged right up to the counter so that I could

peer down and see the rest of him. His jeans were a bit baggy at the knee, and one leg was torn. Some people wore ripped jeans as a fashion statement, but these just looked very old. He wore a truly old style of trainers too – they looked as if they were practically falling to pieces – but he wasn't walking anywhere, he was just standing in his van.

So his clothes were a bit rubbish, but I thought he was still better looking than Sean Godfrey. He didn't have a silly haircut for a start. He had fairish wavy hair and a lovely friendly face, with big brown eyes and a wide mouth  that was always smiling. He was just a nice normal size and build, not all shoulders and six-pack like Sean Godfrey.

If Mum really wanted a boyfriend, then Bill would be perfect. He really seemed to like me too, he wasn't just pretending. He loved Alfie and always gave him his own rasher of bacon as a little treat. If Bill and Mum ever got together, then we could still live in Cooksea and run the shop with Flo.

Why couldn't he ask Mum out? Why couldn't she hint that she'd like that? Perhaps they needed a little encouragement!

Mum and I were walking towards the first row of cars, munching away. I stopped suddenly.

'Won't be a minute, Mum,' I said, turning round. 'I'm just going to put some tomato sauce on my bacon roll.'

'You put some on already,' she said.

'Yes, but I'd like a bit more,' I said, and ran back to Bill's van.

'Are you wanting *another* roll, Jess?' Bill laughed.

'Just some more sauce, if I may,' I said, squeezing the big red bottle. I took a deep breath. 'Do you know something, Bill?'

'What's that, Jess?'

'My mum really fancies you.'

Bill looked startled. 'You what?'

'She likes you. Ever so. Do you like her?'

'Well, yes. She's lovely. But I don't think I'm really her type,' he said awkwardly.

'Yes you are! Why don't you ask her out next Sunday?'

'Out where?'

Bill was very nice, but he wasn't really *enterprising*.

'You could go for a walk, or for a drink, or to see a film. And you could have a curry after – you both like curries, don't you?' I said.

'Yes, I suppose. Well, I do, anyway,' he agreed.

'There you are then. Ask her.'

'Don't you think I'm a bit old for your mum?' he said.

93

I hadn't really thought about their ages. They were both old. What was he on about? I tried to remember what Mum said to reassure Flo when she fussed about being an old lady. 'Age is just a number,' I said.

Bill burst out laughing. 'You're a card, you are, Jess Beaker.'

'So you'll ask my mum out? She's been hoping and hoping that you will,' I said, fibbing outrageously.

'Really?' he said, looking a bit worried. 'Well, I'd better pop round and have a little word with your mum then. OK?'

I nodded hopefully and started back towards Mum, but Alfie dug his paws in, not wanting to leave Gladys. Dogs were so much simpler than people. They sniffed each  other, they wagged their tails and made friends in just a few seconds, with no pussyfooting around.

I'd put so much tomato sauce on my bacon roll it made my cheeks pucker and it was hard to swallow it down, but I didn't care. I felt I'd got a result.

'What were you nattering about to Bill?' Mum asked, sorting through a load of old children's books in cardboard boxes.

'We were just passing the time of day,' I said airily. '*You* nattered more than me.'

'Well, he's such a sweet guy,' said Mum. 'And I think he's a bit lonely, for all he's so cheery.'

Aha! I thought. *Maybe he won't be lonely for long. Maybe he'll get a brand-new girlfriend!*

I knelt down beside Mum and started sorting through the books myself.

'I wouldn't touch them if I were you, Jess. They're all a bit old and manky and they're mostly picture books anyway. Too young for you.'

'Oh, Mum, look, they've got some of those little animal books – *Peter Rabbit* and *Mrs Tiggy-Winkle* and *Jemima Puddle-Duck!* Couldn't I have them – they're so sweet?' I begged.

'Baby!' said Mum, but she asked the price from the lady at the stall.

'I'd sooner sell the whole box. I've inherited all my old grandad's stuff and we're snowed under with it. You can have the lot for thirty-five quid,' she said.

'No thanks!' said Mum. 'Come on, Jess.'

We wandered around the rest of the stalls, but there was nothing special, just a couple of little china jugs with A SOUVENIR FROM COOKSEA on them, and a box of jigsaw puzzles.

'The day trippers will snap up the jugs, and jigsaw puzzles always sell,' said Mum. 'You and Flo can check that there aren't any pieces missing.'

'I don't like doing jigsaw puzzles. I like books,' I said, looking over at the box of children's books again.

'They're massively overpriced!' said Mum. 'We've already got a heap of kids' books in the shop and no one wants them.'

'*I* do,' I said. 'I've read them all.' I'd had a glorious time reading my way through some old school stories, and paperback Noel Streatfeilds, and a whole set of Ladybird fairy stories, and a trilogy set in the future that made me cry because a dog just like Alfie died. I didn't mind a bit if some of the books were too old for me and some too young. I badly wanted the Beatrix Potter animal stories.

Mum sighed. 'Well, I'll see if I can beat her down in price. After you've read the books I could cut out the pictures and frame them.'

She bargained hard and got the box for twenty-five, though she still thought it a ridiculous price. 'I must be daft. I could buy you several brand-new books at WHSmith for that,' she grumbled, but she grinned at me. 'You're spoiled rotten, do you know that, Jess Beaker? And I'm probably going to rupture myself heaving the blooming box back to the van!'

'I'll carry it, Mum!' I said. It was so heavy I could barely lift it, but I insisted on struggling with it all the same.

Another dealer – an old lady – was hauling along

two huge plastic laundry bags of stuff to the car park, with a boy carrying another two for her. A chunky boy in a baseball cap. *That* boy.

'Look, Mum! It's him. The boy who was getting food out of the waste bin,' I said. 'The one you said looked as if he was starving.'

'Is it?' said Mum. 'Oh well, he looks quite chipper now, doesn't he?'

I wondered if the old lady was his granny. He helped her stow all four bags in the back of her battered car. She rummaged around in her bum bag and brought out a little silver coin – a fifty-pence piece, or maybe just a twenty, I couldn't really see properly. The boy looked very disappointed and said something. The old lady shook her head and muttered, waving him away, clearly telling him that was all he was getting.

He said something back and then sloped off. The old lady got into her car and drove off. It wasn't his granny then. The boy's head was down and he looked fed up. I stared after him – and, as if he knew I was watching, he raised his right hand and made a very rude gesture.

I gestured back, even though I knew he couldn't see me.

'*What* did you just do?' Mum said, horrified.

'Nothing, Mum. I was just flexing my fingers – they keep cramping after carrying that box,' I said quickly.

When we got home I sat cross-legged on the floor showing Flo all the books while Mum started on lunch for Cam and Mary. They're both veggies so she was doing a big tray bake of sweet potatoes and eggs and cheese and asparagus and broccoli.

'I'm sure it'll taste lovely, pet, but personally I think nothing beats a roast,' Flo said wistfully, though she perked up when Mum started making an apple crumble too.

I read *Jemima Puddle-Duck*, loving the quaint old-fashioned words and the soft watercolours.

'What's that little book, Jess?' Flo asked, squinting at the picture on the front. 'It's not *Mother Goose*, is it? I was in the pantomime – it was such a laugh! Hard work with all those matinees and screaming kiddies, but it was a jolly cast.'

'Did you play Mother Goose?' I asked.

'No, lovey, the goose is always a man. And the principal boy is always played by a girl. Yours truly in this case, and very dashing I looked in my white tights, even if I say so myself. Dear old Arty was the best Mother Goose in the business, so we made a fine pair,' said Flo, her eyes misty with memories.

'Was he your boyfriend, Flo?' I asked. I knew he'd left her the shop in his will, and she always spoke about him very fondly.

'Not exactly, dear. I wasn't really his type, in a manner of speaking. But we were always the best of pals, and sometimes that's more important. Friendships last for ever, but I'm not so sure about romance.' Flo sighed. 'I've made a few mistakes in that department.'

'Like Mum and Sean Godfrey. That was never going to work,' I said firmly.

'Your mum's still young, sweetheart,' Flo said gently. 'She might fall for someone else one day.'

'Oh, I know,' I said, nodding. I was certainly doing my best to give her a push in Bill's direction.

It was a big treat to see Cam and Mary. They'd been once before, when they helped us move all our stuff, but we were dying to show them what we'd done to the shop since. As soon as they came through the door, Mum and I raced each other to get to Cam first for a big hug. Alfie joined in too, leaping up eagerly and nearly knocking us all over. Cam put her arms round all of us, and for a few moments we were lost in our little family world – but then she broke away to say hello to Flo, and Mum and I said hello to Mary.

We referred to them as Cam-and-Mary, and we were ever so happy that they'd got together – but it was still a little odd that Mary was family now too, when she used to be my teacher. When she was little Mum had always had a bit of a problem with teachers so, although she gave her a hug, it was rather restrained. I felt too shy to hug Mary properly – you'd never, ever dream of hugging your teachers – but she gave me a kiss and seemed really happy to see me.

'I think you've grown, Jess! And you're so brown! It looks as if you really belong here now,' she said.

'And haven't the two girls done wonders with the shop!' said Flo. 'See all the little displays! The takings have gone through the roof since Tracy's been in charge.'

'We're a partnership, Flo. And you're the one

who's kept the shop going all these years,' Mum insisted. She showed Cam and Mary round so they could see for themselves, and they exclaimed and admired everything.

'I just love the way you've arranged everything, Tracy. Who'd have thought you'd be Queen of the Antiques Trade!' said Cam, giving Mum another hug.

'You've done a marvellous job,' said Mary. 'You must have studied an enormous amount about antiques in a very short space of time.'

'I'm not really the sort of girl who likes studying, am I, Cam?' said Mum, laughing. 'It's not the sort of trade you need to read up on. It's experience that counts. I've been haunting boot fairs and charity shops for years. You've just got to have a good eye and a gut instinct. Flo's taught me a lot too. Do you know, we repaired a beaten-up old desk and sold it for a fortune the other day'

Cam had brought a tin of her home-made blueberry muffins, my favourite, so we all ate one with a coffee. (It was lucky Tyrone wasn't  there or he'd have eaten every muffin in the tin.) Then we sat in the shop and had a proper catch-up. Cam told us all about the girls staying with her. Rosie was still not eating properly and Jax was staying out much too late with her new boyfriend.

'Dear goodness, I don't know how you cope with teenage girls!' said Flo. 'Doesn't it do your head in, Cam?'

'Oh, I'm used to it,' she said cheerfully. 'All teenage girls can be a pain at times. I know I was.'

'And she brought me up – all these others since are a doddle compared to that!' said Mum.

'You turned out OK in the end,' said Cam fondly. 'And I'm sure all the others will too. However, now they're older I'm thinking of shutting up shop and relaxing for a while.'

'About time,' said Mary.

'Jax has left school and is starting on a nursery nurse course at college in September. She's so looking forward to it too,' said Cam.

'What about your school, Jess?' Mary asked. 'Do you like it?'

I shrugged my shoulders.

'It's the holidays, Mary!' said Mum.

'Yes, I know, obviously, but you *have* found somewhere for Jess in September?' She was starting to sound like the Miss Oliver of old.

'Well, she'll go to the local primary, won't she?'

'Probably, but you have to enrol her and get everything sorted. They'll need to contact Duke Primary for all her reports. Tracy, you've had weeks and weeks to get it all arranged!' Mary scolded.

'Yes, like I've had all the time in the world,' said Mum.

'Surely you've had time to spend a morning looking at the schools in your area and asking a few questions,' said Mary. 'Jess is very bright. She needs to go to a school where she can flourish. It's vital at this stage – she'll be sitting her SATs this coming year, and thinking about secondary schools.'

'OK, OK, I do get it, you know,' said Mum. 'Stop fussing, Mary. She's my child, not yours. I'll do my best.'

'Of course you will,' said Cam quickly. 'I know it's a bore – I'm a veteran at sorting out schooling for my girls. It's going to be a hard job finding a teacher as good as Mary though. Do you know they're making her deputy head in September?'

She was at her most Cam-like, trying to calm everyone down. Flo started talking about her own schooldays and her first job as a chorus girl at fifteen, and Mum sloped off to finish preparing lunch. I went to help her. She was banging the pots and plates about with unnecessary violence.

'Hey, can I help, Mum?' I offered.

'You could grate some cheese if you're careful. Don't you dare grate your fingers or Mary will say it's my fault,' she muttered. 'Dear goodness, she's such a bossy boots. What is it about teachers? They can't help telling you what to do, even when it's none of their business.' She chopped even harder, pieces of potato bouncing about on the worktop.

'Watch out, Mum.' I paused. 'Mary will say you've got Anger Issues!'

Mum gave me a look but then started laughing.

Lunch was a success. The tray bake was golden and delicious, and Mum had made a tomato salad to go with it. Even Flo admitted it was good, and she raved about the apple crumble. Cam and Mary were very appreciative too. Mum relaxed visibly.

We'd closed the shop over lunch, but when we opened up again we were suddenly inundated with customers, mostly old folk on a coach trip to the seaside. Flo couldn't cope with them all by herself, so Mum helped while I went for a walk with Cam and Mary and Alfie.

I did quite like Mary, but I wished Cam and I could be on our own. We went for a really long walk, right across the clifftops, round the golf course, and then up past Cooksea Manor. The gardens were open to the public on Sunday afternoons.

'Oh, marvellous,' said Mary. 'Look at those hollyhocks! And the poster says they've got a big water lily pond. Let's go and have a look round.'

But the lady at the entrance said she was very sorry, Alfie looked adorable, but unfortunately dogs weren't allowed into the gardens.

'Never mind, Mary. You go and have a look while I keep Jess and Alfie company,' said Cam.

Mary bustled off, and Cam put her arm round me. 'How's it going then, Jessica Bluebell Camilla Beaker? Happy?' she asked, rubbing her cheek against the top of my head.

'Very,' I said, snuggling against her. 'Though I wish I could see you more often, Cam.'

'I wish I could see you more too, love. And your mum. She's happy too?'

'Yes, ever so. She loves it at the shop,' I said.

'Have you both made any new friends here?'

'Flo's our friend. And we've got heaps of other friends. We like Bill best – he does absolutely magic bacon rolls. He gets on very well with Mum!'

'I'm sure he does.'

'I have a feeling Mum and Bill might start going out together!' I said.

'Really? So Mum wants to start dating again? You think she's over the whole Sean thing?'

'Of course she is,' I said. 'He's history.'

'He came to visit you the other day though.'

'Yes, but that was just to bring Tyrone. *He* was desperate to come and see us.'

'Desperate to see *you*!' Cam teased.

'Yeah, well, Tyrone's a friend, I suppose – but he doesn't half get on my nerves at times. And I don't think I'm really friends with Alice and Ava any more. Still, I don't really need a best friend, not now I've got Alfie,' I said, giving him a pat.

'Yes, Alfie's a real pal,' said Cam. 'And you'll make lots of other friends when you go to school. Hey, Tracy said you saw Peter Ingham from the children's home the first day you came to Cooksea. The one who has the same birthday as her. I think she used to give him rather a hard time, but they were good friends too. She said he's a head teacher now. Maybe he'll be head of your new school!'

'No, I think he's head of a secondary school. He was having a peer in our shop the other day, but he didn't come in.'

'I take it he's not your mum's type now?' Cam said.

'Not really! You know she doesn't go a bundle on teachers!' I said – and then blushed because I'd been so tactless. 'But she likes Mary, truly!'

'That's good, because *I* like Mary,' said Cam. 'And

she likes you and your mum. She didn't mean to sound bossy earlier.'

'I know. And I expect Mum knows too. She just doesn't like it when people tell her what to do.'

'You don't need to tell me that!' said Cam.

When Mary came out of the gardens she had a potted plant in either hand, with flowers like great big pink daisies.

'They were for sale and I couldn't resist them. I love echinacea. I'll plant one in your garden and I thought Tracy might like one to plant in hers,' said Mary.

Flo didn't really have a proper garden, just a scrubby patch of grass and a shed where she kept a lot of junk – but maybe Mum and I could make part of it into a flower bed.

'Thank you very much, Mary!' I said. 'What did you say it was called?'

'Echinacea. You can make herbal tea with it. It's supposed to ward off colds,' she said.

Mum was often a bit sniffy about herbal teas but she seemed delighted with the plant and actually gave Mary a kiss. 'I love these big daisies,' she said.

'It's called echinacea, Mum,' I told her.

'Yeah, echinacea, whatever. We'll make a little flower garden out the back. You can sit out and sunbathe in a deckchair, Flo.'

'That would be lovely, sweetheart,' said Flo. She smiled at Cam. 'Your girl doesn't half spoil me!'

While we were out, Mum had been arranging the books from the boot fair. She'd put them in size order on an old school desk, with a teddy reading *Mrs Tiggy-Winkle*. I picked him up carefully to see if there was a copy of *The Tale of Peter Rabbit*.

Mary came and bent down beside me. 'These look interesting. Can I have a look?' She sorted through them with me, getting them out of size order, pulling out a big red book from the bottom. Mum twitched, but managed not to say anything. Mary held the book up in triumph. It was a big volume of fairy tales.

'Oh, this is lovely!' she said. 'I think Arthur Rackham illustrations are beautiful. What a great find.' But when she opened it up she saw that some silly child had scribbled over most of the pages with red crayon. 'Oh no!'

'Shame, isn't it?' said Mum. 'I've gone through pricing them up, but they're all in a wretched state, apart from a couple of those little Beatrix Potters.

I'm hoping they might sell for a tenner each once Jess has finished with them. If not, I might try cutting out the coloured plates and framing them.'

'Oh dear, I hate the thought of ripping books apart,' said Cam. 'Still, it's a good idea, Tracy. Isn't it, Mary?'

Mary didn't react. She was looking at the little books now, first *Jemima Puddle-Duck* and then *Mrs Tiggy-Winkle*.

'They're not as good as *Peter Rabbit* but they're still quite sweet,' I said. 'A bit babyish for me now of course.'

'Yes, young Jess is a brilliant little reader. She tackles all sorts, even great fat books without any pictures at all,' said Flo.

Mary didn't reply to either of us. She seemed intent on looking at the Beatrix Potter books.

'What is it, Mary?' asked Mum.

'You can't sell these for a tenner! I'd say they were worth hundreds of pounds. They're first editions – and in reasonable condition too,' she said. 'I should take them to a specialist book dealer if I were you.'

We all stared at her. Then Flo clapped her hands. 'Well I never! If they're really worth that, we'll make a tidy profit. And you must have your share, Mary. Isn't that right, Tracy?'

Mum nodded, looking stunned. And stricken. 'Of course, I *thought* they might be first editions, but it seemed too good to be true,' she said shakily.

'And books aren't really your speciality, are they?' said Cam, loyal as always.

'It looks like Jess had better be the book specialist from now on,' said Mum. 'She was the one who picked them out, not me.'

It seemed like we were all set for another celebratory meal at the Spade and Bucket after Cam and Mary set off back to London, but we were all too full of lunch. Flo had another portion of apple crumble and said she'd have an early night.

'But you two go and celebrate, darlings,' she told us.

I was up for it but Mum said she didn't really feel like it. So we ended up making do with the last two blueberry muffins. Mum didn't actually eat hers, she just nibbled at an edge and crumbled the rest onto her plate.

I put my arm round her. 'What's up, Mum?'

'Nothing, really,' she said.

'It was great seeing Cam, wasn't it?'

'Yes, lovely.'

'And Mary. Though she *is* a bit bossy.'

'And a bit of a know-it-all.'

'Yes, she is,' I agreed.

'Whereas I'm a know-nothing-at-all,' said Mum flatly, all the bounce gone out of her. 'I was going to sell those books for a pittance when they're worth a fortune.'

'Yes, but you weren't to know. The lady at the boot sale didn't know either, did she?' I pointed out.

'Yes, but she was just selling off her grandad's stuff. She doesn't run an antique and bric-a-brac shop and brag that she's an expert,' said Mum, and she sounded near tears, even though she hardly ever cries.

'Oh, Mum. Don't get upset. It doesn't matter about the silly books,' I said.

'Yes it does. I so wanted to show Cam that I was good at this – and it turns out I'm total rubbish, making the most elementary mistakes. And it had to be blooming Mary who pointed it out. She didn't even crow about it. She was being all nicey-nicey because she feels sorry for me. Tracy Beaker, the care leaver who can't make a success of anything.'

'Shut up, Mum! That's rubbish,' I said.

'Well, what have I achieved so far? I mucked around at school and I didn't stick it out at college. I've never had a proper job. I've never even had a proper long-term relationship.'

'Yes you have. With me! You're the best mum in the whole world!' I said.

She smiled when I said that, and gave me a hug, but there were tears running down her cheeks.

'**YOU AND ME** are going to find a library today,
Jess,' Mum said at breakfast.

We didn't open the shop until ten thirty – people
got up late in Cooksea. We left Alfie with Flo. She
was reading half the paper, and Alfie was happily
tearing the rest of it into strips.

We knew where all the cafés and restaurants
were, and the supermarket and the bank and the
post office, and the promenade and Seacliff Fields,
and the little old cinema and the two other junk shops
and all the charity ones – but we'd never noticed a
library.

'Perhaps Cooksea doesn't have one any more,' I
said, but Mum had looked it up on the internet.

It was in Park Road, which led to a park we hadn't discovered before, with an old wall round it and lots of grass – a perfect park for Alfie to play in. There was a lovely big building overlooking it, pale grey stone with turrets at the top like a castle. It had gilt lettering above the door:

COOKSEA LIBRARY

'Yay!' I said.

I love libraries. Cam used to take me to one when I was little, and helped me select a handful of picture books each week. There wasn't a library near the Duke Estate but in the Juniors I borrowed books from school. The library was quite small, but the books were kept in very good order and nicely displayed. I was the library monitor, actually.

There were thousands and thousands of books in Cooksea library. While Mum spoke to the lady at the desk, I peered around at all the shelves in awe. She filled in forms and showed her driving licence and was then given two library cards, one for me and one for her.

'For you, Mum?' I said, surprised. She didn't read much. She was generally too fidgety to curl up with a book.

'I *can* read, you know!' she said. 'Right, that's the children's section over there. You choose your books while I choose mine, OK?'

The children's library had big boxes of picture books for the little ones, with large squashy cushions and several teddies to cuddle. I couldn't help wishing I was young enough to sprawl on a cushion with a teddy and listen to a story with the toddlers. There were proper chairs and tables here and there for older children, and a cluster of revolving display stands, and shelves of books almost up to the ceiling.

I felt a deep calm happiness as I started browsing. I could choose up to six books – and of course I wanted the full six. I spent half an hour selecting them, reading several pages. Eventually I took my armful to the lady librarian.

'My, you're a keen reader!' she said. 'Oh, good choices!'

I'd chosen *The Hundred and One Dalmatians*, *Little House on the Prairie*, *The Butterfly Lion*,

Rooftoppers, *The Tulip Touch* and *When Hitler Stole Pink Rabbit*.

'They should keep you going all summer,' she said, smiling.

I went to find Mum, hugging the books to my chest. She was checking out *ten* books – but they weren't storybooks like mine. They were reference works about antiquarian and second-hand books, and dolls and china and old toys and paintings and furniture.

'Oh, Mum!' I said.

'I'm going to show that Mary,' she said. 'I'm going to mug up on everything and become an antiques expert.'

'Seriously?'

'You wait. Before long they'll be asking my opinion on *Antiques Roadshow*,' said Mum.

Our combined books were so heavy and unwieldy that Mum had to fork out for two canvas bags emblazoned with the legend NOTHING BEATS A GOOD BOOK!

'I think I'm going to start my own alternative range: NOTHING BEATS A GOOD BEAKER!' said Mum, shouldering a bulging bag. She's strong but she's small and skinny, and it was rather heavy for her. We were having a bit of an argy-bargy on the way out, me trying to take one bag and Mum batting my hands away, so we weren't looking where we were going. We bumped right into a man coming in, who had a handful of books of his own. It ended up with everyone's books all over the doorstep.

'I'm so sorry!' said the guy, head bent, scurrying round to gather them together.

Then he looked up and we recognized each other. It was Peter Ingham again. Weedy Peter. Though he wasn't really at all weedy now. His arms didn't bulge with muscles like Sean Godfrey's, but they were lean and brown and strong.

'Oh, Peter, you haven't changed a bit!' said Mum nevertheless. 'Apologizing away when it's all our fault! You're a scream.'

'You haven't changed a bit either, Tracy Beaker,' he said, separating the last of the books. 'No, wait a minute. *The Collector's Guide to Antiquarian Books*? Oh, of course, your shop!'

'It's not actually *my* shop, it's Flo's, but I run it for her,' said Mum. 'And it's not a hobby job. I'm taking it very seriously.'

'Mum's going to be a world expert on antiques,' I said proudly.

'Well, good for her,' said Peter. He was looking at my books. 'Lovely mixed bunch! I can tell you're a keen reader. What about your brother? Is he a book-worm too?'

'My brother?' I said, baffled.

'She hasn't got a brother,' said Mum, straightening up and repacking her bag.

'Is he your partner's son then?' Peter asked.

'I haven't got a partner either,' said Mum. 'What are you on about?'

'You were with this great big hunk of a man the other day, when I saw you at your shop. And he had a boy in football strip with him,' said Peter.

'You thought *Tyrone* was my son?' Mum said incredulously. 'Are you crazy?'

'And the big hunk – Sean Godfrey – is absolutely, definitely not Mum's partner – well, not any more,' I said.

'Is he famous or something? I saw several kids staring at him,' said Peter. He wasn't winding Mum up. He was serious.

'You're priceless,' she said, laughing. 'I know you're

unlikely to be into sports, but he's a footballing legend.'

'Not any more though,' I chimed in.

'Oh well. I'm the first to admit I know nothing about football. But I *am* quite sporty nowadays, actually. I swim in the sea every day. And I play badminton,' said Peter. 'I'm the team captain.'

'Oh, Peter! You crack me up,' said Mum. 'Badminton, eh? You devil!'

Peter went faintly pink and Mum looked sorry.

'Oh, don't look like that, Pete. You know what I'm like. Can't resist teasing. I bet your foster mum and dad are proud of you,' she said.

'Well. They were, bless them. But sadly Pa had a stroke and died soon after and Ma went to pieces. She couldn't cope,' he said, looking down at the ground.

'Oh, Pete, I'm so sorry,' said Mum, and she threw her arms round him, nearly sending the books flying again. 'Here, let's go for a coffee and catch up properly.'

Peter looked a bit taken aback. 'Well, I haven't changed my library books yet.'

'Do it after. We won't hold you up for long.'

'Well, I don't want to hold *you* up. Shouldn't you be going back to your shop?'

'Flo can hold the fort for a while. Did you see what it's called?'

'Obviously you've renamed it,' said Peter.

'No, it was called The Dumping Ground all along, truly. It was like fate was staring me in the face. It's as if I'm continually reminded of the past. You'll never, ever guess who I bumped into a little while ago! Justine Littlewood, as sneaky and mean as ever,' said Mum.

'She was after Sean Godfrey!' I said.

'And she's welcome to him,' Mum added quickly. 'I soon saw her off though. Watch! Though you'd better stand back a bit!' She put her huge bag of books on the ground, assumed an exaggerated stance, and then suddenly lunged forward, one leg up in the air. Peter jumped back out of harm's way, looking horrified.

'It's OK! I'd never kick *you*. But I toppled old Justine, didn't I, Jess?'

'Yep. Good and proper. No one messes with my mum, Peter,' I said.

'Don't I know it,' he said.

We walked back towards the town and came to a funny little café called The Fat Tummy.

The Fat Tummy

'I love it!' said Mum.

Peter looked a bit doubtful.

'Isn't it posh enough for you, Mr Head Teacher Ingham? OK, it's a bit of a greasy spoon, but they generally have the best grub,' said Mum.

'It's just the name is a bit un-PC,' he muttered. 'We're not supposed to call people fat nowadays.'

'Tell that to Flo!' said Mum. 'She's got a *huge* fat tummy and she's very proud of it – though I hope she doesn't put on any more weight because it's a bit of a struggle heaving her in and out of bed!'

'You look after her then?' said Peter, surprised.

'Well, she's not really up to doing it herself any more. It's part of our deal. I don't mind – Flo's a laugh, isn't she, Jess?'

We went into the café and sat down at a red Formica table. Mum and Peter ordered coffee and I had a banana milkshake. I couldn't help staring longingly at the home-made cakes on the counter, even though I'd only recently had breakfast.

'OK, just one,' said Mum.

'Could I have the cupcake with the pink cream?' I begged.

'Of course you can,' she said. Peter didn't say a word but Mum sighed. 'It's just one little treat. Jess usually has a very healthy diet. Lots of fruit, veggies, salad, salmon, all the stuff that's good for her. Look at her lovely white teeth and clear skin!'

'I think she's inherited them from you, Tracy – though *your* diet used to be burgers and chips and ice cream and sweets all day, every day,' said Peter. 'I bet you didn't even go through a spotty stage when you were a teenager. I ate properly, but I had awful spots that made me desperately self-conscious. That's probably why I just stayed in night after night and studied.'

'Still, look where you are now,' said Mum, suddenly serious. 'You're a great example for all care leavers. You ought to go and give talks in children's homes and show them what they can achieve.'

'I do, actually,' said Peter. 'I mean, I don't go on about myself – who on earth would want to be a boring old teacher like me? – but I try to show that even though you've been in care you're just as good as anyone else – better, in fact, because you've had so much life experience and developed a bit of resilience. I've tried to show that working hard and passing exams might seem totally uncool – but it's the way to get on and achieve something.'

'Wow!' said Mum. 'Sounds as if you're on a mission. I can't imagine you standing up and lecturing. Don't all the little Tracy Beakers take the mick and give you hell?'

'Sometimes,' Peter replied. 'But I'm learning to deal with them. I'm not so concerned about the feisty ones: they'll get by one way or another. It's the sad little kids who don't join in – the little Peter Inghams – that I want to reach.'

'Have you got any kids of your own, Pete?' Mum asked.

He shook his head.

'You should have. You'd make a lovely dad.'

'Well, you obviously make a lovely mum,' Peter told Mum.

'Do you really think I am?' she asked. 'Thanks for saying that, Pete. It means a lot. You're kind of like a little brother to me. Let's keep in touch.'

'Yes, let's,' he said.

He insisted on paying the bill, and then he started walking back to the library and we headed for home.

'Dear old Pete,' Mum said. 'Did he seem a bit lonely to you, Jess? I wonder if he's got a partner? I should have asked him.'

'Mum! You can't go round asking that,' I said. 'You kept embarrassing him enough as it was.'

'I just teased him a bit, that's all. It's the way we always related to each other. He *likes* it,' said Mum. 'Hey, tell you what we *should* have asked him. Stuff about the primary schools in the area. Perhaps we should go back and winkle him out of the library and see if he can help us get you in somewhere really good.'

So we turned round and hurried after him. He was way ahead by this time, almost at the library entrance. There was someone else following him too, a good-looking young guy in tight white jeans. He was calling out him. Peter turned and saw him, and then they had a big hug.

'Oh!' said Mum. 'Oh, I see. Maybe Peter's not so lonely after all! Oh well. We'd better not go interrupting him now. Come on.' She sounded funny. Sort of disappointed.

'Are you OK, Mum?' I asked as we sloped back down the street.

'Of course I am.'

'You didn't hope that you and Peter . . . ?'

'No! I *said*, he's like my little brother. Well, more like a big brother now, I suppose, as he's grown so much taller than me.' Mum sighed.

'Why are you sighing? Do *you* feel lonely now?' I asked anxiously.

'Of course I don't. I've got you, haven't I?'

'I think you might find you've got someone else quite soon,' I said.

'What do you mean?'

'I just have a feeling that there's someone who secretly fancies you who might make a move any day.'

'What are you on about? You sound like a silly old fortune teller. Shall I set you up with a kiosk at the end of the pier? *Roll up, roll up, come and have your fortune told by little gypsy Jess.*'

'You can mock, Mum. But you just mark my words,' I said.

I very much hoped that Bill wouldn't let me down. It still seemed a long time till Sunday's boot fair. I wished I knew where Bill lived. Then I could pop round and give him a few handy tips on how to make a good impression on Mum.

I tried to imagine what life would be like if Bill became part of our family. Lots of excellent bacon rolls, obviously. And funny jokes. And . . . ? I didn't really know him well enough. I thought he'd be quite 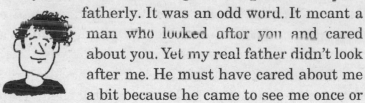 fatherly. It was an odd word. It meant a man who looked after you and cared about you. Yet my real father didn't look after me. He must have cared about me a bit because he came to see me once or twice when we lived on the Duke Estate, but we didn't really know what to say to each other.

Mum had messaged him to say we'd moved so that he'd know where I was – he was welcome to come and see me any time. He sent back a brief reply:

Cheers!

'What's *that* supposed to mean?' she said.

It was pretty obvious what it meant. He didn't really care about me any more. He hadn't come.

I'd actually gone and had a little private cry upstairs with Alfie, though I didn't know why I was so upset – I didn't really *want* him to come. Then Mum came up to find me and gave me a cuddle and said she understood.

'My own dad never, ever came to see me,' she'd said.

So maybe she'd like a fatherly man for a boyfriend. Though none of her previous boyfriends had been remotely fatherly. Especially not Sean Godfrey. Yet he was sort of fatherly towards Tyrone. It was so annoying. People in books were mostly good or bad, but in real life even the worst baddies had a good side, and sometimes the good people could be a little bad.

When Mum and I got back from the library, I discovered that Alfie had been a little bad. He'd sneaked off with an old teddy that had fallen on the floor and played wrestling games with it. One of the teddy's ears and both its legs had fallen off in the process.

'Bad boy, Alfie!' Mum said.

'He didn't mean to be bad, Mum. He was just playing,' I told her. 'He simply got a bit bored.'

'Yes, and I'm a bit bored too, trying to read this dull old book,' she said, turning the page of one of her big library books. 'But I'm not biting the spine and ripping out all the pages, am I?'

I didn't think her resolve to study antiques would last very long. I decided to take Alfie for a run on the beach so he'd calm down a bit. Dogs weren't allowed on the main beach now that it was the summer holidays, but we could go on the rocky part right at the end. I let Alfie off the lead and he ran happily up and down, sometimes dashing right into the waves and then rushing back, woofing joyfully.

There were lots of families with dogs. Lots of fathers throwing sticks and playing ball and taking their little kids paddling. I stared at them, trying to work out which one I'd like for my dad, rating them out of ten. There was one big guy built a bit like Sean Godfrey, playing French cricket with two little boys. They obviously just wanted to mess around but he kept yelling at them to watch the ball and hit it properly. He only got two out of ten.

There was only one other person without a family:

a boy sitting on the pebbles, staring out to sea. He was wearing a baseball cap. *That* boy. The one who'd snatched my ice cream. He was eating an ice cream now. It was covered with rainbow sprinkles, my favourite. Perhaps he'd snatched it from someone else. I kept seeing him everywhere!

A seagull circled over his head. It would serve him right if the bird pooped all over his ice cream. I wished I could turn myself into Gull Girl and teach him a lesson. I wasn't the old timid Jess Beaker from the Duke Estate who let Tyrone and his gang walk all over her. I was the new bold Beaker girl who went out for walks by herself and sorted out her own problems.

I suddenly dashed forward, snatched the ice cream right out of the boy's hand and then charged off with it!

'**H**EY!' the boy yelled. He leaped to his feet to chase after me.

I didn't have time to take a single lick. I ran like mad, Alfie at my heels, barking joyously because he thought it was a game. The boy followed, pebbles crunching. It sounded as if he was getting nearer. He looked much older than me. He could flatten me with one blow! I whipped my head round. He was almost upon me! And he wasn't alone. The big French cricket guy was running after me too, red in the face with fury.

'You cheeky little madam! You might only be knee-high to a grasshopper, but you can't go round nicking other kids' ice creams like that!' he shouted.

He was charging along like a bulldozer, ready to send me flying.

I swerved desperately, and the ice cream wobbled and landed splat on the pebbles, leaving me clutching an empty cone. I threw it down and rushed on, but the angry man was gaining on me.

'You're a wretched litter lout into the bargain!' He lunged forward and caught hold of my wrist. 'Got you! What are you playing at, you naughty little girl? Where are your parents? Take me to them at once!' He gave me a little shake.

The whole beach seemed to be watching. I blushed so deeply that my glasses steamed up. It was so dreadful. And Alfie was making it worse because he thought I was being attacked. His hackles rose, and he started barking furiously at the man, looking all set to bite him.

'Down! Down, I say!' the guy screamed, gesturing with his free arm while hanging onto me with the other. 'Get *down*!'

Alfie chose not to understand. He jumped *up*, baring his teeth.

'No, Alfie!' I screamed. The hateful man might whack him – and if Alfie bit him, he'd probably frogmarch us both to the police station. I didn't think taking an ice cream was a criminal offence, but I knew the police had the power to take your dog away if he bit anyone.

'Hey, Alfie! Here, boy! Down now!' The boy in the baseball cap came running up too. He'd picked up the empty ice-cream cone. 'Look, yum yum!'

Alfie was allowed his own cone only once in a while. It was one of his favourite treats. He didn't leave my side but he wavered, thinking about it. The boy grabbed his collar, taking the lead from me and snapping it on.

'There! He's calming down now,' he told the man. 'Don't be hard on her. She's my friend. She was only messing about.'

'What? You stupid kids! Just learn to play nicely. What sort of an example are you to the others? Now push off!' the guy shouted.

So we walked away, the boy, Alfie and me, past all the staring faces. I glanced across anxiously.

Maybe the boy would turn on me when we were out of sight? Why had I tried to get my own back? I pulled Alfie's lead, ready to run all the way home with him.

'Keep on walking for a bit. He's still watching us,' the boy muttered out of the side of his mouth. It was as if he was playing a gangster in an old movie.

'You're not going to beat me up, are you?' I asked.

'Yeah, I'm gonna bash your brains out,' he said – but I could tell he was joking.

We kept on walking, and I said meekly, 'Thanks for rescuing me anyway.'

'Big interfering bully!' he said.

'My mum used to have a boyfriend a bit like that,' I said, which wasn't completely true.

'So did mine! Well, you know what it's like then.'

'Yeah,' I said, trying to sound tough too. I paused. 'Sorry I snatched your ice cream.'

'Well, I snatched yours. Though you did have three!'

'They weren't all for me. One was for my mum and the other was for Flo, our friend,' I said. 'The one with rainbow sprinkles was going to be for me.'

'The rainbow sprinkle ones are the best.'

'Yeah,' I said. Then I got scared the boy would think I was taking the mick.

Alfie stopped at a bench to have a sniff. I was worried he might decide to do a poo, which would be so embarrassing with the boy watching. Alfie had already been this morning, but excitement sometimes affected his tummy. He seemed calmer now, trotting along on his lead, glancing at the boy every now and then just like me.

'Great dog you've got,' said the boy. 'I like his name. It suits him. Hey, Alfie! Alfie boy! Good dog!'

Alfie nudged nearer, wanting to be petted. It was clear he'd taken a fancy to him. The boy squatted down and made a fuss of him, gently scratching his back, while Alfie nuzzled into his jeans. I couldn't help noticing they were in need of a wash. And his baggy sweatshirt. *He must be boiling*, I thought. I wondered why he didn't simply take it off and tie it round his waist.

'I've always wanted a dog,' he said.

'I always wanted one too. We weren't allowed one in the flat where we used to live,' I said.

'It's the perfect place for a dog. Perfect place for people too. It's my favourite place in all the world.'

'It's my favourite place too!' I agreed.

It was weird finding I had so much in common with this scary boy – though he didn't seem scary any more. We probably couldn't be seen by the fierce dad now, unless he had telescope eyes, but we kept on walking together.

'I'd buy you another ice cream only I don't have any money on me,' I said, digging into my jeans pockets just in case I found some change.

'It's OK. I'd buy you one, but I'm a bit skint too,' the boy said. 'Like, permanently.'

I looked at him carefully. He was still quite bulky but his cheekbones looked sharper. I remembered Mum's comments about the way he'd got the fish and chips out of the rubbish bin.

'You're not starving, are you?' I asked timidly.

'Don't be daft,' he said, but I noticed he kept an eye out each time we passed a bin. Someone had dumped a big cardboard doughnut box in one, and he yanked it out and peered inside. There was just one half-eaten doughnut left.

'Here. You can have it,' he said, offering it to me. 'Go on, I don't want it.'

I loved that kind of doughnut, though I wasn't allowed to have them too often – Mum said they were too sugary. It would be a treat, but I didn't fancy eating someone else's nibbled leftovers.

'No thanks. I don't really like doughnuts,' I fibbed.

'Suit yourself,' said the boy, and gobbled it down in a flash. He really did seem hungry.

I started to wonder where we were walking to. I didn't want to go up on the cliffs in case he started messing about like Tyrone. I'd had enough danger for one day. I pulled Alfie in the direction of Seacliff Fields.

'I saw you at the boot fair,' I said to the boy when we got there.

'It's a good place for picking up a bit of cash,' he said. 'People are always wanting a hand with things.'

'I suppose so,' I said. 'Sometimes I give my mum and Flo a hand but they don't pay me. Still, I'm family.'

'Yeah,' he said, a little bleakly.

The fields weren't as busy as the beach, so I let Alfie off his lead again. He ran around like crazy, and then spotted a small spaniel with a sparkly collar delicately picking her way through the grass. He circled her excitedly, had a polite sniff, and then ran off, looking over his shoulder. She stared at him and then took two tentative steps forward. Alfie tried

135

again, dashing towards her this time. She joined in, getting the idea, and then they both rushed around, playing chase.

The boy and I laughed at them.

'You ever seen that old cartoon film *Lady and the Tramp*?' he asked. 'I used to watch it when . . . when I was little.'

'Yes, they're just like those dogs. I love that scene where they're eating opposite ends of a really long piece of spaghetti and end up nearly kissing!' I said.

'I love that bit too. It always made me laugh and laugh.' The boy sighed, a ghost of a smile on his shadowy face. It didn't look like he did much laughing nowadays.

Alfie and his Lady were circling an abandoned picnic now. There were crumpled bags and drink cans all over the place.

'That man on the beach would go nuts at these litter louts,' I said.

Alfie started sniffing the bags.

'No, Alfie!' I said, running over, scared he might eat something that was bad for him.

The boy came too, and squatted down, delving in and out of each bag. He found a sandwich already curling at the edges, a half-full packet of crisps and a can of Coke. He offered Alfie a crust.

'Don't give him any more. He's not supposed to have snacks between meals,' I said. 'And I'm not either.'

So the boy sat down and ate, drinking the Coke in two great gulps. I sat down beside him while Alfie played with Lady.

The boy burped. 'Sorry!' he said awkwardly.

'You don't get enough to eat or drink, do you?' I said.

He shrugged. 'I do all right. And I'm fat, aren't I? Do me good to lose a bit of weight.'

'You're not supposed to say f-a-t any more. Hey, there's a café up near the library called The Fat Tummy. It's nice there.' I hesitated. 'Maybe another day, when I've got some cash, I could take you there.'

It was hard to see the boy's face because of the long peak of his baseball cap, but he grunted in a pleased sort of way. He lay back on the grass, stretching out. 'Let's do a bit of sunbathing, eh?'

'OK.' I know I should have gone back home a while ago. Mum and Flo would be wondering where I'd got to. They were probably starting to get worried. But I didn't want to leave the boy just yet. He seemed so lonely.

I lay back too. The boy was very quiet. Perhaps he'd fallen asleep. Then I heard a little bark as Alfie leaped on the boy's tummy, startling him.

'Hey! What you playing at, Alfie?' he said, tickling him. 'Want a wrestle, eh?'

He rolled onto his side, and Alfie's paw caught his cap. It fell off – and a long fair ponytail emerged from underneath.

'Oh, you've got long hair!' I said. 'Oh wow, you lucky thing! I've always wanted hair like yours. You look so different! Almost like . . .' And then I realized. 'You're a girl!'

'No I'm not. Boys can have long hair,' she said, sticking her baseball cap back on, making sure her hair was out of sight again.

I looked at her carefully. I realized that, under that baggy T-shirt, she had a proper chest. I looked at her hands and saw streaks of old varnish on her nails.

'You *are* a girl!' I said.

'I'm *not*,' she said furiously. 'I'm a boy.'

'No you're not.'

'OK, OK, I'm a girl, but I'm in disguise, see? You won't tell anyone, will you?'

'No, I promise. But why are you in disguise?' I asked.

'Because I'm on the run,' she said, talking out of the side of her mouth again.

'You're making that up!'

'No, I am. Really. I'm Jordan Whitely.'

I must have looked blank.

'Haven't you heard about me? I must have been on the telly by now. And I expect there are posters up all over the place,' she said proudly.

'Why? What have you *done*?' I asked, wondering if she really *was* a gangster.

'I'm a runaway,' she said.

'You've run away from home?'

'Haven't got a home. My mum couldn't manage and then she got ill. I've been in and out of care, see. Residential. And I've been fostered heaps of times. You've no idea what it's like.'

'Yes I have!' I said. 'My mum was in a home she called the Dumping Ground. And she was fostered. Twice, maybe more.'

'Really?' said Jordan. 'I bet she didn't have such mean, strict foster parents as me.'

'Well, she ended up with Cam, and she's the loveliest person in the whole world,' I admitted.

'And she kept her? Her placement didn't break down?'

'She's family!' I said. 'More like a mum to my mum than her real mum. Hey, that sounds weird, doesn't it, but you know what I mean.'

'Anyway, *my* foster families have all been rubbish. I thought this last lot were OK at first, but they turned out to be even worse than the others. They kicked up a stink if I stayed out late, and they didn't like it when I hung out with the lads — they said I couldn't see them, but they were my *friends*. And then, at school, I lost it: a teacher was winding me up, telling me I'd never amount to anything, so I  punched her,' said Jordan, jabbing her fist in the air.

'You punched your teacher!' I gasped. I knew Mum had been pretty bad at times, and she had often  come to blows with her deadly enemy, Justine Littlewood, but she'd never, ever hit a teacher, not even Mrs Vomit Bagley, who she really hated. I loved hearing Mum's stories about when she was a little girl — but at least they had a happy ending.

'So they excluded me from school without even listening to my side, and my foster mum burst into tears and my foster dad told me off, and they wouldn't hear my side either. So I acted up a bit and they said they couldn't cope. They called my social worker and told these downright lies, saying it was clear I wasn't happy with them — when *they* were the ones who weren't happy with *me*.'

'So has someone else fostered you now?' I asked.

'Nope. That's the whole point. No one wants me now, even though they'd get more cash because I'm "hard to place". My old children's home has closed down, so now they want to send me all the way up to Manchester where I don't know anyone. And I'm not having it. So I walked out. And I didn't go back.'

'You walked out just like that?'

'Yeah – I was so stupid, really, because I didn't grab any of my stuff, not even my phone, and I was wearing my oldest clothes because I was just mooching around the house, and I didn't take any cash. I wish I'd snatched my foster mum's purse – that would have paid her back for not wanting me,' said Jordan.

She was trying to sound big and tough, but her voice had gone wobbly and I could see she had tears in her eyes. I wondered about putting my arm round her but I thought she'd probably just push me away. Alfie sensed her sadness and trotted up. He nudged his head against her and licked her hand lavishly.

'Soppy dog,' said Jordan, but she cuddled him close and hung onto him. 'I wish I had a dog. It would make everything more fun, and he could keep me warm at night.'

'Where do you sleep?' I asked. 'Do you just curl up on the beach somewhere? What if it rains?'

'Oh, I've got that sorted,' she said. 'I've got this little house, see. All mod cons. Well, nearly. I'm OK at night.'

I stared at her, trying to make sense of what she was saying. Then I realized. 'You hide in one of the beach huts!'

'You got it!'

'But they're all locked up at night.'

'Yeah, but one of the locks is broken. Well, I saw it was coming loose so I bashed it about a bit. It doesn't seem to belong to anyone. There's nothing much inside, just an old rug and a cup and a kettle. I hoped the kettle would work but it doesn't. Still, I don't really need one. I just hole up there and I'm fine,' she said, sticking her chin in the air.

'*I* wanted to live in a beach hut when my mum and I first came here. There's a toilet nearby, isn't there, and a tap with running water. I had it all sussed out. But now we live with Flo and we're fine there,' I said. 'So, did you come camping near here from one of the homes?'

'Yes! What are you, a mind reader or something? How did you know that?'

'When my mum was in care, *she* was brought here. Actually, she'll be going berserk now, wondering where I am. Look, Jordan, come back with me. Mum will understand. She'll give you a big meal and let you have a bath if you want one,' I said.

'Oh yeah,' said Jordan. 'And then she'll turn me over to the cops and the care workers.'

'No she won't. She'll try and fix things for you.'

'Yeah, well, people have been fixing things for me ever since I was three. And each time they fix things it's worse than it was before. I don't want anyone fixing things ever again. *I'm* the fixer now.'

'Yes, but you can't stay on the run for ever,' I said.

'Who says? I've managed fine so far. No one's sussed me out,' said Jordan.

'Well, they will if you go around snatching ice creams off kids,' I said. 'And it's summer now. What are you going to do in the winter? You haven't even got a coat.'

'That's easy-peasy. There's heaps of coats at the boot fair. You can get one of them quilted ones with a furry hood for a fiver if you search around. All I have to do is mind someone's stall for an hour or so, or haul stuff in and out of vans and lorries. I earn enough for a coat *and* heaps of bacon sandwiches,' she said.

'Our friend Bill has the bacon-roll van. He's ever so kind. He'd probably let you have a bacon roll for nothing if I explained,' I said.

'Nah, too risky. I don't want any adults knowing about me. No one else. Except you. You're all right. So, what's your name, kid?'

'Jess Beaker.'

'Well, Jess Beaker, swear you won't tell no one about me,' she said, her face so close to mine the peak of her cap was nudging my forehead.

'Not even my mum?'

'Especially not your mum. No one!' She looked really threatening.

'OK, OK, don't get in such a state. I won't tell, I promise,' I said.

'Swear on your mum's life!'

I swallowed. This was getting really scary. 'I swear,' I said, adding inside my head, *But not on Mum's life.*

'Say the whole thing. *I swear on my mum's life not to tell anyone about Jordan.* Go on, repeat it.'

'I don't want to,' I said, trying not to cry.

'Oh don't! I didn't mean to make you cry, kid! Oh please, I want us to be friends. You just have to swear, that's all. To prove you won't tell. To prove we're mates.' Jordan was nearly crying too.

I couldn't bear it. 'OK, I swear on my mum's life I won't tell about you,' I gabbled, hoping it wouldn't really count if I said it quickly enough.

She breathed a great sigh of relief. 'That means we're really mates now! You're a great little kid,' she said, grinning at me.

144

'Thanks,' I said. 'But I really do have to go home now or my mum will come looking for me. I'll come and wait near the ice-cream van tomorrow morning around the same time and I'll bring some cash. OK?'

'Yeah, that'll be great.' Jordan held out her hand, her little finger out. *'Make friends, make friends, never never break friends,'* she said, hooking her finger round mine.

I was surprised, because it was the sort of thing we used to do in the Infants. Still, I said it too – and then I ran off with Alfie.

When Mum and Flo had finished giving me a telling off for worrying them I went on Mum's iPad, pretending I wanted to look up the name of some seabird I'd spotted on the beach.

I looked up the name Jordan Whitely instead. There was nothing about a missing girl who had run away. Poor Jordan. It was such a big deal for her – but no one else seemed to care.

I HAD £3.50 in cash. I had taken a fancy to an old piggy bank in the shop so Flo had given it to me. Whenever someone paid for a little trinket in cash Flo gave me any fifty pences to put in my pig. It rattled in a very satisfactory manner, and I liked hoarding my coins and thinking of the books I'd buy when the pig was full to bursting – but they were needed now.

I couldn't bear the idea of smashing the pig, so I had to hide upstairs in the bedroom and prise the stopper out of his tummy. The poor pig didn't make a sound now when I shook him, but it couldn't be helped.

Now I had to think about food. I'd managed to save a whole slice of fruit cake at teatime, and I snaffled two digestive biscuits when I went to make a cup of tea for Mum and Flo. While I was in the kitchen I cut a big wodge of cheese too, wrapping everything in kitchen foil. Then, in the morning, I slipped half a toasted marmalade sandwich up my T-shirt (marmalade sides together obviously so it didn't make too much of a mess) and asked if I could take an apple from the bowl.

I packed all the provisions in an old canvas bag.

'What do you want with that old thing?' Mum asked, looking up from one of her books on antiques as I headed out. She read all the time in between customers now, sometimes even making notes.

'I thought I might go for a little paddle while I'm walking Alfie so I've packed a towel,' I said, quick as a flash. It was disconcerting to discover I was such a good liar. Mum didn't seem remotely suspicious and just went back to her book.

I put Alfie on his lead and set off for the beach. I hung about beside the ice-cream van. I stood there jingling the fifty pences in my pocket, watching a queue of kids being handed their ice creams. It was very tempting. I wondered whether Jordan would decide to blow all her cash on a giant cone with two flakes. I hoped she'd give me a few licks.

She was a long time coming. She was five minutes late, then ten. I took Alfie for a run along the esplanade, twisting round every so often to keep an eye on the people by the ice-cream van. There was no sign of her. Perhaps she wasn't going to come after all.

I felt indignant when I'd gone to so much trouble to find everything for her. She was supposed to be my friend now! I'd even sworn on Mum's life not to tell on her. I did a little dance up and down the paving stones to distract myself, careful not to tread on any of the cracks.

Then I started to worry. Perhaps something had happened to her. Maybe she'd got locked in the beach hut. Or perhaps someone had spotted her and carted her off to the police. She might assume I'd told on her, which was an awful thought.

'What's happened to her, Alfie, eh?' I asked, giving him a pat.

Alfie gave a sudden bark. I looked round and

there she was, hurrying along, baseball cap pulled down. 'Jordan!' I called, without thinking.

'Shut up,' she said hurriedly, looking round to see if anyone was listening.

'Sorry! But I was getting worried. You're so late!'

'I don't have a watch or a phone, do I? When I woke up I came along to the ice-cream van, thinking it might be round about the right time, and the van wasn't even open and there were hardly any people on the beach and it turned out it was only half past seven. So then I went back and had another kip and I've only just woken up.' She rubbed sleep out of her eyes and grinned at me apologetically. 'Sorry! It's great you came though. Have you got anything to eat? I'm starving.'

'Come to the end of the beach where it's quieter. I've got a huge picnic in my bag. And there's cash too, if you want an ice cream. There's actually all my savings – three pounds fifty – so you could have a ginormous one.'

'I shouldn't spend it all on ice cream,' said Jordan, but she looked tempted. 'What's the smallest size cost?'

'One pound fifty,' I said.

'Will you get one then? I'm scared the man will recognize me.'

It turned out the ice cream didn't cost anything at

all. When the ice-cream man saw me he gave me a grin and said, 'Hello, it's little rainbow sprinkles! Come for your specials, sweetheart?'

'No, I'm just buying one small ice cream with my piggy-bank money,' I said.

'Well, in that case have this one on me, and pop your pennies back in your piggy bank,' he said. He even gave me rainbow sprinkles on top.

'Here you are,' I said nobly to Jordan, handing it over, though my mouth had started watering.

She took one big lick and then offered it to me. 'We'll share it,' she said.

She didn't share it accurately – she took very big licks, slightly more often than me – but I was pleased all the same. I don't think Mum was ever very good at sharing. She hated sharing her birthday cake with Peter Ingham. Why did he have to like guys? He might have been a good boyfriend, though he didn't really seem Mum's type. She liked men with a bit of spark. I wasn't sure, but I thought Bill was quite sparky.

'Have you ever had a boyfriend, Jordan?' I asked.

'Heaps,' she said, breaking off the bottom of the wafer and then digging it into the ice cream. 'Look, I've made a baby cone!'

It was always very irritating
when people did that because
then the ice cream started
melting through the hole
and dripping up your sleeve,
though if you didn't often have
ice creams you mightn't realize.

'I've got a sort of boyfriend,' I said, determined not
to be outdone. 'His name's Tyrone. He's good at football.'

'So's Ryan. He can bore for England about it,' said
Jordan, licking her wrist. I knew that would happen.

'So he's your boyfriend now?'

'No, I've broken up with him. When I ran away I
went round his place first. I hoped he'd do a runner
with me. I wanted it to be romantic – the two of us
against the world. But he wouldn't come. Chicken!'
she said, flapping her arms around. She flapped
a little too violently and ice cream flew into the air.
'Oh rats,' she said. 'Still, we'd nearly finished it,
hadn't we?'

'And I've got heaps of food in my bag if you're still
hungry.'

We squatted down behind a wooden groyne and I
tipped everything out of my bag. The food was a bit
squashed but still edible, and Jordan seemed delighted.

'Oh wow! You're a star, Jess! You nicked all this
for me?' she exclaimed.

'Well, I didn't really nick it – it came from home so it's kind of mine,' I said.

'Did you ask your mum for it then?' Jordan demanded. 'You told her, didn't you?'

'No, of course not! I swore I wouldn't, you know I did. I just took it when she wasn't watching,' I said. 'I snaffled the toast and marmalade right in front of her, but I was quick about it.'

'I'll bet you were,' said Jordan, looking at me appraisingly. 'You ever nicked stuff from shops?'

My heart started thumping. 'No!'

'Don't look so worried. It's easy-peasy. Everyone does it. The big shops put their prices up because they *expect* people to shoplift. Anyway, how else am I going to get all the stuff I need? I haven't got a mum around to give it to me, have I?'

'It might not be so wrong for *you* to do it – but it would be for me,' I said.

'Yeah, but they keep an eye on me because I'm big and I look streetwise. You're little and cute with your curls and your specs. They'd never, ever expect a kid like you to nick stuff,' said Jordan.

'Well, I'm not going to anyway,' I said.

'Because you're chicken.'

'No, because I don't want to.'

Jordan did the silly arm-flapping thing again.

'Stop it!'

152

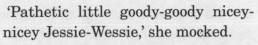

'Pathetic little goody-goody nicey-nicey Jessie-Wessie,' she mocked.

'You can just shut up. I thought we were supposed to be friends! Stop being so mean to me after I brought you all that food! And the three pounds fifty! That was all my savings!' I said indignantly.

'Like three pounds fifty is going to buy me clothes and everything else I need!' said Jordan.

'Well, as if I care,' I said, scrambling to my feet and whistling to Alfie. 'You can push off and do your own shoplifting. I'm sick of you. I'm going home.'

I ran off. I thought she might come after me and apologize, but she didn't. Alfie ran with me, but he wasn't sure he wanted to. He kept stopping and looking back, wondering why Jordan wasn't with us.

'She's a horrid girl. We don't like her any more,' I told him. 'Catch me being her friend now.'

When I got home Mum was in a terrible tizz, marching about the shop. She was supposed to be dusting but she picked up the ornaments and set them down with such fury it was a wonder they didn't shatter at her touch. There were two old ladies in the toy corner having a long, loud conversation about kids today – it was a wonder Mum didn't heave each

153

one up and dust their grey hair and set them back down on their Dr Scholl sandals.

'What's up, Mum?' I asked when they eventually tottered out of the shop, not buying anything. I was worried that she was mad at *me* because I'd been gone so long.

'That wretched Mary,' said Mum through gritted teeth. She picked up a wooden Pinocchio doll and tapped it hard on its long nose. 'She's got a long nose too and I'm sick of her poking it into our affairs. Why can't she mind her own business?'

'Why? What's she done?' I asked, sitting on the sofa beside Flo. She'd started a knitting fad and was busily plaining and purling some odd mustard-yellow garment, needles clicking so busily that I practically bounced up and down. I very much hoped that the jumper or cardie or cape or tunic wasn't for me.

'She's just sent your mum a long email with reports on the three local primary schools, and their SATs results – whatever they are – and the pros and cons of each one, and the names of the head teachers, and probably a detailed account of what they like for breakfast and what they watch on telly,' said Flo, chuckling. 'I dare say it's very helpful of her, but I'm with your mum on this one. None of her business!'

'It's like she doesn't trust me to find a school for my own daughter,' said Mum. 'I wrote an email back right away, telling her as much!'

'Oh, Mum!' I said. 'You weren't rude, were you?'

'Of course not. I was ultra-diplomatic. I was short and to the point, but perfectly polite.'

'You didn't tell her to bog off, did you?' I asked, horrified.

'No! I just said it was nice of her to go to all that trouble, but actually we'd already got you enrolled at a lovely school, thanks very much,' said Mum.

I blinked at her. 'Have we?'

'No, but we'll do it today. We'll have a look round all the schools, and then tell the council which one we want. You'll mind the shop for us, won't you, Flo?'

'Course I will, darling. And I'd better have Alfie too. You can't go barging into schools with him in tow, it'll be too distracting,' she said.

Mum looked me up and down, and then brushed my hair vigorously and made me change my T-shirt and even started cutting my nails.

'Ouch!' I protested. 'Let *me* do it, Mum. I'm not a baby!'

'I'm not having you wandering round like a little scruff. I want you to look immaculate, OK?' She glanced in an old looking glass in the shop. 'Oh help, *I'm* the total scruff. Hang on a minute!'

She charged upstairs. We could hear her rushing around, and the sudden *clonk clonk* on the floor as she discarded her shoes and selected different ones.

'I think we've got time for a cup of tea while she's getting ready,' said Flo. 'Pop the kettle on, Jess, there's a dear.'

We'd drunk our tea by the time Mum came clattering downstairs in her high heels, wearing her best dress, face fully made up, hair in a top knot.

'Right,' she said, chin in the air. 'Off we go.'

She'd printed off Mary's long email. 'I'm only looking at it to get the addresses,' she said. 'I don't care what she's written about them. How does she know what's best for you anyway? You're *my* daughter.'

'But Mary is a teacher, Mum,' I muttered. 'And she taught me. So she does know a bit. Quite a lot in fact.'

I didn't actually say that out loud, not with Mum in this kind of mood. I knew *she* knew that Mary was just trying to be helpful. But Mum's always had a problem with teachers. And now that Mary was Cam's special friend the problem had grown.

I sighed heavily.

'What's the matter?' said Mum. 'Don't worry, Jess. I'll find you a good school, I promise.'

'I know, Mum. I just miss Cam,' I said.

'I miss her too,' she said.

I tucked my arm in hers and we walked to the school nearest our shop.

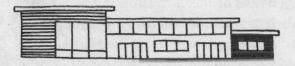

It was a big modern building with a fence painted different colours to make it look child-friendly. There was a big notice in the playground.

LOCKWOOD SCHOOL

Head Teacher Mrs L. Brookes

Lockwood rated OUTSTANDING
IN ALL ASPECTS in
OFSTED report

'Okaaay!' said Mum. The gate was locked, but there was a bell and an intercom on the wall.

She pressed the bell. She pressed it again. And a third time.

'Mum!' I protested.

'Well, they need waking up, dozy lot!'

At last a voice spoke out of the wall. 'I'm afraid Lockwood School is closed for the summer holidays.'

'We know that,' said Mum, raising her eyebrows at me. 'I'm thinking of enrolling my daughter Jess at your school. I'd like to come in and meet the head teacher, please.'

'Oh, you can't possibly do that,' said the voice. 'Mrs Brookes isn't here. Like I said, the school is closed.'

'Well, can you let us in and show us around then?' Mum asked.

'I'm just admin. I'm not authorized. You'll have to come back at the start of term if you want to see Mrs Brookes, but you'll be wasting your time. We're completely full up, with a long waiting list.'

'But Lockwood's our nearest school. We must be in your catchment area,' said Mum.

'That can't be helped, not if we haven't got any places – not unless there are exceptional circumstances.'

'Like what?' Mum asked, quick as a flash.

'If your daughter had serious health issues and couldn't travel very far, for example.'

Mum looked me up and down and had to admit that wasn't the case.

'Or if she'd been seriously bullied at her former school,' the voice continued.

'Yes! She was knocked over by this great big lout!' Mum declared eagerly, choosing to ignore the fact that the great big lout was Tyrone and we were friends now.

'Well, we would need detailed reports from her old school and a letter to say the bullying had been detrimental to her mental or physical health.'

'Oh,' said Mum, deflating. 'She's a very brave, resilient little girl and didn't like to make a fuss. So are there any other circumstances?'

'Only if she's in care, and that's clearly not the case,' the voice pronounced.

'But *I* was in care all my childhood. Won't that count?' said Mum, semi-seriously.

'Of course not. I'm sorry, I have a lot of work to do. I'm afraid I can't carry on this conversation any longer.'

'Well, my daughter is excellent in all aspects, just like your wretched OFSTED report, so you're missing a trick by not letting her into your school,' said Mum. 'Still, your loss. Come on, Jess.' She glared at the wall as if the very bricks had been talking to her, and pulled me away.

'What will we do if all the schools are full up?' I asked.

'They won't be.' Mum tapped the address of the second school into her smartphone. 'Right – Primrose Juniors.'

'That's a nice name,' I said. I imagined a small school painted pale yellow, with a green lawn at the front speckled with primroses all year round.

The actual Primrose Juniors was nothing like that. It was on a big estate on the outskirts of Cooksea. It was even bigger and bleaker than Lockwood and had barbed wire along the top of the fence.

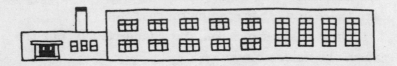

'Is that to keep the children in?' Mum asked. 'It's like a prison camp.' She rang the bell. She rang it lots of times. No one answered. 'Oh well, I wouldn't want you to go there anyway. Horrible-looking place. Don't worry, Jess. We'll try the next school – I bet it'll be third time lucky.'

St John's Church of England Primary seemed much more friendly. It was an old red-brick school with coloured flags over the gateway, left over from their summer fete.

'This looks better,' said Mum. She rang the bell.

Someone answered straight away. 'St John's. Can I help you?' said a cheery voice.

'Yes, I hope so!' said Mum. 'Can we come in and have a chat, please? I'd like to enrol my daughter at your school.'

'Well, our head isn't here but you can come in and I'll take down your details,' said the voice.

Mum gave me the thumbs-up sign. 'Yay!' she mouthed. 'Looks like they can take you, Jess!'

The gate opened and we headed towards the school entrance. A chubby lady came out to welcome us – but her face fell a mile when she saw me.

'Oh dear!' she said. 'I didn't realize your daughter was so big!'

We stared at her.

'What?' said Mum. 'Jess is very *small* for her age!'

'I assumed she was a toddler and you'd come to register her for the kindergarten class,' said the chubby lady. She patted my shoulder playfully.

161

'Unless you're a very, very advanced three-year-old I'm afraid we can't take you!' She laughed merrily.

Mum didn't smile. 'She's ten and we'd like her to start your Year Six in September. Please,' she said.

'I'm afraid that's not possible. We've only got one form per year and there are already thirty in our top class, which is stretching things.'

'Yes, but one little Jess isn't going to make a difference,' Mum argued. 'She's hardly going to take up much room, is she? She's very well behaved and was top of the class in her last school. She'd be a positive asset to Year Six.'

'I'm sure you're right, but I'm afraid rules are rules.'

'Well, could you at least put her on your waiting list?' Mum suggested.

'I could do that, but it would be a complete waste of time. Jess would be thirteen or fourteen by the time she got to the top of the list, and then she'd obviously be needing to attend secondary school,' she said.

'But this is such a mad system,' said Mum. 'Jess can't help being a newcomer. There must be *some* school that has a place for her. Surely it's a legal requirement?'

'Well, I imagine Faraday could take her on,' said the lady. I didn't like the way she said the word *Faraday*, wrinkling her nose.

'Faraday?' Mum glanced at Mary's email. It wasn't on the list.

'I'll give you the address if you like,' said Chubby Chops. I'd gone off her now. 'Though I have to warn you that it's currently in special measures, so it could be closed down soon. They've lost a lot of their pupils to Primrose.'

'How could it be worse than a place with barbed wire?' said Mum.

'It's not worse, exactly,' Chubby replied.

'So why exactly is it in special measures, whatever they are?'

'It's had a lot of staffing problems – and the building isn't really fit for purpose. And some of the children can be a bit wild. There's no parental support,' she confided.

'Maybe that's not the children's fault,' Mum said stiffly. 'Thank you. We'll go and give it a try.'

We set off again. Faraday was back on the other side of Cooksea, near the estate. It was going to be a very long walk.

'Oh God, I'm getting a blister! Why on earth didn't I wear my boots?' Mum moaned. 'What's up, Jess? Are your feet hurting too?'

I was trying to picture Faraday. I didn't like the sound of wild children. I imagined them big and tough, twice my size. They'd be fiercer than Tyrone. Fiercer than Jordan.

'Do we really have to go to this Faraday, Mum? Why do I have to go to school? Couldn't I just get books out of the library and read a lot?' I asked. 'Or maybe Mary could set me lessons. I'm sure she wouldn't mind.'

'Mary's not your teacher any more,' she said. 'And you have to go to school. It's the law.'

'No it's not,' I argued. 'You could home-school me.'

'For goodness' sake, you already know more than me, Miss Clever. I'm pig-ignorant precisely because I didn't settle down and work hard at school. I fell behind and didn't know what the teacher was on about – I had to play the class joker so I didn't look like an idiot. Only the joke was on me. Learn by my mistakes, kid,' said Mum. 'You don't want to end up stooo-pid like me.'

'You're the cleverest person I know,' I said.

Mum had switched to an American accent for comic effect, and it reminded me uncomfortably of Jordan.

'Mum, why did that lady back at Lockwood say they let children in care into their school?' I asked.

'I think it's some kind of rule. It's because you get moved around a lot when you're in care, especially nowadays.'

'Like all over the country, away from all your friends?'

'Yep, it happens a lot,' said Mum. 'I got off quite lightly compared to kids nowadays. Some move twenty or thirty times, even more. You know that! Look at Cam's girls.'

Cam's girls! I was so stupid. Surely Jordan could go there? Cam would look after her and sort her out. She never gave up on anyone. I didn't like Jordan much any more but I still felt sorry for her. I'd go back to the beach tomorrow morning and tell her all about Cam.

I gave a little skip. Mum laughed and skipped too, in spite of her blister.

'That's the ticket. No more long faces. I'm sure this Faraday place will turn out nicer than all the others, in spite of being in these silly special measures,' she said.

She actually turned out to be right too! Admittedly Faraday Primary looked pretty grotty. The school building was very old, with scaffolding at one end.

There were rude words and silly pictures spray-painted all along the walls. It didn't have a proper electronic gate, just an old wooden one that swung open easily.

Mum and I looked at each other, and then walked into the playground without bothering to ring any bell. Then we stopped. At the side of the building there was a man on his hands and knees in the earth, with a cluster of children around him. Some had trowels, some had trugs, and two boys were lugging a watering can. They were gardening!

'Fancy bothering with a gardener when the school is such a mess,' Mum murmured to me. Not quite quietly enough.

'We're gardening because it's more fun watching our tomatoes grow,' said the man. He looked up and smiled when he saw me. 'Want to join in? We're digging up potatoes today.'

I looked at Mum. She was screwing up her face. 'I think she'd better wait till after she's seen the head teacher. I don't want her to get all mucky or they'll think I'm a rubbish mum,' she explained.

'He won't think that at all, I promise you.' The man stood up and brushed himself down as best he could. His hands were filthy so he left dirty smudges on his checked shirt and jeans. He winced a bit as he straightened up, rubbing the small of his back.

'I'm going to need a very hot bath when I get home. I'm getting a bit long in the tooth for gardening. But I've got a few years before I retire from my main job. I'm Jeff Harper, head of Faraday Primary.' He offered his hand automatically and then laughed when he noticed it was crusted with earth. 'I'll let you off shaking it,' he said.

'I'm Tracy Beaker and this is my daughter, Jess,' said Mum. 'So are these all your children?'

'Heavens, no! They're my special gardening club,' he said.

'We're in charge of the gardening, aren't we, Mr Harper?' said a little boy proudly.

'You bet you are, Michael.'

'Haven't you broken up yet?' Mum asked.

'Yep, but the children come in whenever they can to keep the garden going,' said Mr Harper.

'And we get to eat the tomatoes!' said another boy.

'And we pick the flowers. I take them home to my mum,' said a girl.

'And then next week some of the new Year Sixes are coming to help me blast off the graffiti and we'll work on fixing the gate. Michael's dad is in the building trade, and when he's finished fitting a kitchen he's going to see if he and his mate can patch up the roof,' said Mr Harper. 'We're all working together to make Faraday a little palace, inside and out.'

'So how did it get so run down?' Mum asked.

'You ask some very direct questions, Tracy Beaker!' said Mr Harper. 'And rightly so. I expect you've been told that Faraday is in special measures. I've been called in to set it to rights. And I'm going to, I promise you.'

Mum grinned. 'I bet you are,' she said. 'I'm thinking of sending Jess here. I think she'd love all this gardening lark. But I want her to be taught proper lessons too so she gets to pass her exams. She's very bright.'

'Mum!' I said, going red.

'Well, you are. Top of the class at Duke Primary, but we've moved here now.'

'Don't worry, I want all the children here to have proper lessons too. I want them to be ace at English and maths, and little whizzes at IT and football, and great at painting and drama, and able to play an instrument, even if it's just a triangle, so we can have a proper school band. Do you fancy a go on the drums, Jess?'

'Yes please!' I said. 'Mum, can I come here?'

'If Mr Harper will have you,' said Mum. She was smiling at him. I suddenly wondered if Mr Harper was married. He was quite a bit older than Mum, but that didn't really matter, did it?

'Have you got any questions, Jess?' he asked.

Yes, I did! I thought quickly.

'Doesn't Mrs Harper mind you coming into school in the holidays?' I asked.

He laughed. 'She sometimes comes and helps too. And she gives me tips. She's a landscape gardener by profession.'

'Oh, that's lucky,' I said, but I couldn't help feeling disappointed.

Mum gave me a right telling off on the way home. 'You practically asked him outright if he was married! Honestly, Jess!'

'Well, I wanted to know. He'd have been a lovely boyfriend for you.'

'Will you *stop* this! I don't want

a boyfriend! Get the whole idea out of your head,' Mum insisted.

'OK,' I said. I shook my head as if I was getting water out of my ears. 'There! All gone.'

But I was fibbing.

STRAIGHT AFTER LUNCH I took Alfie for a walk because he'd been cooped up in the shop with Flo. I was starting to worry about Jordan now. I wanted to tell her about Cam. I looked for her by the ice-cream van. I walked along the promenade. I hung about the beach huts. I went to Seacliff Fields and wandered around – but there was no sign of her.

'Where's Jordan, Alfie? Let's find Jordan. You know her. The boy in the baseball cap. Be a tracker dog, Alfie!' I said into his silky ear.

He licked me happily, thinking I was simply paying him compliments. We did another circuit, but then I gave up and went home, feeling a bit anxious. I told myself firmly that Jordan had simply taken herself off for a walk somewhere. Perhaps she'd gone right up to the other end of the beach. There was another ice-cream van there. She was probably snatching some other kid's cone right this minute.

She wasn't a very nice girl at all. She didn't really want to be friends with me. She was just using me. But I'd stood up to her! I'd shown her I wasn't a pushover. I wasn't daft enough to go shoplifting with her. I knew it was wrong, no matter what she said. And I also knew Mum would die of shame if I got caught.

I'd make some proper friends when I started at Faraday Primary in September. The children had seemed quite friendly. One girl had even lent me her trowel so I could do some weeding while Mum sorted out my registration with Mr Harper. She was called Natalie. Two of the boys kept calling her *Nit*alie, but she just stuck her tongue out at them and raised her eyebrows at me.

'Boys!' she said.

'I know. Pathetic,' I replied, and we'd grinned at each other.

Natalie seemed to be about my age. I hoped she would be in Year Six too. Maybe we could make friends properly then. I could join the gardening club. When I knew all about digging and planting I could make my own little garden in Flo's back yard.

When we returned to the shop I had a good peer out the back. There was a pile of old junk under the lean-to, waiting to be sorted for stock, and an old bath with wonky legs, and the patch of earth where Alfie liked to hide his bones. I tried to imagine honeysuckle climbing up the lean-to, pansies and snap-dragons growing in the bath, and a little apple tree in the patch of earth, with bluebells growing all around. We could plant Mary's echinacea in the middle, in pride of place.

I went back indoors and drew a picture of my garden ideas. I was still colouring it in when one of Flo's old acting friends, a sweet, pink-faced old man in a checked shirt and red trousers, came to call on her. He was called Lawrence and he was very proud still to be working in one of the long-running TV soaps. He played a vague old grandad, forever forgetting things, but in real life he was as sharp as a tack. He clearly thought the world of Flo and gave her a bunch of scented freesias and a box of Hotel Chocolat assorted creams.

'Oh, Lawrence darling, you know exactly how to spoil a girl,' Flo said, giggling with pleasure. 'Ever the gentleman!'

'Well, my dear Florence, you're ever the lady,' he said, and he picked up one of her plump hands and gave it a kiss.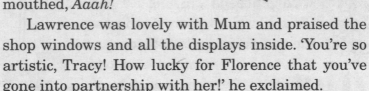

Mum caught my eye and we both mouthed, *Aaah!*

Lawrence was lovely with Mum and praised the shop windows and all the displays inside. 'You're so artistic, Tracy! How lucky for Florence that you've gone into partnership with her!' he exclaimed.

'How lucky for *me*!' said Mum.

'And you clearly take after your mother, Jess,' Lawrence said, looking at my garden picture. 'I love the way you've done all the flowers. You've got such a delicate touch.'

It was Lawrence himself who had the delicate touch, saying just the right thing to each of us. I went into the kitchen to help Mum make tea and we both cooed over Lawrence while the kettle boiled.

'Why can't all men be like lovely Lawrence?' Mum whispered. 'Isn't he priceless? And Flo's blushing and giggling like a schoolgirl, bless her.'

'So you like older men, do you, Mum?' I asked.

Bill was quite a bit older than her, so this was a good sign.

'If they're like Lawrence,' she said.

I couldn't pretend even to myself that Bill was remotely like Lawrence, but I still hoped that they'd hit it off. I was relying on Bill to make a move at next Sunday's boot sale.

But it turned out I didn't have to wait that long. That evening Mum and Flo and I were sitting in the kitchen having a cup of tea. We'd persuaded Lawrence to stay for a quick supper. It was just macaroni, but he said it was the most delicious mac and cheese he'd ever tasted, whizzing him right back to his childhood. He smacked his lips together enthusiastically, and actually begged for a second helping.

He'd only just driven off in his car, and we were all chatting about him.

'Did you ever have a fling with him, Flo?' Mum asked.

'Of course I did!' she said. 'Along with a few dozen other ladies! Lawrence was even more of a charmer in the old days. Though he's still very spry now.'

'Maybe you could have another fling for old times' sake?' Mum teased. 'He seems very keen.'

'Darling, I'm way past flings, though I must admit seeing Lawrence has been a real tonic,' said Flo.

There was the sudden sound of the shop bell. Alfie started barking excitedly.

'Hey, I think he's come back!' Mum went through to the front, singing out, 'Coming!' We heard her open the door and then go, 'Oh!'

A man's voice said something.

'*Is* that Lawrence?' Flo asked. 'It doesn't sound like him. Don't say I've got two gentleman callers in one day!' She gave me a nudge. 'Go and have a peep, Jess.'

I peered round the kitchen door. Mum was standing in the doorway, shifting uncertainly from one foot to the other. I couldn't make out the man standing outside – but I knew his voice!

I went charging back into the kitchen. 'It looks like *Mum's* got a gentleman caller now!' I announced happily.

'Not Sean the Superstud again?' said Flo.

'Ew, not him! It's Bill!' I said, giving her hand a squeeze.

'Bill?' She looked blank.

'You know! He has the bacon-roll van at the boot fair.'

'*That* Bill? I wonder what he wants,' Flo said. 'Better pop the kettle on, Jess, in case your mum invites him in. I hope she does. Nice bloke, Bill.'

'I've got a feeling he's inviting Mum *out!*' I said.

'Never! Oh, Jess, you do get some funny notions in that noddle of yours!'

Mum came scurrying through the shop into the kitchen, leaving Bill standing at the door. She was very pink in the face. 'You'll never guess what!' she hissed.

'What, Mum?' I asked, as innocently as I could.

'It's Bill – you know, Bacon Roll Bill. He's asking me out!'

'Really!' I said, giving Flo a meaningful nod.

'Well I never!' she said.

'He's asking me to the Indian restaurant over the road. I told him I'd already eaten, but he wants me to come anyway, for a beer and a few poppadoms while he has a curry.' Mum sounded bewildered.

Flo burst out laughing. 'That sounds dead romantic – not!' she spluttered.

'Don't be mean, Flo! He can't help not being romantic like Lawrence. He's lovely in his own way,' I said. 'Isn't he, Mum?'

'Well, I suppose. But I don't want to go over the road with him while he has his wretched curry! How can I get out of it without hurting his feelings?' she whispered.

'You've got to go, Mum! You can't let him down!' I said.

177

'Did he say what he wants?' Flo asked. 'Can't we tell him to get his curry and then come and eat it here?'

'He says he'd like to have a private little chat with me,' said Mum. 'He looks very serious, as if he's got something on his mind. Oh dear, I suppose I'd better go.'

She grabbed her jacket and bag. 'If I'm not back in an hour, can you help Flo to bed and then put yourself to bed too, Jess? I'll come and tuck you up when I get back.'

'Aren't you going to brush your hair and put some lippy on, Mum?' I suggested.

'Come on! It's not like I'm going on a date!' she said.

'You might be.'

Mum stared at me. 'What do you mean, Jess Beaker?' she demanded.

But Bill was calling her name and stepping into the shop. 'Are you coming, Tracy?'

'Yes, she is!' I said, grabbing Alfie, who seemed to think that Bill was calling him.

'Oh!' Bill saw me in the kitchen. 'Hello, Jess. Hello, Flo. Hello, Alfie,' he said awkwardly.

Mum turned and pulled a face at me –

but then managed a smile for Bill. 'Right, Bill. Off we go then,' she said.

She didn't look up at him the way she did with Sean Godfrey – but at least she looked friendly. They went off over the road together. Alfie whimpered in disgust. He'd clearly been hoping Bill might have some bacon in his pocket.

It was Flo's turn to stare at me. 'So what's all that about?' she asked, giving me a little dig in the ribs.

'*I* don't know,' I said, opening my eyes wide. 'Presumably Bill likes Mum and wants to get to know her better.'

'Mmm,' said Flo. 'So how come *you* know all about it?'

'Maybe I can predict the future.'

'And maybe you've been meddling, you naughty girl,' said Flo, but she looked amused, not cross. 'Don't get too excited, little Miss Matchmaker. I don't think there's any spark between your mum and Bill.'

'Wait and see,' I said, refusing to lose heart.

Flo and I watched television  together, catching the last quarter of an hour of the soap that Lawrence was in. We gave a little cheer when he put in an appearance right at the end. Then we watched a programme about Battersea Dogs and Cats Home and I tried to get Alfie to pay attention.

'That was your home once, Alfie, look! See all those other dogs and their kennels? Do you remember it?'

Alfie didn't seem interested.

'Oh well, this is your forever home now, isn't it?' I said. 'You and me and Mum and Flo.'

I hadn't even started helping Flo to get ready for bed when Mum came back. She looked even pinker. I hoped Bill had kissed her, but from the expression on Mum's face it didn't seem likely.

'Up to bed, Jess!' she said shortly.

When Mum was in that kind of mood it was best to do as you were told, pronto. I cleaned my teeth and put on my pyjamas, straining my ears to hear what she was saying to Flo downstairs, but there was only a faint rumble of voices. Mum sounded angry – but I thought I heard Flo laughing.

'I'm not sure things have gone to plan,' I said to Alfie, hugging him.

He lay on the end of the bed, thumping his tail. He woofed happily when Mum came into the room, and looked hurt when she totally ignored him. She was concentrating solely on me.

'What on earth are you playing at, Jess Beaker?' she demanded.

'I'm not playing at anything, Mum,' I said.

'Did you or did you not tell Bill that I *fancied* him?'

'Well . . . I might have sort of hinted,' I mumbled.

'Surely you know that's not true!'

'But you like him! And I could see that Bill liked you, so I thought I might just help things along a bit,' I said. 'Don't look like that, Mum! I didn't mean to do any harm. I thought you'd be pleased. And Bill was obviously thrilled because he came to ask you out, right?'

'Wrong on all counts.' Mum sat on the edge of the bed, rubbing her forehead. 'God, it was so embarrassing! It took ages for Bill to tell me. He just kept rambling on about nothing – the weather, Indian beer, boot fairs – it looked like we were going to be discussing the price of bacon any minute. It was all so squirmy that my toes clenched inside my boots and I could hardly sit still. I thought he was just cripplingly shy – I couldn't help feeling sorry for him. But all the time he was feeling equally embarrassed and feeling sorry for *me*!'

'Why, Mum?' I asked, astonished.

'Because of you and your silly meddling! Bill tried to be as tactful as possible. "A little bird told me that you might have feelings for me, Tracy," he said at last. "And I'm immensely flattered to hear that a gorgeous young girl like you likes a boring old bloke like me. If my circumstances were different I'd count myself a very lucky man, but I'm afraid I'm already spoken for." His exact words. I practically fainted into his curry.'

'But I asked him if there was a Mrs Bill and he said he wasn't married. What a fibber!' I said indignantly.

'No he's not. He's a decent, honourable guy. He's got a long-term lady friend he sees every now and then, but she lives with her ancient mother who's got dementia so she can't get away very often. They're waiting till the ancient mum is no longer around. "It's very hard," he said, "but Iris is the love of my life and she's worth waiting for." He looked just like a Labrador when he said it, all big brown eyes and soulful expression. I felt I should be patting him on the head.'

I giggled, which was a big mistake.

'No, it's not funny, Jess Beaker! How *dare* you go round telling some stray guy that I *fancy* them! Surely you're old enough to realize how that could lead to terrible consequences! Suppose you take it into your head to tell the ice-cream man or the guy in the chippy or that bloke who bought the art deco vase today that I fancy them – and then they turn out to be serial killers?' Mum said, getting up and pacing about the room.

Alfie got up and started pacing with

her, hoping she was going to take him for his last-wee walk.

'The ice-cream man is lovely and wouldn't kill so much as a wasp, and it's all really young boys serving in the chippy, and the guy who bought the vase is gay – he was buying it for his boyfriend,' I retorted.

'Oh, you think you're so clever, Miss Smarty Pants,' said Mum. 'But you must promise me never, ever to do anything so criminally stupid ever again. Why *did* you do it, anyway? *You* don't fancy Bill, do you?'

'Oh, Mum! Though I don't see why not. He's quite good looking. Sort of. And he's very kind. And he makes great bacon rolls,' I said.

'Are you trying to be funny? Just cut it out, will you? Why are you so keen to pair me off with someone anyway? You were always dead set *against* me having a boyfriend before. Look how you were with Sean.'

'I know,' I said, and my voice suddenly went wobbly. 'It's *because* of Sean. I'm scared you'll go back to him. I want to fix you up with someone else so you're not tempted.'

'Oh, Jess!' Mum sat down on the bed again and put her arm round me. 'For goodness' sake, it's all over with Sean, I promise promise promise.'

'You still looked kind of pleased to see him when he brought Tyrone,' I mumbled. 'And look how thrilled you were when he sent those flowers.'

'No I wasn't! Well, perhaps I was touched. I *was* in love with him – we were actually *engaged* – so I still feel a bit weird around him. I suppose I'm pleased that he still wants me back – especially as it seems like he prefers me to Justine Man-Snatcher Littlebrain. But I don't want him back. How many times do I have to tell you?' Mum took hold of my head and gently waggled it about. 'Get that into your head, OK!'

'OK,' I said.

Then a message pinged into her mobile.

I looked at her. 'Who's that?'

'Oh, for goodness' sake!'

'It's him, isn't it! It's Sean Godfrey texting you!'

'Don't be so silly. It'll be some message from a shop, a reminder about a gas bill, any old thing,' said Mum.

'Let me see then,' I said, holding out my hand.

'Don't be so silly, Jess. I'm not having you policing my phone! *I'm* the adult here.'

'It *is* Sean Godfrey. I can tell by your face!'

'Oh, for heaven's sake! I'm not going through this rigmarole every time I get a wretched text,' said Mum. She glanced quickly at her phone and bit her lip.

'I'm right, aren't I?' I said, and I leaped up and tried to snatch the phone out of her hand.

'You do that one once more and you'll be sorry!' Mum threatened.

I subsided back onto the bed and put my head on my knees. The room had started to whirl around me, making me feel dizzy. I knew I was right. It really *was* Sean Godfrey.

'Jess?' said Mum.

I didn't answer.

'Really, Jess, stop acting like a baby.' Mum put her hand on my back. I didn't move. She nudged up to me and sighed. 'OK, I think it *is* from Sean. But it doesn't mean anything. I didn't text him. I never reply. He's wasting his time.'

'You promised me it was all over with him,' I murmured into my knees.

'What? It *is* all over. I promised and it's true. I can't help it if he still texts from time to time. It's just a load of rubbish anyway,' said Mum.

'Is it all lovey-dovey?' I asked.

'Sort of. But it doesn't mean anything. He's probably texting the same mush to a dozen other girls. Plus poor stupid Justine.'

I sat up straight and looked her. 'But why didn't you just admit straight away that it was Sean Godfrey texting you?'

'I didn't know for sure. And I knew you'd make a fuss,' said Mum. She put on a silly voice. 'Am I right or am I right?'

'You're not supposed to keep anything from me.'

'Well, I'm sure you sometimes keep things from me.'

'Never!' I said. I thought of Jordan. I wondered if I should tell Mum about her now – but it was so complicated. Mum would be furious if she knew Jordan had tried to get me to go shoplifting with her. She'd even be mad about her snatching my ice cream. She'd be mad at *me* for not telling on her.

'You never, ever keep things from me?' Mum said. 'Come on! What about telling Bill I fancied him!' But this time she suddenly started laughing. 'Honestly, Jess, whatever are you going to do next?'

I was so relieved we were friends again that I didn't want to start complicating things. Mum and I couldn't decide whether Alfie really needed to go out for his last wee or not, but then it started raining, coming down in stair rods so that the window rattled.

'Cross your paws, Alfie, I'm not going out in this!' said Mum, and she changed into her pyjamas and got into bed. 'I hope poor old Bill's got home already. You'd get soaked in seconds on a night like this. Glad we're all tucked up in the warm and dry! Night night, monster matchmaker. Sleep tight.'

I couldn't sleep. The rain poured down steadily.

I wondered if Jordan was in the warm and dry like us. She'd be holed up in that beach hut, but it probably didn't have a bed. Did she even have a pillow or a blanket? Maybe the roof wasn't totally watertight . . .

I imagined her hunched up on the hard floor, drips falling on her head. She'd be hungry too, unless she'd been lucky scavenging in the waste bins, and worried every time she heard footsteps in case it was someone come to cart her off to the far-off residential home.

I had no idea what a children's home was really like. Mum sometimes joked about the Dumping Ground: after her fights with Justine Littlewood she'd often been put in the Quiet Room.

I wondered what the Quiet Room was like. I imagined a dank prison cell with an old mattress and a horrid toilet in the corner. Mum would have yelled her head off if anyone had shut her in there, so why was it called the *Quiet* Room? Maybe they gagged her so she couldn't be heard. Then they'd have to tie her hands behind her back to stop her ripping the gag off. It was such a scary thought that I could barely breathe. Little girl Mum and big girl Jordan kept getting mixed up in my head. It was so awful I couldn't keep still, and tossed and turned.

'Jess! Settle down and go to sleep,' Mum murmured.

'I can't!' I said, and I burst into tears.

'Jess? Are you crying?' She wriggled over and took me in her arms. 'Oh, darling, what's the matter? You're not still upset because I got cross with you . . . ? That's all over now. In fact, I'll probably go and see Bill next Sunday and we'll have a good laugh about it. There's nothing to worry about.'

'I wasn't worrying about you and Bill,' I sobbed. 'Oh, Mum!'

'What is it? You're not still fussing about Sean, are you?' She wiped my eyes with the edge of the sheet. 'There now. How many times do I have to promise? He's not part of our lives any more and he's never going to be.'

'Good! Though I wasn't crying just because of him,' I said, sniffling.

'So what was it? Give that nose a good blow. No, not on the sheet! Find a tissue!'

I couldn't find one so Mum went to get the toilet roll. It gave me a few seconds' thinking time. I so, so, so wanted to tell her about Jordan. I knew it was the only sensible thing to do. But I'd sworn on Mum's life that I wouldn't say a word to anyone. The rational bit of me knew that making a childish oath couldn't *really* have any effect on Mum, but most of me was still too scared to risk it. What if I told Mum and then she dropped dead right in front of me? Or dashed out into the road and got knocked down by a car? Or suddenly clutched her chest in terrible pain and was taken off to hospital and I never saw her again?

'Here, blow!' said Mum, giving me a long length of loo roll. 'Now, cuddle up and tell me what's on your mind, Jessica Bluebell Camilla Beaker.'

'I – I was just thinking about . . . residential homes,' I whispered.

'You what?'

'You know, like the one you were in. The Dumping Ground,' I said, mopping my nose.

'Whatever made you think of that?' Mum asked.

I had a sudden picture of Jordan looking menacing, making a cut-your-throat gesture. Cut-*Mum's*-throat.

'I was imagining what it must have been like for you,' I said quickly. It wasn't really a fib.

'Ah, you sweetheart,' said Mum. 'But there's no need to be so upset. The Dumping Ground wasn't really that bad.'

'What about when they tied you up in the Quiet Room?' I asked.

'They didn't tie me up!'

'But they locked you in . . .'

'I don't think they even did that. It wasn't like a punishment place. It was just a little room where you were taken when you needed to calm down,' Mum explained. 'It had a sofa and some old teddies, and some crayons and paper if  you wanted to draw. I mostly just wanted to yell, so I suppose they should really have called it the Noisy Room.'

'Did you get put in there a lot?' I asked.

'I suppose. I was a bit of a handful. Well, some of 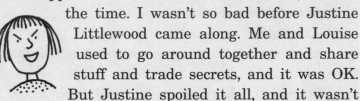 the time. I wasn't so bad before Justine Littlewood came along. Me and Louise used to go around together and share stuff and trade secrets, and it was OK. But Justine spoiled it all, and it wasn't much fun having zero friends.'

'I thought you and Peter Ingham were friends.'

'That was all on *his* side. He used to follow me around and act like I was the bee's knees. It was really irritating,'  said Mum, laughing. 'Funny how he's turned out. He's OK now, isn't he? I hope we bump into him again – I'd like to be proper friends with him.

Shame he's gay – he's someone I *could* fancy now.'

'Really?' I said, surprised. 'But he's a head teacher and you always say you can't stick teachers.'

'I know, I know. But that's stupid. Mr Harper seems a lovely chap. I think you'll love it at his school. Even *I* would have loved it if I'd gone to a school like that when I was little,' said Mum.

'But you still don't like Mary much, do you?'

'She's OK-ish. I just don't like her trying to boss me around and tell me what to do, even though I know she means well.'

I had a sudden flash of insight. 'It's because you want Cam all to yourself,' I said.

Sometimes it's better to keep quiet.

'It is *not!*' Mum said indignantly, and ranted for several minutes about daughters who think they know it all.

'Maybe you need the Quiet Room now, Mum,' I risked saying.

'You cheeky little whatsit!' she said, but she laughed too.

Then we cuddled down together. The rain was still making the windows rattle, so I put my head right under the covers. I started muttering all the poems and song lyrics I could think of to blot out thoughts of Jordan.

'What's with the mumbling?' Mum asked sleepily.

'Just sending myself to sleep,' I said.

'Well, you're keeping *me* awake!' she said, but she gave me a hug. 'Night night, darling.'

'Night night,' I said, and at long last I fell asleep.

10

IN THE MORNING, when Mum went to help Flo get washed and dressed, I sprang out of bed too. We didn't have a duvet, just sheets, a couple of blankets and an old-fashioned silky eiderdown. Two blankets. We didn't need both of them, not in the summer, and Mum said she wanted to get a proper duvet anyway. The blankets belonged to Flo, but I was sure she wouldn't mind if I took one of them.

I untucked it from the rest of the bedding and rolled it up as small as I could. I wanted to take a pillow too. I was willing to sacrifice my own, but Mum would have noticed, and I couldn't find any going spare in Flo's airing cupboard. I made do with an old cushion embroidered with puppies. I thought Jordan might like it, seeing as she loved dogs so much.

I couldn't squash the blanket *and* the pillow into the canvas bag. I hid them in the wardrobe, and then managed to pinch a big black bin bag  from under the kitchen sink. I took a new loaf of bread too, and a tub of cream cheese and a carton of orange juice, managing all this while Mum was helping Flo. I put them in the canvas bag, not wanting to risk them in the bin bag with the bedding.

I charged upstairs with my loot and then ran back down again to make toast with what was left of the old loaf, set some bacon to sizzle in the pan and put   the kettle on. By the time Mum and Flo had come in I'd made us all bacon sandwiches.

'What a little darling,' said Flo, munching appreciatively.

'They're very good.' Mum glanced at me. 'You'll have to set up business with Bill after we're married.'

'*What?*'

'Joke,' said Mum. 'It's just our Jess here got hold of the wrong end of the stick.'

'Ah, don't tease the kiddie. She's a little gem,' said Flo.

'Yes, she's basically a good kid,' said Mum. 'She just gets a bit carried away at times.'

I felt awful – I was stealing their food and bedding, even though it wasn't for me. Still, it couldn't be helped. At least I wasn't stealing from other people.

After breakfast I washed the dishes, and then Flo settled down on her sofa with her newspaper. She called it her *Daily Rubbish*, but said she liked to read all the scandal. Mum was deep in her library books, busily taking notes, as if she was swotting for an exam. Every so often she prowled around the shop, seizing on some toy or piece of china, comparing them with the pictures in her books. Cam and Mary would have been amazed to see her studying so seriously.

'I think I'll take Alfie for a really long walk this morning,' I announced.

'OK,' said Mum, her head in her book. 'But make sure you cross the road at the zebra crossing – and don't talk to any strange men.'

'I won't, I promise,' I said. She hadn't said anything about talking to any strange girls dressed up as boys. And maybe I wouldn't find Jordan anyway. Still, I had to try.

It was a nightmare trying to slip out of the shop with the bin bag in one hand and the canvas bag slung over my shoulder. I hovered on the stairs until Flo was thoroughly absorbed in some scandal about an actress and Mum was kneeling by the bookshelf. Then, double-quick, I charged out of the shop with Alfie on his lead.

It was still raining, but it was just a light drizzle now. It was so grey and cloudy it didn't seem like summer at all. There weren't many people on the promenade and no one was waiting for an ice cream, or for a coffee at the kiosk. No one was setting up deck-chairs and windbreaks for the day. There were still dog walkers, so Alfie trotted along happily, sniffing every canine friend, pulling hard on his lead when he wanted to go and see a favourite spaniel or terrier.

'Careful, Alfie! You'll topple me over!' I said, trying to hang onto the bin bag and the canvas bag as well as his lead. 'Look for Jordan! Where's Jordan? Go get Jordan!'

He woofed excitedly and set off, but it was just to say hello to a girly white poodle.

'Jordan!' I reminded him. 'Go on, be a tracker dog!'

Alfie obviously had no idea what I was talking about, so I had to do the hunting myself. I went along

to the beach huts, sure she'd be tucked up inside one of them. They were all closed up. I peered at the locks, trying to see which one was broken. There was one that looked rusty, with ugly brown stains leaking down the yellowed paint. I juggled my bags and cautiously tried to open the door.

A man a little further up the promenade turned to see why his sons were dawdling – and saw me.

'Hey, you! What are you doing?' he asked.

Oh no! It was the man who had chased me up the beach after I'd snatched Jordan's ice cream! Alfie recognized him too and struggled to get at him. I had to hang onto his lead tightly, which wasn't easy with the two bags.

'Keep that wretched dog under control!' the man shouted. He narrowed his eyes. 'Aren't you the girl who stole the ice cream?'

'What? I don't know what you mean,' I said, acting total innocence.

'Yes, you are! What are you up to now, trying to get into that beach hut?'

'I'm not!' I protested.

'I saw you!'

'It's *my* beach hut,' I said, blurting the words out in a panic.

'Don't be ridiculous!'

'It is,' I insisted, though I knew perfectly well that a ten-year-old girl couldn't own a beach hut. 'It's my granny's,' I added, more rationally. 'She sent me to check she'd remembered to lock it up yesterday. And she has – see?'

It was indeed locked. I'd got myself into this scrape for nothing. This horrid nosy man was never going to let it go. Any minute now he'd be dragging me and Alfie and the bin bag and the canvas one all the way to the police station, and they'd call Mum and she'd die of shame. Well, I knew this was actually unlikely, and I hadn't even done anything, but I was getting in such a state that I couldn't think clearly.

'What's the matter with you?' the man demanded, seeing I'd started shivering.

'You're scaring me,' I said. 'My mum said I wasn't to talk to strange men!'

He stared at me, looking startled. 'What? Oh, for goodness' sake!' he blustered, but when I backed away from him he didn't try to stop me.

I hurried along the row of beach huts, my arms aching, and when I looked back the man and the boys had disappeared from view. I waited a while and then doubled back, going behind the beach huts this time. As I passed each one I called out in a low voice, 'Jordan? Are you there? It's me, Jess.'

I didn't get any reply.

'Oh, Alfie, what am I going to do? Where *is* she?' I wailed.

Alfie didn't seem to be listening. He edged towards the pebbles, his nose twitching.

'What? No, it's not a beach day, silly,' I said. Then I saw someone paddling right by the water's edge.

I stared. The tide was out so I couldn't see properly, but the someone was wearing a baseball cap and jeans.

'Is it Jordan?' I asked Alfie.

He seemed to think so, hurtling forward now. He never seemed to mind the hard stones under his paws but I found it a struggle, the pebbles crunching underfoot. It took me a while to reach the water's edge.

'Jordan?' I called.

The person turned round – and it was her.

'Oh, thank goodness!' I said. 'I've been looking and looking for you! You weren't anywhere yesterday afternoon, and today you weren't anywhere either and I thought I'd never find you again.'

She turned to look at me but didn't say anything. I couldn't see her face properly because her cap was pulled down low, shading her eyes. She just stood there, her shoes in her hand, her feet in the water. She hadn't rolled up the legs of her jeans and they were soaked. Then I saw that all of her was soaked. Her grey sweatshirt was clinging to her. Her hands were clenched, the knuckles white. She was shivering.

'You haven't been *swimming* in your clothes, have you?' I asked.

'What do you think I am, out of my mind?' Jordan muttered.

'You're so wet!'

'Well, duh! It's been raining cats and dogs all night, hasn't it?'

'Why didn't you take shelter in your beach hut?'

'This nosy old guy came along and said no one was allowed to sleep there and I had to push off. He said he'd phone the police so I had to get away quick,' said Jordan. She was shivering so much that her words sounded wobbly.

'So where did you sleep then?' I asked.

'In one of them shelters on the promenade. Only the wind was blowing so the rain came in,' she said. 'Call it a shelter! It was flipping useless.' She sniffed

200

and I looked at her carefully. I couldn't see her eyes but I wondered if those were tears on her cheeks.

'Well, you're getting even wetter now,' I said. 'Look at your jeans. Why are you paddling?'

'Just felt like it,' she said. 'To cool down.'

I stared at Jordan. She couldn't be hot, not when she was shivering. But actually she did smell a bit sweaty. I wondered if she had a temperature. She looked quite ill.

I put the bin bag down carefully out of reach of the waves and took her hand. I thought she'd probably snatch it away but she held onto mine.

'What are you doing here, anyway? You flounced off yesterday,' Jordan muttered.

'Yes, well, I'm back now. And I've brought you some food and a blanket. I wish I'd thought to bring a towel! I'll go back for one if you like,' I offered.

'No, don't go,' she said. She squeezed my hand. 'You really got all this stuff for me?'

'Yes! Come on, let's go back to one of the shelters. It'll be better than nothing. Maybe you can dry yourself a bit with the blanket. And I'll give you my jacket if you like,' I said, shrugging it off.

'Don't be daft! You're a little shrimp. It wouldn't fit a great lump like me,' said Jordan.

'Just put it round your shoulders,' I said. 'Come on. Look, you hold Alfie's lead while I carry this stuff.'

We started walking up the beach, the pebbles scrunching. Jordan winced and had to sit down to put her trainers on. She didn't seem to have any socks. I saw the raw red marks where the shoes had rubbed.

'Your feet look sore!' I said.

'They're OK,' she muttered.

'You're ever so brave,' I told her.

'No I'm not. I get really scared sometimes.' Jordan's head was bent so I could hardly hear her. 'I went up on them cliffs yesterday and stood right on the edge.'

'Well, that's brave, isn't it? Very stupid, but brave,' I said.

She ducked her head and didn't answer. My heart started banging in my chest.

'You weren't going to jump, were you?' I whispered.

'Would anyone care if I did?' said Jordan.

'I'd care!' I said.

'No you wouldn't. You ran off. You don't really want to be my friend,' said Jordan.

'I do, truly! Come on, get up. You can't just sit there, all soggy.'

I tried to pull her up. Alfie thought it was a game and joined in. Jordan tried to push him away, but he licked her hand and then jumped up and licked her face too, liking the saltiness of her tears.

'There, Alfie cares about you too!' I said.

He was caring so much that he knocked off her

baseball cap. Her elastic band snapped and her fair hair tumbled down round her shoulders. She swore and tried to cram it back.

'Don't! It looks lovely now it's loose,' I said. 'I wish I had hair like yours.'

Jordan stared at me. 'No you don't,' she said, but she sounded uncertain. 'Anyway, I've got to keep it up. If I don't it'll be obvious I'm a girl and they'll guess I'm Jordan Whitely.'

She tucked her hair in again and we staggered back up the steep, pebbly slope to the promenade. The rain was getting heavier now and even the dog

walkers seemed to have gone home. There was no sign of Angry Man and his children.

'There! We've got the whole beach to ourselves,' I said, pulling Jordan into the nearest shelter. 'Is this where you spent the night?'

'Yeah. Dead luxurious, isn't it?' she said.

'Total five-star hotel,' I said, and she actually chuckled. I couldn't believe how wet she was. She was shivering violently now, though she held onto her elbows tightly, trying to stop it.

I pulled the blanket out of the bin bag. There was no point in keeping it dry for tonight. She needed it right this minute.

'Look, you ought to get out of those soaking wet clothes,' I said. 'Your sweatshirt and your jeans.'

'What? Don't be daft! I'll be nicked for indecent exposure,' she said.

'No, seriously. The blanket will cover you. Keep your underwear on. It'll just look like you've been for a swim in a bikini. You can't possibly get warm like that. You can wrap my jacket back round your shoulders – that'll cover you up a bit. And if you're sitting down no one will see your knickers. Go on!' I insisted.

Normally she'd have taken no notice, I was sure, but she was so wet and tired that she did as she was told. She looked very white and vulnerable in her underwear, with her baseball cap still on her head. I gave her my jacket and then put the blanket round her. She sat back on the seat, wrapping herself up tight in the blanket so it came up to her nose.

'Is that a bit better?' I asked.

'Yeah,' she said, though her teeth were chattering.

'You should take your baseball cap off too,' I said, but she wouldn't go that far.

'It's my disguise, innit,' she said, talking like a gangster again, making her voice gruffer.

'Oh well, keep it on then.' I picked up her sweatshirt and jeans in turn, wringing them out. Little waterfalls sprinkled the pavement.

'Here, let me do it. You're not strong enough,' said Jordan.

'No, stay under that blanket, you silly girl!' I said, squeezing harder.

'Who do you think you are, Mary chuffing Poppins?'

'We could do with her umbrella,' I said, spreading Jordan's clothes out on the seat to dry, though there was little chance of that.

Then I delved into the canvas bag. 'Here, I've brought you breakfast – heaps of it.'

I handed Jordan the carton of orange juice and started spreading cream cheese on the bread, very pleased with myself for remembering a knife. She gulped the juice down eagerly, drinking half the carton before taking a breath. Then she started attacking the first cheese sandwich. It vanished in four bites.

She gave a great belch and looked at me sideways. 'Sorry,' she muttered.

'It's OK,' I said. I was frightened by her desperation. I'd often complained that I was starving hungry, but Jordan wasn't acting like a greedy child whose tea was ten minutes late. It looked like she really *was* starving. She was still a big girl but she'd already lost a lot of weight.

She was holding the orange juice carton out to me. 'Your turn,' she offered.

'No, I'm fine, thanks. It's all for you,' I said, preparing another sandwich for her. 'Are you a bit warmer now?'

'Yeah,' she said, though she was still shivering. She saw I was as well. 'You come under the blanket, Jess. You're cold too.'

So I sat down beside her. Alfie stood on his hind legs, begging to join us, so we hauled him up between us. He sprawled happily over both our laps. He was damp and smelled of wet fur, but he was warm too, like a wriggly hot-water bottle. I made Jordan another sandwich, and then another and another, and ate one myself to keep her company. Alfie had his own little dog-size sandwich, though I warned him not to tell Mum.

'I'd forgotten what it's like to feel *full*,' said Jordan, patting her stomach under the blanket. 'Can I have another?'

'You might give yourself a tummy ache,' I said anxiously. 'Remember what it's like to stuff yourself at Christmas so that all you can do is lie on the sofa and groan.' Then I put my hand over my mouth. 'Oh, sorry! That was tactless. Perhaps you've never had that sort of Christmas, with turkey and roast potatoes and pudding and as many chocolates as you want.'

Jordan shrugged. "'S OK. I've had heaps of Christmases like that. With different people. Only they're all much the same.'

'Did your foster parents give you presents?'

'Yes, of course. One couple gave me a smartphone – can you believe it? And there was a label on the package: *To our new daughter Jordan with lots of love*. But that was rubbish because by the New Year they were saying they couldn't keep me any more!' said Jordan. 'Just because I drank some of their booze and was a bit sick. I mean, everyone gets drunk on New Year's Eve, don't they?'

'Not children.'

'Well, I've always been old for my age. I said I was sorry, sort of, but they said they couldn't handle me. The woman cried when the care worker came to cart me off. She said she'd miss me dreadfully. Well, if she was going to miss me that much, why was she sending me away?' Jordan sniffed contemptuously.

'That sort of thing happened to my mum. She was in and out of care. But then Cam fostered her and kept her, and now they're family. Listen, Jordan, you'd love Cam, everyone does. She still fosters – older girls like you – and I'm sure you'd like it at her place,' I said.

'No I wouldn't. I'm not having anyone look after me any more. I can look after myself,' said Jordan.

'You're soaking wet and starving!' I pointed out.

'I'm getting dry under the blanket and I'm not starving any more,' she said. 'Stop preaching at me. I'm not listening – see?' She put her hands over her ears and started humming.

'But, Jordan—'

'I can't hear a word,' she said, in between hums.

'Jordan is sitting here in just her bra and pants!' I sang.

'Shut up!'

'See, you *can* hear.'

Jordan dug me in the ribs.

'Ow! That hurt!'

'Sorry! I didn't mean to hurt you. You're such a skinny little thing. I keep forgetting you're only a kid.' Jordan swallowed. 'Jess, about the other day – when I wanted you to shoplift –'

'I'm not going to,' I said. 'I'd only get caught and then you'd scarper.'

'I wouldn't. I stuck up for you when that guy started ranting at you because you nicked my ice cream,' she said.

'Well, I'm still not doing it because it's wrong, and I don't care if you call me chicken again. There's nothing wrong with being a chicken anyway. They come in all different colours and their feathers are soft and they make funny little clucking sounds when they lay eggs.' I flapped my arms and clucked to demonstrate.

'You're nuts,' said Jordan, laughing. She tried being a chicken too. We were both clucking like crazy when a woman in a rain cape marched past with two little chihuahuas. They had weeny rain capes on as well. The woman stared at us, astonished, and the dogs gave high-pitched barks. Jordan and I collapsed into giggles and Alfie poked his head out of the blanket and gave the chihuahuas a warning woof not to take the mick.

We went on giggling for ages after they'd gone. It helped warm us up a bit.

'Anyway,' Jordan said eventually, 'you don't have

to worry. I'm not going to make you shoplift, not if you don't want to. I'm not a bully. When I was little some big girls made me do it, and I know it's really scary if you get caught.'

'Well, good. Because I wouldn't do it anyway.' I took a deep breath. 'Even though you're my friend.'

Jordan didn't say anything, but she put her arm round me under the blanket. Alfie snuggled closer too. The rain pattered on the top of the shelter but we stayed dry. I could hear the sea sucking at the pebbles on the beach, and a seagull screaming overhead. No more footsteps. It was weirdly peaceful.

Jordan was breathing deeply. I squinted at her in the shadowy shelter. It looked as if she'd gone to sleep. She had her thumb in her mouth, one finger stroking her nose. I smiled at her – big tough Jordan sucking her thumb like a baby.

I wondered what the time was. Mum would be wondering what had happened to me. I knew I should be getting home but I didn't like to disturb Jordan, not when she was looking so peaceful. I decided to give her ten more minutes and then I'd have to get going.

I didn't have a watch so I started counting the seconds. I got to sixty – one minute – and then the numbers started jumbling up in my head, and I fell asleep too.

Then I heard someone calling.

'Jess! Jess! Where *are* you, Jess?'

It was Mum! Alfie woke with a start too, and barked at the sound of her voice. I heard the padding sound of Mum running in her high-tops. Alfie barked again, and she came dashing right into the shelter – and then stared at us, her mouth hanging open.

'Jess?'

'Hello, Mum,' I said in a tiny voice.

'What in God's name are you up to?' she said. 'Who's *this*?' She shook Jordan's shoulder roughly.

'Leave off,' Jordan mumbled, not properly awake.

'No, I won't leave off, matey!' Mum said furiously. 'I know you, don't I? You're the boy who was scavenging for fish and chips! What the hell are you doing with my little girl? How *dare* you! She's ten years old and you're a great big lout nearly twice her age! Cuddling under a blanket together!'

She seized a corner of the blanket and pulled it right off – then gave a great shriek when she saw that Jordan was in her underwear. And then another shriek when she realized: 'You're a *girl*?'

Jordan jumped up, grabbed her wet sweatshirt

211

and jeans, and started running, but Mum was hot on her heels. Jordan was bigger than Mum and much broader — but my mum's Tracy Beaker. She can get the better of anyone in a scrap. She launched herself at Jordan and had her on the ground in a second. Then she grabbed hold of her, twisting her arms behind her back.

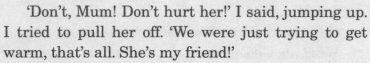

'Don't, Mum! Don't hurt her!' I said, jumping up. I tried to pull her off. 'We were just trying to get warm, that's all. She's my friend!'

'Some friend!' she said, jerking Jordan's arms.

Jordan swore at her and tried to get away, but she was weak and tired and still very wet. 'Get off, you're hurting me!' she mumbled.

'Stop struggling or I'll *really* hurt you!' Mum threatened. 'Now, tell me who you are and exactly why you're huddling up with my daughter in your underwear!'

'I *told* you, Mum! She was soaking wet. I made her take off her clothes because she was shivering so. She was out all night in the pouring rain,' I said.

'Why's that? Haven't you got a home to go to?' Mum said, shaking Jordan.

'No, she hasn't!' I shouted. 'That's the whole point! She ran away. Surely *you* can understand, Mum. She's in care near London and they want to send her to a home hundreds of miles away because no one wants her here. Oh!' I suddenly realized I'd told Mum all about Jordan, even though I'd sworn on her life that I wouldn't. 'Oh, Mum, don't die! *Please* don't die! It'll be all my fault if you do!' And I burst into tears.

'What? I'm not going to *die!*' Mum peered at Jordan. 'What have you been saying to her? Are you really in care?'

'No! Not any more. I can look after myself,' said Jordan. 'Leave go of me, will you?'

'Well, stop struggling. And if you try and do a runner, I'll flatten you. So how old are you then?'

'Eighteen.'

Mum peered closely at her. 'No you're not! What are you, fifteen?'

Jordan nodded sulkily.

'And how long have you been hanging around here?'

Jordan shrugged. 'I don't know. A few weeks. This is my place. I'm not going anywhere else.'

'Did you use to live here then?'

'No, I just like it here. I came camping here once,' Jordan muttered.

'You didn't! So did I!' said Mum. 'It was the best

holiday ever. That's why we came here, isn't it, Jess?'

'Yes! And we're going to stay here for ever, aren't we, Mum?'

'Yes, we are.'

'Well, so am I,' said Jordan.

'I understand the way you feel, kid, but you can't manage by yourself, not when you're too young to get a job or a room to live in. If you stay on the streets you'll get in with the wrong crowd,' said Mum.

'I *am* the wrong crowd,' said Jordan. 'I'm the one who's the worst kid ever. No one can cope with me.'

'No, that was *me*,' said Mum. 'I was considered legendary in the care system, I'll have you know. You're a rank amateur compared to me.'

'Ha ha,' said Jordan. She looked at me. 'A bit full of herself, your mum, isn't she?'

'Yep,' I said. 'But she's OK. Mum, do let *go* of her. You won't run off, will you, Jordan?'

'No.' She didn't look as if she could run anywhere actually. She was still shivering and her face was ghostly white.

Mum pulled her up and led her back to the bench. She stared at her, nibbling her lip. 'You don't look too clever,' she said. She put one hand on

Jordan's forehead, under the peak of her cap. 'I wonder if you've got a temperature. Come on, back to my place. You need a hot bath and some aspirin and a warm bed, no matter who you are or what you've been up to.'

'I'm not coming! Do you think I'm daft? You'll call social services,' Jordan protested.

'No I won't. We'll get you sorted first. You'll go down with pneumonia if you stay out here, soaking wet. You'd better put your soggy clothes on again just till we get you home.' Mum started helping her into her jeans.

'Home?' said Jordan.

'Our home. Up you get then. Keep the blanket round you.' Mum peered at it. 'Hey, that's our blanket, isn't it, Jess? And the cushion! You little devil! How on earth did you smuggle them out?'

'She brought me food too. She's been great to me,' said Jordan.

'Well, why didn't you *tell* me, Jess?' asked Mum.

'I wanted to tell, but I promised I wouldn't. On your life,' I said as we set off, Mum holding Jordan's arm – though it was more to support her than anything else.

'Oh, I see! *That's* why you were scared I was going to die,' said Mum. 'Oh, Jess, you've no more sense than a Pot Noodle at times. Swearing on someone's life can't possibly have any effect on them. It's just a load of superstitious nonsense.'

Yet two minutes later, as we turned into our road, we saw a window cleaner's ladder leaning right across the pavement. There was heaps of room for us to go underneath, but Mum led us out into the road to avoid it.

'Mum! *You're* the one who's superstitious, thinking that going under a ladder is bad luck!' I pointed out.

'Nonsense, I just didn't want him to drop his damp rag on us,' she said. She gestured to our shop. 'Here we are, Jordan.'

'What, the junk shop?'

'There's no junk here, girly. Only the finest antiques and bric-a-brac.'

'Then why is it called The Dumping Ground?' Jordan asked.

'It's just a fun title, that's all. Though it just happens to be the name we all called the children's home where I grew up,' said Mum.

'The Dumping Ground. I get it!' said Jordan, and she actually smiled.

11

WE WENT INTO the shop, Mum keeping a firm hold on Jordan just in case. Flo was on her feet, staggering backwards and forwards on her sticks, pacing up and down.

'Thank the Lord!' she said. 'Your mum and I have been going nuts, Jess! You've been gone such ages! Are you all right, pet? And Alfie? And, my goodness, who have we here?' She peered over her glasses at Jordan. 'Cor blimey, it's the ghost of the Ancient Mariner!' she said in her cockney accent.

Jordan was staring back at her.
'I know you!' she said. 'You're the old bat off the telly! I've watched you on Gold. *Life with the Lilliputs.*'

Flo looked utterly delighted and came out with her catchline again: *'Allo, dearies, let me slosh a bit of disinfectant in all your murky corners!'*

'Yeah!' Jordan seemed delighted too. 'You didn't tell me your nan was famous, Jess!'

'Well, bless you, dearie!' said Flo. 'A little fan! How marvellous! But what's happened to you? Did you take a dip in the sea, you poor boy?'

'Poor *girl*,' said Mum, fetching a towel from the kitchen. She flicked up the peak of Jordan's baseball cap, tipping it onto the floor. Jordan's wet hair fell to her shoulders, but Mum quickly wrapped the towel round her head like a turban. 'I found her cuddled up with Jess under a blanket, would you believe.'

'Oh I say!' said Flo. 'You're a bit young for canoodling under blankets, aren't you, Jess?'

'We weren't *canoodling*,' I said, but I think they were teasing me.

'Jess, take Jordan upstairs and run a piping-hot bath for her. Then bring her clothes down and I'll put them in the washing machine,' said Mum. She steered me to the stairs. 'Fetch a towel for yourself too, and change into dry clothes – you look a bit soggy round the edges and all. What a pair!'

Jordan stood her ground. 'You'll call social services the minute I go upstairs, won't you?'

'No. I wouldn't do that. I don't know what we're going to do with you, but we'll discuss it later. I won't do anything behind your back, I promise.'

'Swear on Jess's life.'

'Oh for goodness' sake. You and your swearing,' said Mum. 'OK, I swear on Jess's life I won't. OK?'

'OK,' said Jordan, and she came upstairs with me.

I turned on the taps while Jordan peered around the poky bathroom in surprise. 'It's dead old-fashioned, isn't it?' she said. 'Why doesn't your nan have it all done up with one of them roll-top baths? And why hasn't she got matching fluffy towels and posh smelly stuff, seeing as she's a famous actress?'

'I don't think she earned that much even when she was on telly – and she hasn't acted for years. Look, I've got some bubble stuff – you can squirt that in if you like,' I offered.

'But it's Matey – that's for little kids,' Jordan protested.

'Look, stop being so fussy!' I said, giving her a little push.

'Sorry. Your mum won't tell, will she?'

'No. She swore on my life!'

'Yeah, but she says that's all superstitious nonsense,' said Jordan, struggling out of her soaking jeans.

'Look, I know my mum,' I said.

'Turn round. I don't want you gawping at me. She's ever so fierce, your mum.'

'Only when she's protecting me,' I said, not entirely truthfully.

'And she can't half rugby-tackle! She decked me just like that.'

'Yes, she's good at fighting. She can do kick-boxing and all.'

There were splashing sounds and then a little shriek as Jordan got into the bath. 'It's boiling!'

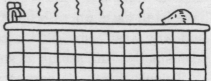

'You need it hot,' I said. 'Stop moaning.'

'You're just like your mum,' said Jordan, giving little gasps as she slid slowly down into the water.

'What, because we've both got mad curly hair?' I asked, turning round to look at her.

'Well, yes – but you're both pretty fierce too.'

I was thrilled. Maybe I'd stopped being sad, wussy little Jess for good!

'Do you think your mum would teach me?' Jordan asked.

'Teach you how to be fierce?'

'How to kick-box!'

'Maybe. You'd better ask her,' I said. 'How's the bath now?'

'I'm getting used to it,' said Jordan, sinking lower until I could only see her face, her hair floating around her head.

I took another towel and started drying my own hair. By the time I'd finished, Jordan's eyes were closed and she was breathing deeply.

'Hey, Jordan!'

'Mmm?'

'You're going to sleep! Watch out or you'll drown. Come on, time to get out now!'

'First you nag me to get *in* the bath, then you nag me to get *out*,' Jordan grumbled sleepily, but she started slowly sitting up.

I scurried around upstairs, wondering what she could put on. My night things and even Mum's were out of the question. In the end I had to plump for one of Flo's nighties, a voluminous full-length white affair that she called the Victorian Nightmare.

'I'm not wearing that!' Jordan said when I showed it to her.

'Well, it's that or go stark naked, take your pick,' I said.

She picked the nightgown. It actually looked amazing on her. She was like a giant version of a little Victorian girl, all white ruffles and long fair hair, her face pink from the hot bath. She was still shivery, but Mum had already popped upstairs and put a hot-water bottle in our bed, even though it was summer.

'An actual bed at last!' said Jordan, and climbed in straight away without moaning.

It wasn't the most comfortable bed in the world. It was very old and creaky and the mattress was lumpy. Mum was saving up to get a new one – or at least a new mattress – but we were making do for now. Still, Jordan stretched out like a starfish and gave a deep sigh.

'Bliss!' she said, but then she propped herself up on one elbow. 'You won't let your mum phone social services, will you?'

'She won't – she *said*. Stop going on about it.'

'Yes, you tell her, Jess,' said Mum, coming into the bedroom with a mug of hot chocolate. 'Here, Jordan, drink this down, and have a couple of aspirin. We'll let you have a kip for a while. Come on, Jess. Your hot chocolate's downstairs.'

'Thanks,' said Jordan. She looked at us both. I wondered if she might cry again. 'Why are you being so nice to me?'

'Goodness knows,' said Mum, but she gave her shoulder a little pat.

'Night night, Jordan,' I said. 'Well, actually it should be day day.'

'You're a weird kid,' she told me, but she said it fondly.

'Well!' said Mum when we were downstairs. 'You've got some explaining to do, Jessica Bluebell Camilla Beaker.'

We all had hot chocolate, Mum and Flo and me, and I told them all about Jordan and how we'd met. I had to relate the story in little chunks, because suddenly we had a flurry of customers and I didn't want them to hear anything while they were poking about.

'Are you sure Jordan's not telling a few porky pies?' Flo asked. 'I mean, she couldn't really have had all these different homes, could she? And why on earth would they want to send her so far away now?'

'It happens,' said Mum. 'You should hear the stories some of the girls at Cam's tell.'

'That's what I wondered, Mum. Couldn't Jordan go and live with Cam?' I asked eagerly.

'Well, I don't think Cam's taking on anyone else. She's waiting till all her current girls are independent and then she's stopping fostering. She'd like more time with Mary, especially in the summer when Mary isn't teaching,' said Mum.

'But Jordan's nearly grown up. She can mostly look after herself. She wouldn't be much trouble,' I said.

'Oh, come off it, Jess, that girl has trouble written all over her. *I* should know!'

'But Cam still took you on,' I persisted. 'And you've turned out lovely.'

'Oh, Jess!' said Mum, and she gave me a hug.

'She seems quite a nice kid, all things considered,' said Flo. 'She's got a lot of attitude, but what teenager hasn't nowadays? And fancy her being a *Lilliputs* fan! That really tickled me. Shall we watch those old episodes again, Jess?'

'Oh yes!' I tried to sound enthusiastic.

'Perhaps I'm getting a whole new fan base,' said Flo. 'You'll be sloshing disinfectant in many more murky corners!' said Mum. 'Oh well, while we think what to do with Jordan I'd better attend to our own corners. Someone's been rummaging in our Book Nook and left half the stock on the floor!'

She headed over to the bookshelf and I went to help her. Mum sorted through the paperbacks and I started on the picture books, though I quickly got distracted by *The Tiger Who Came to Tea*. I had to read it through for old times' sake.

'I love these old green Penguin paperbacks – the crime series,' Mum said. 'Hey, I'll put a little pile in the window beside those Indian daggers! I'll make my own little crime scene! What else?' She wandered around the shop looking for sinister objects, collecting a doll with no eyes and a skull-and-crossbones ring. Then she crawled gingerly into one of the windows to set up her creepy display – and suddenly gave a shriek.

'Mum?'

Someone was peering through the window at her, his forehead against the glass.

'Peter! Dear goodness, you didn't half make me jump!' Mum shouted. She beckoned wildly. 'Come in! Have a proper look round!'

'Sorry. I was just passing and . . .' he said apologetically, putting his head into the doorway. 'Don't worry, I won't hold you up. I can see you're busy.'

'Oh, don't be daft,' said Mum, backing out of the window. 'Jess, run and put the kettle on. Flo, this is Peter Ingham, one of my oldest friends from the past. Peter, this is my dear friend and colleague Florence Garland, famous actress and now antiques dealer.

Did you ever watch *Life with the Lilliputs?*'

'*Allo, dearies, let me slosh a bit of disinfectant in all your murky corners!*' Flo said hopefully.

Peter looked at her nervously, clearly not realizing that she was quoting her famous line, and murmured, 'How do you do?'

I washed out our hot-chocolate mugs and made coffee. I crept upstairs to see if Jordan wanted one, but she was fast asleep, snoring a little. She was holding something to her cheek. I peered – and realized  that it was Woofer. I tiptoed away, shaking my head.

When I got downstairs and handed out the coffees, I found Mum and Peter in deep discussion about Faraday Primary.

'Is it a really ropy school?' Mum asked.

'Well, it used to be – but now they've got a new head and he's already making a huge difference,' said Peter.

'Mr Harper,' I said. 'I like him.'

'Me too,' said Peter. 'Faraday is one of our feeder schools so I've got to know him quite well this past year.'

'So does this mean you could be Jess's head teacher when she goes to secondary school?' Mum said, giggling. 'Good Lord!'

'Well, let's hope Jess doesn't take after her mum too much,' said Peter, smiling.

'Hey, what's that supposed to mean?'

'Cheeking the teachers, never sitting still, telling fibs, writing your own funny stories instead of sticking to the subject, fighting in the playground—' Peter chanted.

'OK, OK! But I've changed now, haven't I, Jess?'

'Well . . .' I floundered. 'Tell you what, you're dead studious now, Mum.'

'Yes, she's always got her head in those blooming great library books,' said Flo.

'I'm learning my trade,' said Mum. 'It's actually quite interesting, finding out what all the little marks and squiggles mean, and the history of everything.'

'And we all watch *Antiques Roadshow* and *Celebrity Bargain Hunt* and *Any Old Junk*,' said Flo. 'Plus we have our specialities. Tracy's great on china and furniture and toys. I've got an eye for jewellery and clothes.' She rattled her amber necklaces and rearranged her Spanish shawl. 'And young Jess here is our literary specialist, aren't you, sweetheart? Always got her head in a book, that one.'

'Then you make a magnificent team,' said Peter. 'And I love the way everything's displayed!'

'That's the fun bit.' Mum put her head on one side.

'Are there any fun bits about being a head teacher, Peter?'

'Ha! Well, sometimes. The kids can crack you up, the funny things they come out with. And I've got a fantastic bunch of staff. We socialize quite a lot,' he said. 'You saw us at the Spade and Bucket on my birthday, remember?'

'*My* birthday!' Mum corrected him. 'But do you actually enjoy the *work* work? Striding about the school bossing everyone around?'

'Oh, come off it, Tracy. You know me. I'm definitely not a bossy kind of guy. I suppose I'm more the quiet but persuasive type. I find the paperwork a bit of a trial, but I love running the school, dealing with the kids.'

'Even the naughty ones like me?'

'They're my speciality. I had all that experience growing up with you! So what about you, Tracy? Have you always been in the antiques trade?'

'I've only just started, but this is my dream career, Pete. I've messed around doing all kinds of jobs – I ran a wine bar, worked in a car showroom, did a bit of nannying—'

'Mum was a dog walker once – that was the best!' I added.

'She was even a WAG, and that's a job and a half!' said Flo.

Peter looked blank.

'Wives and Girlfriends,' I explained, pulling a face. 'Footballers have them.'

'I wasn't a wife but I was a girlfriend for a while,' said Mum. 'Still, that's all in the past now.'

'Thank goodness,' I said.

'Was this footballer the guy I saw you with – the big chap with the shoulders and the swagger?' asked Peter.

'That's him,' said Mum. 'He's got a new girlfriend now. You'll never guess who! Justine Littlewood!'

And at that exact moment Justine Littlewood walked in the door, as if Mum had conjured her out of thin air! She marched in, slamming the door behind her so violently that all the china jingled. She wore a shiny black mac and shiny black high-heeled boots, and her hair shone in the light of the chandelier.

She pointed at Mum, her long fingernail gleaming like a stiletto. 'I want a word with you, Tracy Beaker!' she said.

'Oh my, it's the Wicked Witch of the West!' Flo gasped.

'Well said, Flo,' said Mum.

'Good Lord, it *is* Justine!' said Peter. 'Hello there!'

Justine glanced at him witheringly. 'Do I know you?' she asked.

'Of course you do, Justine. Don't you recognize him?' said Mum. 'Think back to our childhood.'

Justine gave Peter a proper look. Then she folded her arms and shook her head in disbelief. 'Peter Ingham!'

'How do you do,' he said, standing up and offering her his hand in an authoritative head-teacherly way that took her by surprise.

'Well, you've certainly changed!' she said. 'Last thing I remember you were wetting the bed and bursting into tears, Weedy Peter.'

I gasped at her cruelty, but Peter didn't seem thrown.

'Oh, the golden days of our childhood in care,' he said calmly. 'But here we all are, happy and successful – here's to us!' He raised his coffee mug.

Mum laughed and raised hers too.

230

'It's all right for you, Tracy Beaker,' said Justine. 'Yes, laugh your silly head off at me, make it worse. You couldn't be content, could you? You walked out on my Sean, turned your back on him, and now, out of sheer spite, you've decided to lure him back.'

'No she hasn't!' I cried, but my tummy turned over. Mum *couldn't* go back on her word, could she? *Oh please please please*, I prayed, *don't let her go back to Sean Godfrey.*

'It's all right, Jess,' Mum said quietly, coming and putting her arm round me. 'Don't take any notice of her. She's talking nonsense.'

'*I'm* the one talking nonsense, am I?' said Justine.

'Yes, you are. And you're upsetting my daughter and embarrassing my friends.'

The shop bell pinged again and a trio of elderly ladies in flimsy rain capes came into the shop, shaking their umbrellas, seeking shelter from the rain.

'Well, you should have thought of the consequences, you jealous cow!' Justine said. 'You couldn't bear it when Sean chose me over you! You've done your damnedest to get him back again – and I bet you don't even want him. You just want to take him away because you can't bear seeing me happy. You have to spoil everything. You haven't changed since we were kids and you deliberately broke my Mickey Mouse alarm clock, the one my dad gave me!'

The three old ladies stood there, dripping, their mouths open. It was as if they'd walked straight into a soap opera.

Flo heaved herself up from her sofa. 'I know this is riveting, ladies, but I'm afraid this is a private show. I'm shutting the shop just now — but please come back another day,' she said politely, stumping over to the door and opening it.

They filed out reluctantly, heads turned, desperate to see what happened next.

'Now then,' said Flo, shutting the door behind them and hanging the SO SORRY, WE ARE CLOSED sign on the glass. 'I don't think we've been introduced. I gather you are Miss Justine Littlewood. I am Miss Florence Garland, Tracy's business partner.'

Justine sniffed scornfully. 'Call this old junk shop a business?'

 Mum sprang across the room. 'Don't you dare be rude to my friend! And yes, it *is* a business, a very successful one, and for all the problems faced by independent shops nowadays we're actually making a big profit,' she said.

'I believe *your* so-called beauty-product business went bust.'

'That wasn't my fault! I couldn't travel because my dad started to get ill and couldn't cope without me,' Justine explained.

'Well, you've travelled all the way here, haven't you – and you can travel all the way back, pronto, because this is a totally wasted mission. I'm *not* trying to get Sean back. I've told him straight. So off you go, back to Daddy,' said Mum.

'You shut your mouth, Tracy Beaker. You're a liar and you know it. And don't you dare talk about my dad,' said Justine. Then her face screwed up. 'He's so ill he doesn't even recognize me now.' Tears suddenly spilled down her cheeks. She wiped them away fiercely, smearing her make-up and leaving black smudges under her eyes.

There was silence as we all stared at her.

I swallowed. 'Would you like a coffee, Justine?' I asked timidly.

'As if a coffee is going to help, you silly little kid,' she sniffed.

'Don't start picking on Jess. She's only trying to be kind,' said Mum.

'Oh yes, Mummy's little helper,' said Justine. 'You've got it all, haven't you, Tracy? Your happy new life and your sweet little girl, and my Sean texting you constantly, rushing down to see you every five minutes, and sending you flowers and chocolates.'

'What? He sent flowers once – to Flo and Jess as well as me. He hasn't sent any more since then. He did text for a bit but he's stopped now. He doesn't come here every five minutes. He came just the once, and that was because he's taken that weird kid Tyrone under his wing and *he* was desperate to come and see Jess,' said Mum.

'And he's never sent any chocolates,' I said.

'More's the pity,' said Flo. 'Chocolates are my little weakness – as you can see,' she added, patting her very big tummy.

'You can all stop the little comedy act,' Justine said furiously, still crying. 'I'm not a fool! I've seen the florist's bill on his bank statement. And one of your texts pinged in just this morning. He left his phone behind while he was at the gym. *Last night was wonderful – you're a guy in a million!!!*'

'What? Are you crazy? You're making it up. I never sent that!' said Mum. '*A guy in a million* with three exclamation marks? Really?'

'Of course you never sent it, Tracy. But of course you read the text, Justine,' said Peter. 'You're both bright women. Can't you see? This Sean is involved with someone else now.'

'What do you know about it, wimp?' said Justine, but she started crying in earnest now.

Peter put his arm round her and sat her down on one of the armchairs. 'How about making that coffee now, Jess?' he said, offering Justine several folded tissues from his pocket.

'Oh, Pete! The only guy alive who has a clean tissue at the ready!' said Mum.

'It's my stock in trade,' he said. 'All head teachers carry them. I've lost count of the number I've needed to hand over – to kids, to parents, to my staff.'

'You're a head teacher!' said Justine, and she snorted with laughter in the midst of her sobs.

I rushed out to the kitchen to make more coffee for Mum and Flo and Peter, and a new cup for Justine. It didn't seem quite the moment to ask if she liked milk and sugar.

When I came back Justine was still sniffing, but she'd recovered enough to peer into her powder compact and wipe away the panda rings. Alfie was standing anxiously beside her, trying to give her face an earnest lick. Justine tried batting him away but he became even more attentive. He licked her shiny black mac as if she was a giant stick of liquorice.

'Alfie! Stop it, you daft boy,' said Mum. She came and perched on the arm of Justine's chair. 'So your dad doesn't recognize you any more?' she asked softly.

'No!' said Justine. 'When I visit him at the care home he thinks I'm just a member of staff. He begs me to get in touch with his daughter – he wonders why she's stopped visiting him! And I keep telling him that *I'm* Justine, but I can't get him to believe me and it's so upsetting. It's not his fault – he's got dementia. He'll never get better.'

'I'm so sorry,' said Mum. 'I know how much he meant to you. Remember when we used to hang out by the window on Saturdays, you watching out for your dad and me looking for my mum. At least your dad generally turned up.'

'Do you see your mum now?' Justine asked.

'Once in a blue moon. She came running when Jess and I moved in with Sean, but I haven't seen her since,' said Mum. 'Justine, it's really and truly all over with him, I promise you. I'm not in touch with him in any way. I certainly don't have any feelings for him any more.'

'I drove down here to find you the minute I saw that text. I was going to have it out with you once and for all,' said Justine. 'I still don't know whether you're telling the truth or not.'

'She is, I swear it,' I said as I handed her a coffee – but even I wasn't a hundred per cent sure Mum wasn't telling a tiny fib.

'Why wouldn't you want Sean back?' Justine asked.

'Because . . .' said Mum, searching for words.

Because he's a lying, cheating pig who swaggers about and shows off! I said inside my head, trying to will Mum to say something similar.

'Because – because I'm involved with someone else,' said Mum.

We all stared at her.

Justine was looking at me. She must have seen my astonishment. 'If so, it's clearly news to Jess,' she said. 'You're just making it up! You're acting all nicey-nicey but secretly you're laughing at me.'

'I've kept it a secret because I know Jess has problems with my relationships. I was waiting until the time was right. It's hardly that now, but here goes. I'm in love with . . .' Mum paused.

'It's never Bill!' said Flo. 'You said he had a long-term lady friend.'

'No, not Bill. It's . . .' I saw Mum's eyes flicking to and fro. She was certainly fibbing now, trying to conjure up someone convincing.

'It's me!' said Peter.

'What?' said Justine.
'What?' said Flo.
'What?' I echoed. 'You and Mum?'

'Yes, Jess. I do hope you don't mind too much,' he said. 'I couldn't believe it when we met in the pub on our joint birthday! I've thought about her so often, wondering what she was doing. I've been crazy about her ever since we were in the children's home. And I'm still crazy about her now. We've been secretly seeing each other.'

He looked so sweetly serious I had to believe it – and yet it didn't make sense. *How* could he have been secretly seeing Mum when I was nearly always with her?

'Oh my goodness, you dark horse, Tracy Beaker!' said Flo, clapping her hands, clearly convinced.

I stared hard at Mum.

'I'm sorry I kept quiet about it, Jess,' she said. 'Will you forgive me?'

'Well, I suppose so,' I said, bewildered.

'Bless you, darling,' Mum said, giving me a kiss. Then she went over to Peter *and gave him a kiss too.*

'Oh my God!' said Justine. 'You and Weedy Peter!'

'If you call him that one more time I'll stop being Ms Nicey-Nicey, I'm warning you,' said Mum.

'Not so weedy now,' said Peter, flexing his arm and showing off a sizeable muscle. 'Otherwise all that swimming and badminton have been totally wasted!'

'Well, you've certainly changed.' Justine shook her head. 'I still can't believe it!' Yet as she looked at Mum, and then at Peter, I could see that she believed it.

I believed it too, though I didn't see how it was possible. Mum and Peter somehow looked so right together, side by side. They really did look like a proper couple – and Mum had never, ever looked completely right with Sean Godfrey.

Justine sighed. 'I've come all this way to have it out with you, Tracy – and now there's no point. Do you really think he's seeing some completely new girl?'

'Probably. I don't know. But it won't necessarily be serious. He was clearly really keen on you, Justine,' said Mum.

'Maybe. At first. But when you cleared off he went to pieces,' said Justine. 'I still think it's you he really loves.'

'No he doesn't. He just hated me leaving. If I went back to him he'd soon be playing around with someone else. He can't help it. He doesn't feel good about himself unless he's got new girls falling at his feet. Do you really want to hang around and get hurt?' asked Mum.

'Yes. No. I don't know,' said Justine.

'You could have anyone, a stunning-looking girl like you,' said Flo. 'I'd give anything to be young enough to wear that shiny mac and those amazing boots! Talk about the Killer Queen look!'

Justine smiled wanly. She blew her nose and then looked at herself in her powder compact again. 'Oh God, I look such a mess! Have you got a proper mirror?' she asked.

'Sure,' said Mum, and pointed up the stairs. 'The bedroom's on the right.'

'Jordan's in there, Mum!' I reminded her.

I wasn't quite quick enough. Justine was already halfway up the stairs.

'Oh Lord, I forgot. Oh well, she'll still be sound asleep.' Mum looked at Peter. 'You were incredible, butting in like that, sounding so convincing! You're such a sweetheart – it was about the only way I could get her to believe that I don't want Sean back.'

'And you really don't?' Peter asked.

'No! Never. Not in a million years,' said Mum.

'Hang on a minute,' said Flo. 'So you two were just acting for Justine's benefit?'

'Of course we were,' said Mum.

'Well—' said Peter.

'Oh my stars, you certainly had *us* convinced – didn't they, Jess?' said Flo. 'I've seen more acting in my time than you've had hot dinners, but I've never seen such a genuine performance. There seemed to be a real connection – total Romeo and Juliet time! I was already imagining hobbling up the aisle on my Zimmer frame, the oldest matron of honour in the world. Were you wondering what colour your bridesmaid's dress was going to be, Jess?'

I was still in such a muddle I didn't have an answer. Bridesmaid's dress? Mum and Peter weren't really in love. They weren't a couple. They hardly knew each other. Though of course they had actually known each other for twenty-five years or more.

'Mum?' I said.

But then there was a great scream from upstairs.

12

JORDAN CAME CHARGING down the stairs in her borrowed nightdress. Her face was red with rage.

'You liar!' she shouted at Mum. Then she looked at me. 'How could you have let her, Jess? I thought you were my *friend*!'

'I am!' I said.

'Don't give me that! I'm out of here!' said Jordan as Justine came clattering down behind her, nearly tripping in her high-heeled boots.

'You might have warned me there was the girl from hell sleeping in your bed!' she said. 'She actually tried to take a swing at me!'

'I hate social workers!' Jordan said furiously.

'What? You think I'm a *social worker*?' Justine demanded, outraged.

'The new Elaine the Pain,' said Mum, and she doubled up laughing.

Peter joined in. Even Justine snorted.

'Don't you dare laugh at me!' said Jordan. 'You give me my clothes back, Tracy, and then I'm out of here, and none of you can stop me, see.'

'We're not laughing at you, Jordan. We're laughing at you thinking Justine was a social worker. I had this poor woman called Elaine as my social worker and we all used to take the mick – she was pretty useless. Well, I suppose she was simply doing her best. *I* was the pain,' said Mum.

'You sound as if you've done self-awareness therapy,' said Peter, gently mocking her.

'Are *you* the social worker then?' Jordan demanded.

'No. He's an even worse figure of authority – he's a head teacher, believe it or not,' said Mum. 'Sit yourself down, Jordan. Flo, lend us your shawl, darling, I don't want her getting cold again.' She leaned forward and put her hand on Jordan's forehead.

'Get off me!' Jordan snarled.

'I'm seeing if you've got a temperature. Have you got a thermometer anywhere, Flo? Jess, make Jordan another hot chocolate. Jump to it!'

'I guess I'm just the waitress around here,' I said.

'You haven't changed one bit, have you, Tracy Beaker?' said Justine.

'That's my girl,' said Peter.

'I don't want a hot chocolate! Just give me my clothes!' Jordan yelled.

Mum held her by the elbows. Jordan struggled, but Mum hung on tightly. She's got a very firm grip. I should know.

'I can't give you your clothes,' she said. 'They're in the washing machine, soaking wet. I can stop the cycle and fish them out, but if you go round Cooksea like that, then people will think you've tried to drown yourself and they'll have an ambulance on your tail in minutes. And I can't lend you my clothes because they won't fit, and apart from her shawl Flo's clothes will be way too big.'

'Charming,' said Flo, draining her coffee. 'I can't help being a Two-Ton Tessie. It's my glands, I'll have you know. Is it hot chocolate for everyone? Could you make me one too, Jess, lovey, with a dollop of whipped cream on top?'

'If you wander off in that nightie you'll get stopped too,' Mum continued. 'In fact, you can't wander off anywhere because I'm pretty sure you *have* got a temperature – if you're not careful you'll develop pneumonia and end up in hospital anyway.'

'I don't *care*,' said Jordan. 'I don't care if I end up *dead*. And no one else cares either. Who's come looking for me since I ran away? I might just as well chuck myself off a cliff.'

'Well, you've got plenty to choose from round here,' said Mum. 'But I'm not going to let you, see. Because *I* care about you. I know what you're going through. And so does Peter here. And even Justine.'

'I ran away when I was your age,' said Justine. 'I thought I could fend for myself. I had it all sussed out. I ran off with a boyfriend.'

'I wanted *my* boyfriend to come with me,' said Jordan, more quietly now, 'but he was too chicken.'

'My guy stuck around a while. Long enough to get me into drugs and all sorts. I thought I was being so tough and daring. But it was a nightmare, living in a squat, never getting enough to eat, not even having a proper wash. Is that what you want?' Justine asked.

'But look at you now. You seem so cool and smart,' Jordan pointed out.

'Because I got nicked stealing something, and then I was back in care, and then I did a course at college and got a job in an office – even did a bit of modelling,' said Justine.

'Yeah, like that's going to happen to me,' said Jordan.

'She's got her own business now – well, she *did* have,' said Mum. 'And a famous boyfriend.'

'Ha!' said Justine.

I didn't want to miss a word of this, but I went to make the hot chocolate. I was still worried that Jordan would rush off in her borrowed nightdress. I could see her running wildly down to the seafront, clambering up the cliff path, teetering on the edge . . .

But when I came back in, I saw that she was sitting in Peter's chair and he was squatting beside her, talking quietly. She looked much calmer now.

Mum was squeezed up beside Justine and they seemed to be chatting like old friends. Mum even patted her on the shoulder – and she didn't push her away, she just smiled wanly.

Flo was leaning forward, craning her head this way and that, as if switching madly between two fascinating soap operas.

I handed round hot chocolates, giving the creamiest one to Jordan. She nodded at me and sipped it gratefully. She was already looking a bit better.

I sat down cross-legged on the floor beside Alfie. He nudged against me happily, his soft head burrowing into my neck. I put my arms round him.

'Are you OK, Jess?' Mum asked, looking over at me. 'You're a little star.'

'I wish *I* had a daughter,' said Justine.

'Well, there's still heaps of time.'

'If I had a baby, do you think Sean would stop playing around and be a proper father?' Justine asked.

I tried to imagine a Sean Godfrey baby daughter, with his silly haircut and huge shoulders and a too-tight babygro. It was a pretty scary thought.

'I think Sean would be a good father,' Mum said thoughtfully.

'No he wouldn't!' I said quickly. 'He was ever so mean to me. He wouldn't even let me feed Alfie.'

'He wouldn't let you feed Alfie titbits while you were eating, that's all. He did try with you, Jess. And he's been great with Tyrone,' said Mum.

'Why are you sticking up for him when you don't want him any more?' I asked.

'I'm just being truthful, that's all. He'd probably be a great father. But I don't think it would stop him playing around, Justine. That's just the way he is,' said Mum. 'If you think he'll change, it'll break your heart. But you could look the other way and try not to mind. Lots of women do. But not me.'

'I can't see Peter playing away!' said Justine, turning to look at him. 'It's weird seeing him so kind of grown up and sensible and – and *headmasterly*!'

'I know,' said Mum.

'And you're a serious item?' Justine had lowered her voice, but I still heard her clearly.

I strained forward.

'Well, it's early days yet,' Mum murmured, glancing over to see if I was listening. 'We'll have to see.'

'But you'd like it to be serious?'

Mum hesitated and then nodded.

I clutched Alfie tightly, peering across at Peter. I tried to imagine him as Mum's boyfriend. What if they really did get serious and we lived with him? It would be a serious squash upstairs. I hoped I wouldn't be sent downstairs to sleep in Flo's room. For all I'd been longing to find Mum a boyfriend, I really liked it best when it was just Mum and me, the way it used to be.

Even so, I liked Peter. I liked him a lot. He was kind and friendly and he loved books. You'd feel safe with him. He'd be a lovely head teacher, not scary like Mrs Michaels at my old school.

Mum thought he liked guys instead of girls – but she was clearly wrong. She had always joked about him when she talked about her childhood. She was the one who'd given him the nickname Weedy Peter

Peter himself was still talking to Jordan, discussing placements and residential homes and all sorts of other stuff. He said several children at his school were in care and they were all doing well, though a couple had had various issues at first.

'Yeah, I've got plenty of them issues!' said Jordan. 'OK, if I stick around here, perhaps I'll come to your school and sit exams and stuff, if you think it's important.'

'Well, let's see if it's possible,' said Peter. 'If your local authority wanted to send you all the way to Manchester, I can't see why they wouldn't support you here – but it's going to be very difficult to find you somewhere suitable.'

'No it isn't,' said Jordan. 'It's easy-peasy. I'll stay here!'

'Here in Cooksea?'

'Here with Tracy and Jess and the *Lilliput* lady.'

'Bless!' Flo murmured.

'I don't think that would be possible,' said Peter.

'Yes it is!' Jordan raised her voice. 'Tracy?'

'Yes, Jordan?' said Mum.

'*You* can foster me!'

'What? But I'm not a foster parent, sweetheart. Jess is my daughter,' Mum pointed out.

'And I could be your foster daughter,' said Jordan.

'I'm afraid that isn't going to happen, Jordan, much as I'd like to,' said Mum.

'Why isn't it?' she demanded.

'Well, for starters, there aren't any spare bedrooms here.'

'There's a little box room full of junk next to your bedroom – I looked. I could squeeze in there. I could have one of them camp beds. Anything would be more comfortable than a beach shelter,' said Jordan.

I blinked. Mum and I had made plans.

'That's going to be Jess's room,' Mum said gently.

'We could share. We'd love that, wouldn't we, Jess?' Jordan was looking at me, her eyes wide and pleading. I didn't know what to say.

'It's not up to Jess,' said Mum, trying to get me off the hook.

'But we're best friends,' said Jordan. 'Aren't we, Jess?'

I'd always longed for a proper best friend, but it hadn't been easy to find

one. When Mum and I lived with Cam, all
her girls were much older than me. Then,
when I went to Duke Primary, my
classmates already had best friends and I
was a bit left out. I ended up with Tyrone for a mate,
even though he'd started off being my worst enemy.
All things considered he didn't really qualify as a
best friend. I'd thought Alice was a true best
friend. We used to have fun together – but
when she came to Cooksea she seemed to
have changed. We didn't really know what to
say to each other. And she'd found a new best friend
at her posh school anyway.

In my head I had an ideal best friend –
a girl just like me, who was shy inside
even though she was learning to stick up
for herself, a girl who liked reading and
drawing and playing pretend games. But she was
imaginary. Jordan was real. We didn't have a thing
in common and she was a bit tough and scary and
she was older too – but somehow we'd become really
close. You couldn't help it, huddled under a blanket
together.

'Yeah, we're best friends,' I said. 'Sort of.'

Jordan's eyes went all watery and she smiled at me.

'Well, that's great,' said Mum, 'but I still couldn't
be a foster parent. You have to be vetted and do all

kinds of special training and go to interviews where they delve into your background. Given my history I'd be the last person they'd want.'

'I think you'd actually make a great foster parent, Tracy,' said Peter. 'You've got a lifetime's experience of the care system.'

'Speak for yourself, Peter!' said Mum.

'Well, I've sometimes wondered about fostering myself, but I'm always so tied up at work – and it's harder if you're a single guy,' he said.

'But you're not a single guy now you and Tracy have got together,' said Justine. She chuckled. 'You two could start your very own children's home. You could be the new Mike and Jenny. The Peter and Tracy Dumping Ground.'

'Well, I know we wouldn't call it that. I'm sure that nickname would be frowned on nowadays. What do children call residential homes now, Jordan?' Peter asked.

'Prison,' she said shortly.

'Well, Cam's girls call it home,' I said.

'I'm going to phone her,' said Mum. 'Where is your children's home Jordan?'

'No! Don't phone her,' said Jordan.

'Listen . . .' Mum went over and held her by the shoulders. Jordan told her and Mum said, 'I think that's quite near Cam. I'm pretty certain she can't take you and, even if she agrees, there'll be all kinds of boring procedures. But let's try, because it's your best option – way better than being shipped off to Manchester or wherever. I *know* you'll like it there. Cam's my *mum* – and if she hadn't fostered me, goodness knows where I'd have ended up.

'Settle down with her and stop running away, OK? And meanwhile I'll have a serious think about fostering. I'll talk it over properly with Jess and Flo, and I'll have a chat with the fostering service, and then, you never know, you *might* be able to come and live with us. What do you think?'

'I don't like all this *might* stuff,' said Jordan. 'Why won't you promise and say definitely?'

'Because I don't want to make any promises I can't keep,' said Mum. 'I want to be straight with you. We don't know each other properly. We only met this morning! But if you're at Cam's we'll come and visit you – and you can visit us – and, even if the fostering idea falls through, you can still be our friend. We're kind of alike, you and me.

'Will you teach me how to kick-box?' Jordan asked.

Justine snorted. 'You don't want to do that. I'm sure I've still got the bruises on my bum from when Tracy floored me,' she said. Her phone bleeped and she fished it out of her bag and stared at the screen. Her face went pink.

'Is it Sean?' said Mum.

'Yes! He's wondering where on earth I am. And he says – well, never mind what he says. But he sounds like he cares.' Justine texted rapidly, a little smile on her face.

'Really?'

'I know, I know. But maybe I was getting the wrong end of the stick before. That's what he says. And I don't always get it right. After all, I was convinced he was still seeing you, and you swear he's not. You do swear, don't you?' said Justine.

'I swear,' said Mum.

'She's definitely *not* seeing him,' I assured her.

'She's seeing *me*,' said Peter.

Another text pinged on Justine's phone. She read it, her smile getting wider. 'Looks like *I'm* still seeing Sean!' She looked at Mum. 'I know you think I'm a fool, but I don't care. He's the man of my dreams. And I'm going to start trusting him.'

'What was it my old granny used to say?' said Flo. 'Never trust a man, a shilling's your best friend.'

Jordan looked at me, screwing up her face. 'What are they on about?'

'Just boyfriends,' I said.

She came over to me. 'Do you think your mum

means it when she says she might foster me?' she whispered.

'I think so,' I said.

'And what do you feel about it, Jess? You wouldn't mind?' she asked huskily.

'Of course not,' I said, though I wasn't exactly telling the truth.

I really wanted Mum all to myself, even though I knew that was probably very selfish. But if Mum and Peter were going to be an item, maybe it would be good to have a friend to hang out with. A foster sister. You didn't have to get on with your sister all the time. Alice was always falling out with Ava. But deep down, even when they were yelling at each other, they cared.

'Maybe it would be fun,' I said.

'You're as bad as your mum. *Might* this, *maybe* that. It would be great!' said Jordan.

'You wouldn't try to make me shoplift?' I whispered.

'Well, there would be no need, would there, because Tracy would give us lots of make-up and designer clobber.'

'No she wouldn't. We're dead poor! Mum's always saying we can't afford stuff. And I don't wear make-up or designer things anyway, I'm too young.'

'Yeah, I keep forgetting you're just a little kid. I'll be like your big sister,' said Jordan.

'That doesn't mean you can boss me about.'

'It means I'll look out for you and make sure no one picks on you.'

'What if they snatch my ice cream?' I said, grinning.

'I'll flatten them,' said Jordan, grinning back.

Alfie came and wagged his tail, happy to see us smiling. Jordan rubbed his head, making his ears waggle. He usually dislikes it when people do that and backs away, growling – but he seemed happy enough when Jordan did it.

'Can Alfie be my dog too?' she asked.

I wasn't ready to go that far. 'You can have your own dog. Alfie would love a playmate,' I said.

'Can I really?' said Jordan. 'Oh wow! I'm going to get one of those amazing huskies with blue eyes just like mine.'

'No huskies,' said Peter firmly. 'I know they're beautiful, but they're pack animals. They were bred to pull sledges. They need to live with other dogs and go for really long runs every day.'

'My husky could join up with Alfie and pull Jess and me along the seafront in a sledge,' said Jordan. 'That would be so cool.'

'Cruel, not cool. You need a huge garden to keep a husky happy,' Peter insisted. 'They need the right environment to thrive, otherwise they cause havoc.'

'I've only got a little back yard,' said Flo. 'Though Jess has plans to turn it into a garden, haven't you, pet?'

'Are you saying I can't have a dog then?' said Jordan.

'Perhaps a small one. A little rescue dog from Battersea Dogs and Cats Home. But we'll have to make sure it gets on with Alfie,' said Mum.

'*Perhaps!* That's another *might* and *maybe* word,' said Jordan, but she was smiling. 'Hey, I'm a rescue girl and I have to have the right environment to thrive otherwise *I* cause havoc. I'd be as good as gold if I could live here with you guys.'

'That's it, kid. You tell them,' said Justine. 'Well, I'm off.'

'Stay for lunch,' Mum said surprisingly.

'Thanks, but I need to get home.'

'Sean's home?' asked Mum.

'It's my home now,' said Justine.

'Well, I think you're mad,' said Mum – and she suddenly got to her feet and rushed towards her.

Justine took a step backwards in alarm, but Mum

simply threw her arms round her and gave her a big hug. Justine teetered in her high-heeled boots, but then gave Mum a wary pat on the back.

'Good luck,' said Mum.

'Well, thanks,' said Justine. 'I suppose this was a bit of a wasted journey, eh?'

'No it wasn't. I know we've always been worst enemies – but maybe it's time to be friends. We're kind of family, you and me and Peter. I bet old Elaine the Pain would be proud if she could see us all now,' said Mum. 'Keep in touch, Justine.'

'Maybe,' she said. 'See you, Tracy. Bye, mini Tracy. Bye, Flo. Bye, Jordan – I hope everything works out for you.' Then she fist-bumped Peter. 'Bye, you! I still can't get over it – you and Tracy!'

She stalked out of the shop, waving her hand in the air.

'I don't get it,' said Jordan. 'Isn't her bloke playing around with someone else?'

'Yes, but she's decided she doesn't care. Just so long as it isn't me,' said Mum. 'I used to live with Sean Godfrey, her boyfriend. I was engaged to him, actually. And then she came along and— Well, it's history now.'

'Wait a minute. Is this *the* Sean Godfrey you're talking about? Sean Godfrey the famous footballer?' asked Jordan. 'The really hot one?'

Mum pulled a face. 'I wouldn't go that far.'

'I would,' said Flo.

'And you'd sooner have *him* for a boyfriend?' Jordan asked with supreme lack of tact, nodding at Peter.

Luckily Peter smiled. 'Yes – weird, isn't it,' he said.

'Oh, Pete, you were so brilliant!' said Mum. 'We really convinced her, didn't we? You were so clever, making out we were madly in love!'

'But you're not, are you?' I asked, feeling dizzy. I couldn't keep track of what was true.

'No, darling – I *said*, we were just pretending. Of course Peter and I aren't an item. Peter's gay, you know that,' said Mum.

'Oh yes,' I said, remembering him hugging the young guy at the library.

'What makes you think I'm gay?' he asked.

'Well, I wasn't sure at first, but then Jess and I saw you with your friend after we'd had coffee together,' said Mum.

Peter looked puzzled – and then he laughed. 'That was Pat! I tutored him last year and he got a place at Cambridge. He loves it there. He wanted to tell me all about it. He's all hugs and happiness at the moment, bless him.'

'Oh!' said Mum.

'I wasn't acting, Tracy. You know I've been madly in love with you ever since I was a little kid.' Peter was trying to say it in a casual, throwaway manner, but he went very red.

'You're joking, right?' said Mum uncertainly.

'I'm not the joking sort, you know that. Deadly serious, that's me,' he said. 'I couldn't believe my eyes when we met up on our birthday. And then we kept bumping into each other!'

'But why didn't you *say* anything? You could have asked me out!'

'I was sure you'd say no. You've always made it very plain what you think of me!'

'Well, you happen to be wrong this time, Mr Know-it-all Head Teacher. I was actually pretty thrilled to see you. Maybe if you were to ask me out, then I might say yes,' said Mum.

'*Maybe! Might!* Ask her out then!' said Jordan.

'Would you like to go out with me sometime, Tracy?' Peter asked obediently.

'Not *sometime*! Ask her out *now*!'

'OK. Will you come out with me right now, Tracy Beaker?'

We all stared at Mum. She went very pink too! I'd never seen her look embarrassed before. But she nodded.

'Yes, please,' she said. 'Just let me make a quick phone call first.'

13

M UM WENT RIGHT outside the shop to have a private phone conversation with Cam. Peering through the shop window, we saw her pacing up and down, talking and talking. It was a very long phone call.

'It's not going to work, is it?' said Jordan, heaving a huge sigh and standing up.

'You wait. You don't know my mum,' I told her.

'Where's the washing machine? I'm going to see if my clothes are ready,' she said.

'Oh no you don't! You're not doing a runner. And they'll still be soaking wet – we don't have a dryer,' said Flo.

'You've got to wait to see what Mum says anyway.'

I patted the sleeve of the voluminous nightgown. 'Patience!'

'Yeah, but I don't have any, do I?' said Jordan. 'At school they said I was ADHD.'

'What's that?'

'She can't sit still and concentrate,' said Peter.

'Ants in my pants, that's what my last foster mum said,' said Jordan.

'We're going to need her name and details. And your social worker's, of course. And there'll have to be a conference. Maybe several.' Peter sighed too.

'How come you're getting involved?' said Jordan. 'You don't even know me.'

'I know your situation. I'm a head teacher. I know the routine. And I know Tracy. We're old friends.'

'And now you're going to be my mum's boyfriend!' I said.

'Maybe. Though she might change her mind.'

'*Might* and *maybe* again,' said Jordan. 'You're nuts. You're obviously mad about her and she likes you, so what's the problem?'

'Tracy's going to get fed up if you dither around,' said Flo.

'Yep, you're right. Thanks for the advice, ladies,' said Peter. He looked at me. 'How do you feel about me and your mum, Jess? Does it seem a bit weird?'

'It felt a whole lot weirder when she was seeing Sean Godfrey,' I told him.

He was looking at me earnestly, as if it really mattered to him what I thought.

'Actually, it's weird in a nice way,' I said. 'You're much nicer than any of Mum's other boyfriends. It just feels odd that you're actually that little boy from her children's home. She often talked about you, even before we met you again.'

'Yes, and I bet I know the sort of things she said,' Peter replied. 'I bet the word *weedy* cropped up a lot.'

'You're not a bit weedy now,' I said. 'It's only a silly nickname. I used to get called all sorts at my old school.'

'Me too,' said Jordan. 'Though I used to slap them.'

'That's not a great way to deal with it,' said Peter.

'You're right – I ended up being excluded, even though it wasn't my fault. Well, not always,' said Jordan. 'But don't tell Tracy or she'll think I'm too much of a handful.'

'I think she's probably guessed that,' said Peter. 'And I know for a fact that Tracy was a huge handful herself when she was young.'

'Was she really, really bad?' I asked, fascinated.

'Come on, tell us,' said Flo, leaning forward eagerly.

'Well, there was the time she set the classroom gerbils free – and the time she pretended to be a ghost – and the time she tried to make chips in the middle of the night and set off the smoke alarm – and the time she inked tattoos all over her arms and legs when the inspectors were coming – and the time she kicked her social worker on the shin – and then of course there were the endless times she got into fist fights with Justine . . .'

'*Seriously?*' I gasped, round-eyed.

'Oops!' said Flo, chuckling.

'That's nothing,' said Jordan. 'They're just little-kid pranks.'

'She *was* a little kid at the time. She was a lot worse when she got older,' said Peter. 'She was really pretty awesomely terrible when she was ten or eleven – and then she got fostered by Cam. We were so envious. We all loved Cam. She came to the home to do an article about us for some magazine – and then she kept on coming and made a fuss of us.'

'But she liked my mum best,' I said proudly.

'Well, your mum pestered her most!' said Peter, but I think he was joking. He peered out of the window at her. She was still talking on the phone. 'It looks as if she's *still* pestering her.'

But at last Mum came back indoors, and she was smiling.

'Has she said she'll take Jordan?' I asked eagerly.

'Well, not exactly. She wavered for ages, but I think it helps that your local authority will know her. I could hear Mary going on at her in the background. *She* thinks we should get you checked out by a doctor, and then call your social worker, and then there'll have to be endless checks and discussions. She has to do things the boring proper way. Typical teacher!'

'She's right, Tracy,' Peter told her.

'Oh. Sorry. I forgot you're one too. But that way Jordan will be whisked off to this place in Manchester and we'll never get her out. I think we should check Jordan's OK health-wise, and then drive her straight up to Cam's. She says she's willing to have her as an emergency placement, if the local authority approves it – she'll see how things pan out. We'll tell the social worker and I don't see how she can possibly object: it'll be much cheaper if Jordan's with Cam, and *she's* the star of the care system because she's so good with her girls,' Mum said breathlessly.

'Yeah, well, I bet I'll be her first failure,' said Jordan. 'I still don't see why I can't stay here with you.'

'I'm not an approved foster carer. Yet. But I said I'd think about it seriously. And *you've* got to do some serious thinking too, Jordan. If you do a runner again, then they really will put you in some kind of secure care home.'

'Yeah, I've heard about them – all the rules and regulations and being locked up at night.'

'Well, if you end up here in a few months' time, you'll find *we've* got rules and regulations too, missy,' said Mum. 'And I'll certainly lock you up if you try staying out at night. And likely handcuff you and put you in leg irons.'

'Ha ha,' said Jordan. 'I know you're joking.'

Mum folded her arms and looked at me, eyebrows raised. 'Tell her, Jess!'

'She's joking about the handcuff stuff. But she *is* very strict,' I said.

'And I'm an old tartar too,' said Flo. 'See this walking stick? Give me any cheek and I'll whack you on the bum.'

Jordan laughed uncertainly. 'Not sure I want to come here after all,' she said, but she was joking too.

'So, it's all settled then,' said Mum. 'I suppose I'd better rustle up a late lunch and then we'll hit the road.'

'If you don't mind keeping the shop shut, come out for lunch at the Spade and Bucket,' said Peter, 'seeing as we've got something to celebrate.'

'This chap is growing on me,' said Flo.

Mum rescued Jordan's clothes from the washing machine and, taking Alfie for company, I ran off through the rain to the old launderette to give them a spin in the big tumble dryer. I usually had a book with me when I was being the laundrymaid, but this time I simply sat there, my thoughts spinning around my head as rapidly as the wet washing in the dryer.

So much had happened in just one morning! It was hard to take it all in. I'd been bold and rescued Jordan! Mum might foster her! She'd also made friends with Justine Littlewood! And she wanted to go out with Peter Ingham! All these astonishing statements lit up before my eyes like neon signs.

'What do you think about everything, Alfie?' I asked.

He wagged his tail enthusiastically.

'Do you think it will all work out OK?'

He butted my knees and then laid his head lovingly on

my lap. He seemed to be telling me that of course it would.

When we got back to the shop, the same three old ladies were clustered outside the door, frowning at the CLOSED sign.

'They're still inside, I can see them!' said one.

'I wonder what they're up to now,' said another.

'They're meant to be open! Call themselves shopkeepers! We want to come in out of the rain!' said the third.

I sidled past them and tapped on the door.

'Ah, are you opening up now?' asked the first old lady.

'No, I'm sorry. We're going out for lunch. But there's a warm launderette just up the road if you want to be in the dry,' I said politely as Mum let me in.

Jordan looked a lot better when she put her clean dry clothes on. She wanted to wear the baseball cap too, but now that it had been washed the peak hung down limply, flapping on her forehead, so she threw it off in disgust. I lent her my brush so she could sort her tangled hair.

'I should have chopped it all off,' she said impatiently.

'Then you'd have been bonkers. Your hair's lovely,' I said. 'I'd swap you any day.'

'Here, look in the mirror!' Jordan stood above me and let her hair flop around my face.

'I look so different!' I said.

'I wish *I* looked different. Still, I don't suppose it matters if I'm recognized now, seeing as I've been caught.'

I didn't like to tell her that no one seemed to realize she was missing. It must be awful, no one bothering whether you were there or not.

'You belong to us now,' I said suddenly.

I glanced up at her face in the mirror. She looked as if she was going to cry, but I think she was happy rather than sad.

'Are you all right?' I asked.

'Course I am,' she said, sniffing.

Her trainers were still sopping wet. My shoes were obviously much too small. Mum's too. So Jordan had to wear Flo's flowery wellies to the pub, though she protested bitterly.

'I look a right berk in these,' she complained.

'There's gratitude!' said Flo, giving her a nudge. 'You mind your manners, young lady, or I'll slosh a bit of disinfectant in all *your* murky corners!'

Jordan burst out laughing. She had a funny laugh,

more like a cackle. Just hearing it made you smile. 'I loved it when you said that on the telly.'

'In my glorious soap-opera days! Tell you what, my whole life's turned into a blooming soap opera since Tracy and Jess came to live with me!'

'Sorry, Flo! I suppose things have been a bit hectic, especially today,' said Mum.

'Don't apologize, darling, I'm absolutely loving it,' said Flo. 'I don't want to miss any juicy developments while you're down the pub!'

'What do you mean?' said Mum. 'You're coming too. We'll take the van again.'

'You don't want all that hassle – it's a bore for everyone. You lot toddle off down the road and have your lunch. You can bring me back a bottle of beer and a bag of crisps.'

'As if!' said Mum. 'You're part of the family.'

'Is Flo *really* part of your family, like an old aunty or something?' Jordan whispered to me.

'Well, she seems like one now, but she's just a lady we started living with,' I explained.

Jordan thought about it. 'So it's like she's fostering both of you?'

'Sort of.'

'And you're all proper family now,' said Jordan. 'So I could be too, couldn't I?'

'It seems like you already are,' I told her.

When we went to have lunch at the Spade and Bucket, we really did seem like one big family – Mum and Peter and Flo and Jordan and Alfie and me. Mum and I had spaghetti bolognese, because that's what we'd had the very first time we went there on our first day in Cooksea. Peter had sausage and mash and onion gravy. Flo had fish and chips and mushy peas. Jordan had burger and chips. And Alfie had a whole sausage and couldn't believe his luck. Peter immediately became his favourite – after me, of course.

Then we drove back to the shop and opened up at last.

'Can I leave you in charge, Flo, if I drive Jordan up to Cam's?' Mum asked.

'Course you can, darling,' she said.

'Jess will help you, won't you, baby?'

'Oh! Can't I come to Cam's too?' I pleaded.

'Yes, she's got to come with me!' said Jordan. 'I won't get so fussed if Jess is there.'

'I'd quite like to come as well, if you don't mind my barging in. I'm used to dealing with social workers,' said Peter. 'We could take my car so the girls don't have to rattle around in the back of the van.'

So we ended up with Peter driving us in his Volvo, Mum in the front with him, and Jordan and me in the back. Alfie curled up on my lap and went to sleep. At first I showed Jordan my favourite places and she asked all sorts of questions, loving the hills and fields and meadows, but when we reached the main road to London she grew quiet, and soon she wasn't saying anything at all, just staring straight ahead, twiddling a lock of her hair.

'What's the matter?' I asked. 'Do you feel sick? Shall I get Peter to stop?'

Jordan shook her head. 'I'm OK,' she said, though she clearly wasn't.

'Are you . . . scared?' I whispered.

'A bit,' she murmured.

'There's nothing to be scared of,' I told her. 'Cam's lovely, honestly.'

'Yeah, but I don't know her, do I? And she's got other girls too, hasn't she? I'll be the new one. They'll all gang up on me. That's what happens. And then I kick off and I get the blame. And anyway, they probably won't let me stay with her. I'll have to go to the place in Manchester and I know it'll be a nightmare. How would you feel if you were me? Wouldn't you be scared?'

'Yes,' I said, feeling stupid. 'Very scared. I suppose you'll just have to be brave. You are, you know. I wouldn't dare run away or scavenge for food or stay out by myself all night.'

'Yeah, well, that was a bit scary too. Especially last night in the rain. I felt so awful this morning. I couldn't believe it when you appeared, bringing the food and the blanket and stuff. I might be a bit braver, but you're the clever one. You think of things, Jess. I just *do* things and then get into trouble.'

'But you mustn't any more,' I said anxiously.

'I won't, not any more,' she told me.

I didn't feel very reassured. It was like Mum promising she'd never get mouthy with anyone ever again. She meant it at the time, but then she forgot.

I think Peter might have been listening because he put on the car radio to distract us, flicking through the stations until he found some cool music. It was a good move. I didn't know any of the songs – I'm not really into that sort of thing – but Jordan was word perfect on most of them. She sang along in her husky voice, sounding really good.

'You're a great singer,' I said admiringly.

'You sing too,' she said.

'I can't. I don't know any of the words,' I admitted.

She was amazed. 'How come you don't know *this*?' and, 'You can't seriously not know *that*!' she exclaimed. It made her feel very superior, which would have been annoying at any other time but now I was quite pleased.

However, when we got to the outskirts of London she got quieter again, and said she didn't feel like singing any more. I suggested playing a car game like I-Spy or Famous People but she gave me a withering look.

'All right, it was only a suggestion,' I said.

'What are these games anyway?' she asked. 'I bet they're babyish.'

'*I* like car games,' said Peter. 'OK, let's play just for a bit. I'll start. I spy with my little eye something beginning with T.'

'Oh, *I* get it,' said Jordan. 'And it's *Tracy*, obviously, because you can hardly keep your eyes off her. It's a wonder you haven't crashed the car.'

'Less cheek, please,' he said. 'And you're wrong. Try again.'

I think he *had* chosen T for *Tracy*, but had now changed it just to be awkward. We all tried and tried and got nowhere, and then eventually he said it was *terrace*.

'You what?' said Jordan.

'Terrace. As in a terrace of houses,' said Peter.

'I love these old Victorian terraces. My foster parents lived in a little terraced house. It was so cosy and old-fashioned. It didn't even have an inside loo, but it didn't matter a bit. Well, it did if you were taken short in the middle of the night, but I didn't really mind. The first year I lived with them Ma would get up too and wrap a blanket around me.'

'So you called her Ma?' Mum asked.

'Yes, Ma and Pa,' he said.

Mum looked round at Jordan. 'If you start calling me Ma you'll get a thick ear,' she warned her. 'I always call Cam *Cam*.'

'This Cam – she's really OK?' Jordan asked me in an undertone.

'I keep saying, she's lovely. She's my second favourite person in all the world after Mum,' I said.

Jordan fidgeted. 'Can't I be your second favourite if I'm going to be your foster sister?'

'Well, maybe second equal,' I said, to keep the peace.

'You said your pa died, Peter?' Mum asked.

'And Ma died soon afterwards. I still miss them a lot. They were great parents,' he said.

So maybe he didn't have any favourites himself, unless it was Mum. I went a bit quiet then. I liked the idea of Mum having Peter for a boyfriend, though obviously they hadn't even gone out on a proper date together yet – but I knew I'd hate it if *he* became her favourite. I felt it had been touch and go with Sean Godfrey at times.

I-Spy was a bit boring with Peter playing because he kept choosing the most obscure words and winning over and over again, which irritated all of us, especially Mum. So we played Famous People instead – that game where you think of a famous person and the others ask you questions to see if they can guess who it is.

Jordan was great at guessing celebrities, but we found it hard work guessing her famous people as we'd often never heard of them. She loved this game and said she was cleverer than all of us. We were totally stumped on her last choice. We established that she was thinking of a female, still alive, not a YouTuber or a singer or an actor or a model, and we tried endless possibilities, but Jordan kept on shaking her head.

'Come on, it's easy-peasy!' she said.

'Are you *sure* we've heard of her?' Peter asked.

'Yes!'

'Oh come on, Jordan, we give up. Tell us,' said Mum.

'It's you,' she said.

'What?'

'*You*. Tracy Beaker!' she declared triumphantly.

'But I'm not famous.'

'Yes you are, Mum,' I said. 'Everyone knows you.'

'See!' said Jordan.

'Yes, but I'm not really famous,' said Mum. 'I'm not famous for anything. I wish I was! I used to want to be a writer, but that's never going to happen.'

'It's already happened, Mum. You wrote that book about yourself,' I pointed out.

'*Did* you?' Peter sounded extremely interested.

'Yes, but my friend Marina, who's a publisher, said it wasn't much good. And I'd probably be sued simply because I told the truth about people,' said Mum.

'You mean you wrote an actual autobiography?'

'Yes, and I thought it was brilliant,' I said loyally. It was true. I'd really enjoyed it, especially the parts where Mum was *ultra* truthful. 'You should read the chapter about Justine Littlewood!'

'I want to!' said Peter. 'So, did you write about me too, Tracy?'

'I might have. Just a bit,' said Mum, sounding awkward.

Peter had had a whole chapter to himself. Mum hadn't been exactly flattering. I'd felt very sorry for the poor weedy little boy she kept bossing about.

'Can I read it?' he asked eagerly.

'I think I chucked it out after Marina turned it down,' Mum said quickly.

'Yes, she did,' I said, backing her up. I was pretty sure Peter wouldn't like what she'd written.

'I might write a book about myself one day,' said Jordan. 'So long as my story has a happy ending,' she added meaningfully.

Then we stopped playing Famous People because we were nearly at Cam's, and Mum had an argument with Peter's satnav because she felt it wanted to take us the long way round — but eventually we drew up outside.

'Is that it?' Jordan asked, peering up at the tall, shabby grey house.

'Hey, I never realized, it's a terrace house!' I said. 'Mum and I used to live up at the top where those blue curtains are. Look at the window boxes, Mum! They're new. Don't they look lovely?'

They were full of bright red geraniums, which cheered up the house enormously. Someone had been working hard in the garden too, planting rose bushes on either side of the path, and a honeysuckle beside the door.

'I bet that's Mary,' said Mum.

We must have made a noise walking up the path because the door opened before we'd rung the bell.

Jordan stared. 'Nope! I don't like her. It's not gonna work,' she muttered, stepping backwards.

'She's not Cam, she's Mary. She's been approved as a foster carer too,' Mum said, nodding at the pin-neat figure in her crisp shirt and white jeans and immaculate trainers. Alfie gave her a happy woof and strained at his lead, because she and Cam used to take him for long interesting walks.

'She used to be my teacher,' I whispered. 'But she's Cam's partner now. She's OK, really.'

She was joined on the step by Cam, whose hair was sticking up like a lavatory brush, her T-shirt and jeans crumpled because she hates ironing, her canvas boots grey with age. Alfie broke free and hurled himself at her, jumping up excitedly.

'*That's* Cam,' I said, and I heard Jordan breathe a sigh of relief.

Mum rushed up too, and gave
Cam such an enthusiastic hug she
nearly knocked her over. I always
get a lump in my throat when I
see Mum and Cam together. It's
as if Mum whizzes back to my age
for a few seconds.

Then Cam freed one arm and
held it out to me, so I joined in.

'Thank you, thank you, thank
you,' Mum breathed in Cam's ear.

'Calm down, love, it mightn't work out,' she
muttered. She peered over Mum's shoulder. 'Hi! So
you're Jordan,' she said.

'So you're Cam,' said Jordan, trying to sound cool
and couldn't-care-less.

'Me and Jordan are friends,' I said.

'Jordan and I,' Mary murmured, automatically
correcting my grammar, but she held out her hand to
Jordan and smiled. 'Welcome to the fun house.'

Then she looked at Peter, who was hovering
politely halfway up the path. She put her head on
one side enquiringly. 'And you're Tracy's friend?'

'Yes, you could say that. How do you do. I'm
Peter – Peter Ingham.'

'Oh my goodness!' Cam was grinning all over her
face. 'Tracy said she'd met up with you again but

I didn't know you were actually . . .'

'We're not. Yet. But I have high hopes,' said Peter. 'Hello, Cam. It's good to see you again. You haven't changed a bit!'

'But you've changed enormously! You really *look* like a head teacher now,' she said.

'A head teacher?' said Mary, looking impressed.

'Anyway, come in, come in,' said Cam. 'Jess, how about showing Jordan round?'

Cam and Mary and Mum and Peter went into Cam's study. I took Jordan to the sitting room, with Alfie at our heels. There were two girls there. Jordan tensed.

'They're OK,' I murmured. 'I know them all.'

The bigger girl was lounging on the sofa, checking her phone. She looked up and held her arms out wide. 'Alfie!' He jumped right on top of her, licking her face.

'That's Jax,' I said.

'Hey, Jess,' she said, laughing. 'Alfie's washing my face!'

'He does that to me too,' Jordan said gruffly.

'So you're the new girl?'

Jordan shrugged. 'It depends.'

'On what?'

'Mind your own business,' Jordan said.

'Last chance?' said Rosie, a painfully thin girl who looked as if her skinny arms would snap any minute. She kept playing with her ponytail, fiddling with the ends and flicking it backwards and forwards like a girl playing with her unicorn doll. 'Have you often done a runner then?'

'She's doing a runner right now,' I said. 'And if she can't stay at Cam's, they're going to lock her up somewhere.'

'I get it,' said Jax. 'Don't look so worried. All the social workers love Cam. They'll let you stay here.'

'They were going to lock me up again too,' said Rosie.

 She wouldn't eat properly. Perhaps, I thought, she'd put on just a little bit of weight since I'd last seen her. I knew better than to tell her that though, or she'd get frantic and stop eating again. Cam had explained it. Rosie was all mixed up in her head and was sure she was fat.

I couldn't help wondering if big Jax was mixed up too and thought she was thin. She was pretty massive and looked tough, so Jordan was acting tough back, but she didn't need to. Jax was as soft as butter – I liked her best of Cam's girls.

She started chuckling at something on her phone.

'Ah, the pet!' she cooed. 'Look!' She handed her phone to Jordan and me. It was a video of a kitten jumping up into a doll's cot and snuggling under the covers. It looked so sweet that Jordan couldn't help smiling.

'Do you like kittens?' Jax asked.

'Course I do. Who doesn't?' she said.

'Ask Cam if you can have one, eh? She always lets the new girls have a treat, something special to make them feel good. She let Rosie have a rabbit, but then it died. Forgot to feed it, most likely.'

'I did not!' Rosie protested.

'Joking, joking!' said Jax. 'Sorry, Your Royal Thinness.'

'Cam got me a Saturday job down at the hairdresser's,' said Rosie. 'It's good there. Soon as I've finished school I'm going to be an apprentice. Antoine's ever so nice – he's already learning me how to style hair.'

'*Teaching* you,' Jax corrected her, doing a wicked imitation of Mary's clipped voice.

'What do you all think of Mary?' I asked.

'She's OK. Ish,' said Jax. 'I don't quite get what Cam sees in her – still, whatever floats your boat, that's what I say.'

'She used to be my teacher,' I said.

'I know, poor you,' said Rosie. 'She's ever so bossy, even though *she's* not our main foster carer, Cam is.

She keeps trying to coach me in maths and stuff, just so I can get good GCSEs. Says I'm bright and could go to university. As if I want to do that. I want to be a hairdresser – that's what I'm good at.' She looked at Jordan. 'Do you want me to put your hair up in a ponytail?'

'I can do it myself,' said Jordan, but then she nodded. 'Thanks though.'

'I wish you could put *my* hair in a ponytail,' I said, and they all laughed.

'I wish I had your curly bonce,' said Jax, ruffling my curls. 'You're the dead spit of your mum, Jess. Where is she, anyway?'

'She's with Cam, in her study,' I said.

'Having a chinwag?' asked Jax.

'About me,' said Jordan. 'And, like I said, she won't want me here, I just know it.'

14

CAM *DID* **WANT** Jordan once they'd had a private talk together. She managed to persuade Jordan to provide her social worker's name and mobile number. After an hour or so she turned up. Jordan had told me she was awful, and called her Megan the Muppet, so I'd pictured her like Miss Piggy, with a round pink face, silly curls and a high-pitched voice. The real Megan was a pale woman with dark circles under her eyes and a quiet voice.

'Oh, Jordan, we've been so worried about you,' she said wearily.

'Really?' said Jordan. 'So where were the search

parties? And the newspaper interviews and the tearful appeals on the telly?'

'We can't go to the press every single time a teenager in care goes missing.'

'Yeah, because no one *cares* about children in care,' Jordan said, working herself up. 'I bet if Jess here went missing Tracy would create a huge fuss and there'd be posters of her everywhere and she'd be on the front page of every tabloid.'

'Yes, good point – but we're here because *we* care,' said Mum. 'Now there's no point in you having a total meltdown. You're here to prove to Megan that you'll sort yourself out living with Cam, just like I did, and that you won't run away again.'

'Is that OK?' said Cam.

'No offence, and I *do* want to stay with you, but only until Tracy gets herself approved as a foster carer. Then I want to be with her, and Jess and Flo and Peter and Alfie,' said Jordan.

Megan blinked. 'Are they more children?' she asked uncertainly.

Jordan sighed theatrically. 'See, I told you she was thick,' she murmured.

'Hey, attitude! That's not going to help your case,' said Mum. 'And I know that from experience.'

'Don't worry, I'm used to Jordan. She can be a

very fierce young lady,' said Megan. 'I know she doesn't really mean it, she's just upset. I do understand, truly. But we can't let every young person in care decide for themselves where they're going to live. *We* have to make that decision, finding the most suitable placement. It's all been fixed.'

'Then unfix it,' said Jordan. 'I'm not going to no residential home in Manchester, and you can't make me. I'll run away again even if they handcuff me to the wall.'

'It's not a medieval prison, Jordan,' Megan sighed.

'I imagine it's pretty expensive keeping a child there,' said Peter. 'More than living here in a family situation, where Jordan has a better chance of flourishing.'

'And you are . . . Ms Beaker's partner?' Megan asked.

'*Are* you, Peter?' Cam asked with interest.

'I am a friend of long standing,' he said. 'And a head teacher with a wide experience of dealing with foster children. I see how they flourish in the right circumstances. As I know from experience. Ms Beaker and I were in the same care home when we were children. Then we were both successfully fostered.'

'Cam brought me up from when I was ten,' Mum said. 'And I was just as much of a handful as Jordan. More so in fact. Cam can vouch for that. But she stuck it out, and now she's more of a mum to me than my real mum.'

'And she's like my granny,' I said. 'Only better, because she's my friend too.'

Cam went pink and ducked her head. Mary looked at her proudly.

'*I* can vouch for that,' she said.

'And you are . . . ?' Megan asked, confused.

'I'm Mary Oliver, Cam's partner. I was also Jess's teacher when she was at primary school here,' Mary explained.

'So we're all old friends,' said Mum.

'And . . . was it Alfie?' Megan went on.

Alfie pricked up his ears at the sound of his name and came trotting forward eagerly.

'Here he is. He's a friend too,' said Mum. 'So surely you can see that we all belong together and we want to be there for Jordan. It's simple.'

It wasn't quite *that* simple. Megan said she'd have to talk things over with her team, and Mum would have to be properly assessed if she was serious about fostering Jordan herself. However, the local authority had agreed that while all these decisions were being made Jordan could stay with Cam as an emergency placement. She suggested that Mum and I see Jordan regularly to make sure it worked out if she eventually came to us.

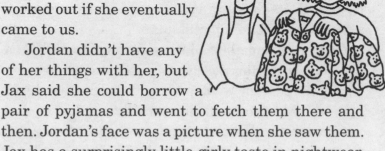

Jordan didn't have any of her things with her, but Jax said she could borrow a pair of pyjamas and went to fetch them there and then. Jordan's face was a picture when she saw them. Jax has a surprisingly little-girly taste in nightwear. The pyjamas were bright pink, patterned with teddy bears. I held my breath, willing Jordan not to say what she was clearly thinking.

She managed a nod and a tiny smile. 'Thanks, Jax,' she said.

I breathed out. Jordan was clearly determined to get on with the other girls. Especially Jax. In fact, they started chatting away together, Jax showing Jordan all her favourite accounts on Instagram. I felt a bit left out.

However, when Mum said we'd better get going, Jordan suddenly grabbed hold of me and gave me a big hug. 'Thanks for everything, Jess,' she said. 'Hanging out with me and bringing me all that food and everything.'

'That's OK,' I said, hugging her back.

'You really will come and see me if I'm stuck here for a bit?'

'Yes, of course. I won't need to bring you any food though. Cam's a great cook. You wait till you try her muffins!'

'And you'll message me too? I haven't got a phone now, but I bet Jax will let me use hers sometimes,' said Jordan.

'Yes, of course I will,' I promised.

'Your mum's not kidding about fostering me, is she? She's really going to go through with it?'

'Yes, she is. She *said*.'

'And you won't go off me meanwhile? I've had friends who've promised they'd keep in touch when I got moved away, but somehow they never did,' said Jordan.

'I know. I've had friends like that,' I said, thinking of Alice. 'But I'll be your friend for ever, honest.'

Mum was listening to us. 'She means it, Jordan. She's a Beaker. We're the Beaker girls. You can trust us.'

'So can I be a Beaker girl too?' she asked.

'Yep, Definitely. See you soon then, kid. For real,' said Mum.

I felt a bit sad on the journey back to Cooksea. I knew just how lovely Cam was, and Mary was really kind too even if she fussed a bit, and Jax and the others wouldn't be mean – but, even so, they were all strangers. Jordan might feel lonely and left out. She might not remember to be tactful all the time. She might get stressed and lose her temper. She might even have a total meltdown.

'Do you think Jordan will be all right, Mum?' I asked.

'Don't worry, Jess. She'll be fine with Cam,' she said.

'But what if she kicks off?'

'Cam's used to it. She coped with me!'

'And that requires a lot of strength and tenacity!' said Peter. 'When your mum kicked off back at the Dumping Ground, the whole street could hear her. Screaming, shouting, hitting, kicking!'

'Really?' I said. 'Mum!'

'I know,' she said, laughing. 'And that was on a *good* day.'

'Weren't you afraid of her?' I asked Peter.

'Sometimes. I think even poor Elaine was frightened of her,' he said. 'No, I'm just teasing. I *liked* her. I really missed her when Cam fostered her. We all did. Even Justine!'

'But you got fostered too.'

'Yes, I did,' said Peter. 'And they were lovely parents, like I said.'

'But you've never had your own family?' Mum asked.

'Well, I've had partners from time to time,' said Peter. 'And lots of good friends. I'm not a total Billy-no-mates.'

'You've got us now anyway, Jess and me, whether we're just friends or something more.'

'Something more would be good.'

They started nattering on, and I curled up with Alfie on the back seat and we both fell fast asleep when we were still in the outskirts of London. We didn't wake up until we were home again. Peter came in with us for supper.

Flo was desperate to hear how we'd got on. She was very perky because her friend Lawrence had phoned.

'There, he's clearly sweet on you,' said Mum, making us cheese on toast with baked beans and bacon – exactly the sort of meal you want when you've had a very long and eventful day.

'I don't know about that,' said Flo – though she looked as if she did know and was very pleased about it. 'But he gave me a bit of good news. His agent got in touch to say that he's been asked to go on one of those afternoon antiques shows – you know, they have celebrities choosing stuff from junk shops all round the country. It's called *Antique Memories*. He's quite tickled by the idea, bless him. Anyway, he says he's going to tell the producer about our shop and see if she'll feature it.'

'That would be great!' said Mum. 'Fantastic publicity!'

'So will you two be on the telly?' I asked.

'Maybe,' said Mum. 'You're used to performing in front of the camera, Flo. You'll have to give me a few tips. It might be the start of a whole new career for me. Good job I've been studying so hard. I'm practically an antiques expert. Tracy Beaker, television star! Wow, two new careers in one day! Foster mum and TV celebrity!'

'Just so long as you're still my mum too,' I said.

After supper we got out an old Monopoly board. I loved the little metal playing pieces, Mum liked to be in charge of the bank, Peter proved to be a demon

player – but Flo turned out to be the champion. We toasted her in hot chocolate. I wished Jordan had been there to share in the fun.

Mum helped a triumphant Flo to bed and then sent me upstairs too. I couldn't get in touch with Jordan yet so I texted Cam instead.

She called straight back. 'Jordan's just fine, Jess, honestly. She's been having a good laugh with the other girls and a long chat with me. I'm hoping she'll settle down here for a while. Don't worry so, sweetheart.'

'Can I speak to her? Just to say goodnight?' I asked.

'Sure. Hang on.' There was a pause – and then I heard her calling Jordan, telling her someone wanted to speak to her. I waited, and then I heard Jordan's husky voice.

'Yeah?'

I was suddenly struck dumb – I didn't really know what to say.

'Who is it?' She sounded very gruff and suspicious.

'It's me,' I said in a very small voice.

'Jess!'

I breathed out. She sounded pleased. Very pleased.

'I just wanted to check you're all right.'

'Yes, I am. Well, sort of.' She lowered her voice. 'She's OK, your Cam.'

'I know! Well, I just wanted to check, that's all.'

'Why, did you think I might have kicked off already, my first night?'

'No. I was just kind of missing you,' I explained.

Jordan was quiet for a second, and then she started making funny little sounds. I wondered if she was having a laugh at me. Then I realized she was crying.

'Nobody's ever said they missed me before,' she said. 'Miss you too, Jess. We'll see each other soon, won't we?'

'You bet. Well, night then.'

'Night, Jess.'

'Say night night to all those little bears on your jimjams too,' I said.

'Cheeky!' said Jordan, and this time she *was* laughing.

Mum came in to tuck me up as I was switching off my phone.

'Just checking on Jordan,' I told her.

'Good plan.'

'You do like her, don't you, Mum?'

'Yes, I do – though, like I said, we don't really know her properly yet.'

'*I* know her,' I said. 'You will foster her, won't you, Mum?'

'Well, I'll give it serious thought,' she said. 'Though

I don't suppose Cam gave it serious thought when she fostered me. I just bamboozled her into it.'

'And look how well that turned out,' I said.

'Yes, it did. For me at least! I'm sure Cam's had a few regrets over the years,' Mum joked.

'I bet she thought it was the happiest day of her life, meeting you,' I said loyally.

'I don't think so. I was bawling my head off! Still, I suppose the day she said she'd foster me was the second happiest of my life.'

'*Second* happiest?' I asked, waiting expectantly.

'You know perfectly well that the happiest day of my life was the day you were born. Maybe not the few hours when I was actually *having* you, but as soon as you were in my arms I just fell in love,' said Mum.

'Even though I was bawling too?'

'No, you didn't cry, you just looked up at me with those big eyes, as if you were thinking, *That's my mum.*'

We hugged each other and Mum gave me a goodnight kiss.

'Aren't you coming to bed too?' I asked, snuggling down, with Alfie curling up in his usual place at the end of the bed.

'Not just yet. Peter's still downstairs. We're going to have a nightcap together and reminisce about old times.'

'Oh yeah?' I said.

'I won't be long,' said Mum.

She was *ever* so long. I stayed awake for a while as I'd slept in the car on the way back from Cam's. After half an hour or so I crept out of bed, careful not to disturb Alfie, and tiptoed onto the landing. I could hear Mum and Peter chatting away, laughing fondly. I went down the stairs and peeped at them. They were sitting on Flo's sofa. Peter had his arm round Mum's shoulders and she had her head tucked into his neck – her curls must have been tickling him dreadfully, though he didn't look as if he minded.

I watched them for a little while, and then I went back to bed. When Mum slipped into our room I was fast asleep.

'Mum?' I mumbled.

'Shh now. Go back to sleep, sweetheart,' she whispered.

'What time is it?'

'Late.'

'Has Peter gone home?'

'Yep.' She paused. 'He's probably popping back tomorrow. Are you OK with that?'

'Course I am. I like him,' I said.

'Truly?'

'I like him more than Bill. And a hundred thousand times more than Sean Godfrey,' I said.

'Well, I do too.' Mum chuckled as she climbed into bed. 'I can't get over it. Me and Peter Ingham! I knew I liked him when we first saw him at the Spade and Bucket. I mean, I always liked him deep down when we were little kids, but he got on my nerves then.'

'He's always liked you,' I said.

'I know. I led him a terrible dance. I bossed him around and kept telling him what to do. I never expected him to grow up so . . . so . . .' Mum struggled for the words. 'I want to say quietly masterful, but it sounds like a phrase from a soppy love story.'

'Well, maybe it *is* a love story. Just not soppy,' I said.

'We were such idiots though, him thinking that Sean was my bloke and Tyrone my son, and then me thinking he was gay because he was hugging another guy.'

'But now you've fallen for each other,' I said, yawning. 'And we're all going to live happily ever after.'

'I used to get really irritated when fairy tales ended like that – I didn't think there was any chance of things ending happily ever after for me,' said Mum. 'I'd have been astonished if I'd known I'd end up getting all lovey-dovey with Weedy Peter.'

'*And* making friends with Justine Littlewood!' I said.

'I certainly didn't dream I'd have my own lovely daughter – and maybe foster another,' said Mum.

'No *maybes*,' I said, copying Jordan. 'Definitely.'

We went back to see Jordan a week later. Mum and I had chosen some new clothes for her. We didn't know her exact size but we had a good guess. We knew she wouldn't like girly clothes – short skirts and high heels – so we bought her a bigger version of what we liked: jeans and two T-shirts, one stripy and one with stars. Mum got her a big denim jacket too, and I chose some badges to pin on  it. One had a smiley emoji, another had a seashell, and the third said *Best Friend* in red letters.

Jordan was thrilled with her

new clothes, especially the denim jacket, and liked the *Best Friend* badge best of all. She dressed up in her new outfit and Mum took a photo of her, and then Cam took a photo of Jordan and Mum and me.

'Big smiles, Beaker girls!' she commanded.

'I should dye my hair black and make it go all frizzy and then I'd look like a real Beaker girl,' said Jordan.

Then Jordan's social worker, Megan, came round, and she took a photo of the three of us with Cam and Mary and Alfie and Jax and Rosie. It was a job getting us all in, but she managed it. She had put Mum in touch with the fostering service. Mum had had a visit from a lady called Elaine – she was terrified that it might be her old social worker, but it was another Elaine entirely, and she wasn't a pain at all, she was very relaxed and friendly.

'I've made a formal application to be a foster parent,' Mum told Jordan, 'but it'll be ages before they give us the go-ahead.'

'Weeks?' said Jordan.

'Months! It's crazy, isn't it? But I suppose they have to check up on me and get all these references. You'll vouch for me, won't you, Cam?' said Mum, looking anxious.

'Of course I will!' she said. 'You're my big success story, Tracy. I know you'll be a really great foster mother.'

Mum looked at Mary, who was hovering. 'Mary would say I'll have to deal with a few Anger Issues first.'

'I'd say you'll always have a problem with bossy authority figures like me,' said Mary, grinning. 'But I think you'll prove to be a star at fostering.'

NOW IT WAS a waiting game. Mum and I cleared
out the little junk room upstairs and painted it,
ready for Jordan. We asked her what colour she liked
best and she said blue. I chose the lovely sky-blue
shade I'd had back at Marlborough Tower. At the
paint shop I saw some stick-on seagulls and we
bought them too. When the paint was dry I put them
all round the walls, with the smallest right above the
space for Jordan's bed. I wondered about inking black
curls and little glasses onto the bird's head to turn
her into Gull Girl, but I didn't want it to look too
strange.

We bought Jordan a new bed from Argos – a small
double because she was a bit big to find a single bed

really comfortable. We found
a blue-and-yellow quilt
and some yellow curtains
at a bric-a-brac fair, but
decided to let her choose
her own ornaments and
pictures when she came
to live with us. It looked
very fresh and pretty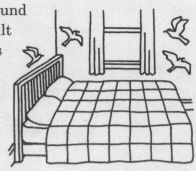
even so. I often crept in to admire it. I couldn't help
feeling a little jealous. I wished I had my own room
now, though back at Marlborough Tower I'd usually
gone to cuddle up with Mum.

Still, I had my own garden. I'd cleared out the old
junk – well, Mum and Peter did that for me, but I dug
the earth and mixed in some compost. It was hard
work, but fun too, like making mud pies. I wanted to
plant bluebells because Bluebell is one of my middle
names, but the lady at the garden centre said it was
the wrong season for bluebells, so I chose some
agapanthus instead, because they're blue too. Mum
treated me to a little fuchsia with red and purple
flowers, and Flo bought me a bluey-pink rose bush.

Cam and Mary sent me lots of hyacinth and miniature iris bulbs 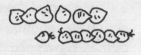 to plant for the spring.

You'll never guess what Peter bought me! A little white statue of a girl reading a book. She looked so beautiful sitting beside the rose bush. When I told Jordan, she said Peter was just trying to keep in with me so that I wouldn't mind him being Mum's boyfriend. Maybe she was right, because Sean Godfrey had bought me heaps of things when he first visited me – but I didn't usually like them. Peter had chosen the statue very carefully, specially for me.

I often squatted down beside the girl and gently stroked her pale stone curls. She looked several years younger than me, but she was actually much older, maybe nearly a hundred. Peter had found her in an antiques shop in a town further along the coast. Mum and I had been to check it out. It was also going to be featured on *Antique Memories*, Lawrence had told Flo.

'It's bigger than The Dumping Ground,' I said.

'And it's got some lovely stock,' Mum sniffed. 'But we've got better displays.'

The television people had phoned and said they wanted to come on Friday, if that was all right.

'Of course,' said Flo, but when she
got off the phone she panicked. 'Why
didn't Lawrence tell me it was
going to be so soon? I was planning
to have my hair cut and set – and, dear Lord, what on
earth am I going to wear? And they haven't sent the
script yet! It'll take me weeks to learn my lines. Oh
dear heavens, I can't let you all down and forget my
words on screen!'

'It's OK, Flo darling,' said Mum, giving her a hug.
'I'll phone and see if your hairdresser can fit you in
today – and if not I'll give your hair a trim. You don't
need to fuss about clothes. Wear what you've got on
now, it looks perfect. And I don't think there *is* a
script – we just have to act naturally.'

'I can't act without any lines!' said Flo, but she
calmed down a little.

Mum took her to have her hair done and I
pretended to be Lawrence coming into the shop so
that Flo could practise serving me. I limped a bit and
used a walking stick and put on a very fruity voice,
but Mum told me off – she worried that Flo might
think I was taking the mick.

Mum was good at calming Flo, but by Thursday
she was in a bit of a state herself. She changed the
window displays twice, and kept looking around the
shop, a book under her arm, her phone in her hand,

researching each item so she could sound as knowledgeable as possible. She had found another little Victorian desk on eBay, and had oiled and polished it until it shone, and  then written more manuscript pages on tea-stained paper, displaying them with another quill pen.

Then, late on Thursday afternoon, just as we were closing, a customer came in and fell in love with it.

'I'd like to buy that desk, please,' he said happily.

Mum glared at him. The desk had been given pride of place and she'd speed-read an entire book on Victorian furniture so she could show off on camera. 'I'm afraid that desk isn't for sale,' she said.

'Yes it is!' the man argued, holding up the display ticket. 'And at a reasonable price, seeing as it's in such fabulous condition.'

'I know,' said Mum. 'But I can't sell it to you.'

'What kind of a shop *is* this?' he said, getting irritated.

'It's a shop full of treasures, dear, and it's going to be featured on the television tomorrow!' said Flo excitedly. She looked a little alarming now – she'd had her hair dyed a jaffa orange colour, which didn't quite go with her red lipstick. (Flo herself wasn't quite sure about her hair, but Mum and I had told her she looked lovely.)

'If you could come back on Saturday, I'll sell you the desk with pleasure,' said Mum.

'But I need it *now*!' he said. 'It's my wife's birthday *on* Saturday.'

Mum had to take ten per cent off the asking price *and* offer free delivery, just so she could hang onto the desk. Then, when Lawrence and the television people arrived on Friday, they didn't give the desk a second glance!

'We want Lawrence to pick the pieces that resonate with *him*,' said Amanda, the director. She wore a baseball cap very similar to Jordan's, but it looked very different on her. It was set at a rakish angle, with her hair in a long golden plait. She wore a very skimpy T-shirt that showed her bare midriff, with low-slung baggy jeans and canvas Docs. She was trying to look very street, but whenever she opened her mouth it was clear that she was ultra posh. She opened her mouth a lot, telling the camera crew how to do their job. They didn't argue with her, but there was a lot of eye-rolling behind her back.

'Hadn't we better wait till Adele gets here?' the cameraman said.

'Well, we don't know how long she'll be, do we?' Amanda turned to us. 'Adele is our producer. She seems to have got lost driving from Hastings, bless her! Oh, the shop we featured there was a picture, wasn't it, Lawrence? Such unusual pieces! We were spoiled for choice!'

Her voice was starting to grate. Alfie seemed enchanted with her though, and followed her as she paced up and down, wagging his tail.

'Nice doggy,' said Amanda, giving him a vague pat. 'Is there anywhere we can put him when the cameras start rolling?'

'Can't he stay with us?' I asked.

'Well, I think he'll be a bit of a distraction, don't you? I want the viewers to concentrate on Lawrence and the shop,' she said.

'But Alfie's *part* of the shop. He always greets our customers,' said Mum. 'They love him.'

'I'm sure they do, but this is *Antique Memories*, not *For the Love of Dogs*,' Amanda said crisply.

'And I'm definitely the antique today,' said Lawrence, trying to lighten the mood.

'Me too, darling!' said Flo. '*I'm* the poor soul with the murky corners nowadays.'

Amanda clearly didn't get the reference to Flo's character in *Life with the Lilliputs*, but she sat down beside her and asked about her acting background.

'This is a nostalgia show, you see, and Lawrence tells me you were a soap star in your heyday. The viewers might remember you. I'd like to see you and Lawrence chatting as he wanders around your shop. Maybe a bit of flirty banter? That would be fun,' she said.

'I'm game!' said Flo.

'Perhaps you could hint at past romance?'

'Never mind the past,' said Lawrence gallantly, and kissed Flo's hand. 'An ongoing romance, if you please!'

Mum pulled a face at me. It was all getting very cheesy. We didn't need to say a word. We were united in our loathing of Amanda. She ignored us completely, and wasn't even interested in Mum's clever displays. She kept picking up a china ornament here, a soft toy there, showing them to Lawrence and then putting them back in the wrong place.

Mum sighed meaningfully and rearranged them.

'How about Mr Teddy here as one of your choices, Lawrence?' Amanda asked, plucking a bear from Mum's teddy bears' picnic. 'I'm sure you cuddled up with a teddy just like him when you were a little boy.'

'I wasn't really keen on teddies. I preferred an elephant called Currant Bun who went everywhere with me. But I can always pretend an affection for stuffed bears if you think it a good idea, Amanda,' Lawrence said obligingly.

'I could show Lawrence the whole bear display, and we could have "The Teddy Bear's Picnic" playing on the gramophone,' said Mum.

'I think that might be a little twee,' said Amanda. 'And we'll be concentrating on Lawrence and Flo, as they've got such a splendid rapport.'

'Oh!' Mum's mouth stayed in an O shape, as if she was about to say more.

Flo said it for her. 'Tracy's my business partner and dear friend. She's made the world of difference to the shop. She *has* to be part of the show!' She grew so heated that her face matched her glasses.

'Well, I dare say we can fit her in somewhere. I'll think of a line for her to say,' said Amanda.

'I can think of my own line, thanks very much,' said Mum.

'I know!' Amanda picked up a pink cup and saucer from a display Mum had called 'Pretty in Pink', with china in rose and candy and shocking pink, and little toy flamingos dipping their heads in to drink. 'You can offer Lawrence a cup of tea in this, and he can look down and say he remembers his mother having that exact tea set back in Edwardian days.'

'I'm not quite *that* old, my dear!' said Lawrence.

'And it's not Edwardian anyway, it's mid-Victorian,' added Mum.

'But you get the gist,' said Amanda impatiently. 'Actually, do you think you could be an angel and rustle up a few actual cuppas? I'm sure these guys are parched. I know I am.'

I knew Mum felt like *throwing* a cup of tea at Amanda, but she liked the camera crew so she headed for the kitchen.

I followed her. 'That lady! She's *awful*!' I hissed as Mum filled the kettle.

'You're telling me,' she said.

'Why don't you tell her where to get off?' I asked.

'She's leaving you out completely, when you found all the stock and made everything look so pretty!'

Mum sighed. 'I know. But it *is* Flo's shop, not mine, and it means so much to her to be back on the telly with dear old Lawrence. Let her have her moment.'

I blinked at her. She suddenly seemed a meek and mild stranger! She even *looked* like a stranger: she'd put on lots of make-up for the television cameras. She wasn't used to wearing it so it was a bit smeary.

'Hang on, Mum, let me wipe that little smudge away,' I said, advancing on her with the tea towel.

'Oh, what does it matter if I'm just the tea lady for a while?' said Mum. 'There I was, kidding myself this could be the start of a whole new career. I might just as well be back at the Silver Spoon caff.'

We heard the shop bell jangling as someone else came in.

'Hey, guys! Sorry I'm a bit late. I stopped off at a transport café to get everyone cups of tea and bacon sandwiches,' a cheery voice rang out. 'Help yourselves.'

'And now I'm a *redundant* tea lady,' Mum said. 'That'll be the producer, Adele.'

'At least she sounds nicer than Amanda,' I whispered.

We made more cups of tea anyway, and carried them into the shop, along with some special white chocolate and hazelnut cookies. Adele was busy handing round the bacon sandwiches and making a fuss of Flo, telling her she was a big fan. She was older than Amanda, a curvy woman in a brightly patterned dress and little boots. Her hair was beautifully cut and her make-up was immaculate, her eyebrows, eyes and lips all clearly defined.

She was smiling. 'I absolutely love the name of your shop,' she said to Flo. 'When Lawrence told me, I knew we had to come here. The show's all about reminding people of their childhood. Well, your entire shop reminds me of mine. I was in a children's home for a while and we all called it the Dumping Ground.'

Mum very nearly dropped her tea tray. I gasped. Adele stared at me, looking totally astonished.

'Tracy Beaker!' she said to me. 'No, you can't be. She'd be nearly my age. But you're the absolute spitting image of her!'

'That's because she takes after her mum,' said Mum, coming forward.

'I don't believe it!' said Adele, rushing up to her.

She gave her a big embrace, so the mugs were in danger all over again.

'You two *know* each other?' Amanda said, asking the obvious.

'Tracy was my little pal! Remember when you pinched all my make-up? You were hopeless at putting it on though!' Adele looked closely. 'You still are!' she said, dissolving into peals of laughter. 'But you're looking great otherwise.'

'I can't believe it's you, Adele!' said Mum.

'And you have a daughter!'

'Jess, come and meet my friend Adele! She was the oldest girl at the Dumping Ground and I used to think she was dead sophisticated,' said Mum. 'Still do!'

'I am!' said Adele, laughing. 'My goodness, Jess, this is weird – you're *so* like your mum! Do you have massive tantrums if you don't get your own way?'

'I'm a bit quieter,' I said.

'She's more artful than me!' Mum put her arm round me. 'She gets her own way without having to kick off.'

'And is this your dog?' said Adele, bending down and making a fuss of Alfie.

'He's Alfie,' I told her. 'I'm afraid he's not quiet at all.'

'He's got great character!'

'Could he possibly be on television for just a split second?' I asked. 'I don't mind if I'm not in it, but I'd be so proud if Alfie was.'

'I'd like to be in it too!' said Mum. 'You'll *all* be in it,' said Adele.

We glanced at Amanda, who was looking peeved. 'I thought it would be more effective if we concentrated on the old lady and Lawrence,' she said.

'Hey, less of the *old*, thank you,' said Flo.

'I see your point, Amanda, but we'd be mad not to make the most of this set-up. I think we'll need to stretch it to a ten-minute slot and skimp on the other three shops – maybe cut one out altogether. We've got everything we need here: great personalities and a wonderful setting. I absolutely love the window displays and the quirky ways the stock is arranged. We'll start with Lawrence coming in and wandering around like he's Alice in Wonderland, astonished by everything, and there'll be Flo here smiling like the Cheshire cat, and Tracy and Jess the absolute spitting image of each other like a big Tweedledee and a little Tweedledum, and Alfie here charging around like a March Hare, bumping into everything. Perfect!'

It *was* perfect too, though we had to do the filming over and over again. It wasn't because we kept

making mistakes, it was because of camera angles and sound problems and customers ringing the shop bell. Amanda bobbed about being bossy, telling Lawrence to act more surprised and Flo to be more flirty – until they were hamming it up like actors in old silent movies, Lawrence gesturing dramatically and Flo pulling faces and fluttering her eyelashes.

'Shall we try just one more take, Amanda – a little less mannered, to see how that works?' Adele suggested tactfully.

She had Alfie and me in a corner, with me 'reading' him an old copy of *Where's Spot?* I felt very self-conscious, but Alfie turned out to be a marvellous actor and pretended to be thoroughly engrossed in the story. However, Mum was the star of the show. Lawrence might not be interested in the little desk, but she'd displayed all kinds of things to remind him of his past. She'd Googled him and found out that he'd been a child actor in the 1950s, so there was an old

Picturegoer annual, with a statuette of Marilyn Monroe in a skimpy white dress leaning against it. Lawrence gently set her aside and leafed through the pages, suddenly stabbing one excitedly.

'There we are! Look, it's me! *Little child star Lawrie acts the Little Prince!*' he read. 'Oh my, look at my mop of golden curls!'

He also liked the crimson smoking jacket Mum had hung on the vintage clothing rail, saying he'd always fancied himself in one. 'What do you think, Flo? Do you think I could get away with it?'

'Of course, darling. *I'd* fancy you in it,' said Flo, and he blew her a kiss.

Then he bent down to examine a pair of black-and-white gentlemen's shoes, angled as if they were going to do a little Charlie Chaplin walk all by themselves. 'I like these co-respondent shoes too. Very flashy!' said Lawrence. 'And practically good as new.'

Amanda suggested Lawrence look at the china cabinet, and he obligingly found a Clarice Cliff teapot to add to his collection. Making the most of her new knowledge, Mum told him that it was the popular crocus design, but if he wanted Clarice's Bizarre teapot it would probably set him back £2,000.

Best of all, Lawrence spotted the little Beatrix Potter *Jemima Puddle-Duck* and opened it lovingly, quoting passages and sighing because Jemima was so gullible. 'My mother used to read me this night after night,' he said, shaking his head fondly at the memory. 'I must have this little book too!'

He glanced at the price and looked surprised. 'Oh dear! Such a lot for such a little book!'

'I know, but it's a first edition – and it has its original glassine dust wrapper, which makes it worth even more,' said Mum. 'But I dare say we can arrange a special price for you, Lawrence, as it means so much to you – or maybe I can find one without a dust wrapper. Jess will hunt one out for you. She's our book expert. She found this copy – a bargain at a car boot sale!'

I looked up and smiled as the cameraman focused on me for a few seconds. Alfie licked my face as if he was proud of me.

'Perfect!' Adele breathed at the end of the take. 'I'm tempted to alter the format of the show and simply concentrate on this shop. You're all star performers – and you really know your stuff, Tracy!'

'Doesn't she just!' said Flo proudly. 'She'll be on *Antiques Roadshow* next.'

'No, we don't want her on a rival channel!' said Adele. 'Still, maybe we should think about her own show. Let's think – I know, *Beaker's Bargains!'*

We all laughed, but Adele seemed semi-serious. She spent a happy half-hour with Mum, reminiscing about life in the Dumping Ground, but then had to go on to another shop in Brighton.

'But I'd love to come back and have a proper catch-up,' she said.

'That would be great,' said Mum. 'And I'll invite Peter round too. Remember him?'

'Little Peter Ingham? You're still in touch?' Adele asked delightedly.

'Well, we're sort of seeing each other,' said Mum, and she actually blushed.

'Oh, how sweet! I can't wait to see the two of you together! This is amazing. You'll be telling me you're best friends with Justine Littlewood next!'

'Well, not exactly *best* friends,' said Mum. 'But we have met up a couple of times.'

'And everything's worked out OK for you, Tracy?

Did you stay with Cam?'

'Of course I did,' said Mum. 'She's our family, isn't she, Jess?'

'Of course she is! She's coming tomorrow, and she's bringing Jordan, who's going to be my foster sister,' I said proudly.

'No!' Adele looked at Mum. 'You're going to start fostering?'

She shrugged. 'If it all works out. Jordan's not going to be the easiest kid to look after, but then I wasn't either, was I?'

'You're telling me!'

The next morning Jordan came running into the shop, looking great in her new clothes. She was carrying a big tin.

'I've made you all cakes!' she said excitedly. 'Cam showed me how to bake and I've really got the hang of it, haven't I, Cam? Look! You can choose between brownies and flapjacks and muffins. Help yourselves!'

'You can be the chief cake maker when you come to live with us then,' said Mum. She took a big bite of muffin.

'Mmm! Even better than yours, Cam!'

I felt just a little twinge of jealousy then, because I'd once tried to make muffins with Cam and something had gone wrong and they hadn't risen at all, ending up more like biscuits than cakes.

Jordan saw my face. 'I'll show you how to bake if you like, Jess. Here, try one. See what you think of my muffins.'

She handed round her cakes proudly. I saw Mum give a quick thumbs-up sign to Cam.

'Tell us all about the telly thing. Did it go well?' Cam asked.

'It went splendidly!' said Mum. 'Where's Mary? I've got something to say to her!'

'She's just parking the car. Jordan leaped out the minute we got here. Why? What have you got to say to Mary?' Cam looked a little anxious.

At that moment Mary came in and was startled when Mum flew across the shop towards her. She actually took a step backwards. But Mum gave her a huge hug.

'Tracy?' she gasped, scarcely able to breathe. 'What's all this about?'

'I am just so enormously grateful to you! You made me feel a bit of a fool, setting myself up as an antiques dealer with Flo without knowing a thing about it. I still don't, actually, but I've started getting books out of the library, and I made sure I knew about every item in the shop. It meant I could show off on camera, and Adele, the producer – who just happens to be an old friend of mine from the Dumping Ground, would you believe? – but anyway, that's not the point – the *point* is that I knew my stuff, and it was all down to you! No wonder you're a teacher. You've certainly taught me a lesson!'

Mary had gone bright pink, partly because she was squashed, partly because she was pleased. 'Thanks, Tracy! You've made my day! That's what us boring old teachers love – praise and gratitude!' she said, giving Mum a hug back.

'Oh my!' said Flo, from her sofa. 'This is like the very last episode of *Life with the Lilliputs*. Everyone was suddenly ultra-sweet and we all went round hugging each other.'

'Can I have a hug?' Jordan said to Mum. 'My social worker Megan says you're really and truly serious about fostering me. Is she right?'

'Yep,' said Mum, releasing Mary and hugging Jordan instead. They looked a bit comical, because Jordan's much bigger than her.

'You won't regret it, I promise,' said Jordan. 'I've turned over a new leaf, haven't I, Cam? I've been as good as gold, honest. I haven't kicked off once and I've been ever so helpful. And Jax and I are really good mates now, aren't we? I'm not telling porkies, am I?'

'No, you're telling the absolute gold-star truth,' said Cam.

'It's called the honeymoon period,' said Mum. 'It lasts a few weeks, and then the foster child kicks off royally. It's the testing time. I know. I did my fair share. But you belong with us, Jordan, no matter what, OK?'

'Even if . . . if I smashed up all the things in this shop?' said Jordan.

'Well, that wouldn't be wise, girl, because I'd beat you with my walking sticks,' said Flo. 'Only joking.'

'Yeah, I was only joking too,' said Jordan. 'Have another cake. All of you.'

I took Jordan out the back to show her my garden. I thought she might mock, because it was only a very *little* garden, and still a bit bare, but she said she loved it.

'You've made it really pretty. You take after your mum, Jess. You've got the knack,' said Jordan, flinging herself down on the little patch of grass. 'Hey, we can sunbathe here. I don't even have to wear my baseball cap because I'm not on the run any

more. No one's looking for me now,' she said.

'That's cool,' I said, starting to dig up a few weeds. 'But if you run away again, then Mum and me and Flo and Cam and Mary and Jax and Rosie will be looking for you big time. Alfie will act like a tracker dog and hunt you down, and then we'll capture you and bring you back home. Right?'

'Right!' said Jordan, grinning. 'Here, do you want a hand with that digging? You're not very strong, but I am.' She grabbed my trowel and started on another patch. Unfortunately she started digging up a newly planted agapanthus.

'Not that one! It's a flower!' I protested.

Jordan screwed up her face, and just for a moment I thought she might get cross. But then she shrugged. 'Sorry! You be the gardener, I'll be the cake maker. Deal?'

'Deal!'

When we went back into the shop we found Peter there, asking all about the television show. He seemed really pleased to see Jordan and me.

'He isn't just trying to impress Mum by making a fuss of me like Sean Godfrey did,' I whispered to Jordan. 'He's soooo much nicer.'

'Yeah. Shame he's not rich and famous like Sean Godfrey though,' she said. '*I* wouldn't have minded him for a stepdad.'

'I don't want *any* kind of stepdad,' I said, but I didn't think I'd mind *too* much if Mum and Peter became a serious item.

Later that morning Lawrence came in to mull over *Antique Memories* with Flo. We were starting to get more visitors than customers.

However, the guy who'd wanted Mum's little Victorian desk soon came back again, this time with his wife. She absolutely loved the desk – and Mum and Flo gave her an extra discount because it was her birthday. Even so, we made a good profit.

'We've all got to celebrate!' Mum said when they'd gone. 'How about the Spade and Bucket tonight?'

'We've got to be back for the rest of the girls by teatime,' said Cam.

'That's not fair!' exclaimed Jordan.

'Life's not fair, chickie,' said Cam cheerfully. 'And I was hoping you'd help out with the cooking, Jordan, because I'll be knackered after all the driving.'

'Well, I suppose. OK then,' she said, looking pleased.

'I was actually hoping you'd come round to my place for supper tonight,' said Peter. 'I want to show off my cooking skills. I've got a chicken marinating as we speak.'

'Just you and Mum?' I asked.

'No, you too, Jess, of course. And Flo as well.'

'I might have other plans,' said Flo coyly, looking at Lawrence.

'So let's shut the shop now and go down to the Spade and Bucket for a celebration lunch!' said Mum.

'Good plan!' I said, and everyone agreed.

We didn't have time for a proper meal, but we had baguettes and chips and they were very good.

'Shall we have a look at the pudding menu?' Peter asked. 'Perhaps Lizzie could even rustle up a cake again . . . It was so weird, meeting you here, Tracy, and sharing a birthday cake. It was just like we were little kids again, both of us holding the knife and wishing! What did you wish for then, Tracy?'

'That would be telling,' said Mum, smiling.

'Maybe it was the same wish as me,' he said, smiling back.

327

'We can have some cake now!' said Jordan. 'There was one of my muffins left. I brought it along in case anyone was extra peckish.' She produced a rather squashed muffin from her jacket pocket.

'Who's going to have it then? How about sharing it with Jess?' Cam suggested.

'Of course I'll share with Jess. She's like my little sister already,' said Jordan.

So we set the muffin on a plate and took hold of a knife together and wished. I'm pretty sure I know what Jordan wished. I looked around at her and Mum and Peter and Alfie and Cam and Mary and Flo and Lawrence, and decided that I loved having a big family. I wished we'd all live happily ever after, like in a storybook.

THE FOSTERING NETWORK

There are 65,000 children and young people –
just like Jordan – living with foster families
across the UK. There is a need for thousands
more foster families each year.

To find out more about fostering, visit
thefosteringnetwork.org.uk/allaboutfostering

WHO CARES? SCOTLAND

If you are Care Experienced and would like to
connect with others who have experience of care,
you can do so alongside Who Cares? Scotland.

Who Cares? Scotland is an independent charity led
by Care Experienced people, campaigning for
change in the care system and in societal attitudes
towards Care Experienced people.

Find out more at
www.whocaresscotland.org

ABOUT THE AUTHOR

JACQUELINE WILSON wrote her first novel when she was nine years old, and she has been writing ever since. She is now one of Britain's bestselling and most beloved children's authors. She has written over 100 books and is the creator of characters such as Tracy Beaker and Hetty Feather. More than forty million copies of her books have been sold.

As well as winning many awards for her books, including the Children's Book of the Year, Jacqueline is a former Children's Laureate, and in 2008 she was appointed a Dame.

Jacqueline is also a great reader, and has amassed over twenty thousand books, along with her famous collection of silver rings.

Find out more about Jacqueline and her books at www.jacquelinewilson.co.uk

☆ ☆ ☆ ☆ ☆ ☆ ☆ ☆ ☆ ☆

ABOUT THE ILLUSTRATOR

NICK SHARRATT has written and illustrated many
books for children and won numerous awards
for his picture books, including the Children's
Book Award and the Educational Writers' Award.
He has also enjoyed great success illustrating
Jacqueline Wilson's books. Nick lives in Hove.

⭐ ⭐ ⭐ ⭐ ⭐ ⭐ ⭐ ⭐ ⭐ ⭐

TEN FACTS ABOUT JESS BEAKER

*Meet Jess, Jacqueline Wilson's
sparkiest new heroine . . .*

Jess's full name is Jessica
Bluebell Camilla Beaker –
Bluebell, for Tracy's old
cuddly toy, and Camilla, for
her foster-grandmother, Cam.

Jess is super smart and at the top of her class at school.

Before living in Cooksea, Jess lived with Tracy in
Marlborough Tower, a block of flats in the city.

Bill, the bacon-roll van owner, calls her
Baby Curly because she has dark curly
hair just like her mum, Tracy.

She has a toy dog called Woofer,
but a real one called Alfie.

Alice used to be her best friend but they lost touch when Jess moved to Cooksea.

Jess's sworn enemy used to be Tyrone, but they later became very good friends, even though he worships Sean Godfrey.

Jess has met her dad a few times but he hasn't come to visit her in Cooksea.

Cam's partner, Mary, used to be Jess's teacher. Tracy once shouted at her!

She is going into Year 6 at school.

TEN FACTS ABOUT TRACY BEAKER

Meet Jess's Mum Tracy, the funniest,
fiercest mum in Cooksea . . .

Tracy's birthday is
8 May – the same day as
Peter Ingham's!

Her lucky number is 7.

Her favourite film genre is horror. Scary!

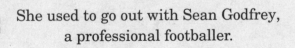

She used to go out with Sean Godfrey,
a professional footballer.

She is really good at Monopoly.

Tracy's sworn enemy is Justine Littlewood,
although it looks like they might not have to be
enemies for ever . . .

 Her birth mum is called Carly and
her foster mum is called Cam.

At The Dumping Ground, Tracy is fantastic at
arranging antiques in ways that tell stories.

Tracy has written an autobiography about her life
with some (not so complimentary) chapters on
Justine Littlewood and Peter Ingham.

Tracy's favourite name is Camilla after a little
girl she knew who was fostered, and after Cam,
her foster mum.

WHICH BEAKER GIRL ARE YOU?

Tracy, Jess and Jordan – the Beaker girls!
Take this amazing quiz to find out which of the
Beakers you are most like . . .

What are you most likely to be doing on the weekend?
a) Arranging antiques into elaborate displays
b) Gardening and planting flowers
c) Baking lots of cakes, muffins and brownies
   for your friends

What's your favourite ice cream?
a) A whippy covered in strawberry sauce
b) Rainbow sprinkles, but a banana split also
   goes down a treat
c) Not too fussed – any ice cream is good with me!

What is your best quality?
a) Caring and fierce
b) Thoughtful and kind
c) Independent and bold

Do you believe in romance?
a) I'm not sure if there is someone special
   out there, but I'd like to hope!
b) Yuck – no thanks!
c) Only if they don't like football

What is most important to you?
a) Sticking up for my family
b) Helping other people
c) Feeling like I have freedom

What do you want to be when you're older?
a) An actress or a TV presenter on an
   antiques show
b) I do quite well at school so maybe a teacher
   or a writer
c) I don't really know – I'm only just starting
   to realize that I might be able to achieve
   my dreams . . .

Do you have a special toy?
a) A doll
b) A plush dog
c) No way! I'm too old for them

If you said mostly a, you're Tracy! Fiercely caring, you'd do anything for your family. You sometimes find it hard to control your emotions but, deep down, you have a super soft centre and are a great friend to boot!

If you said mostly b, you're Jess! Intelligent, kind and selfless, you'd put anyone above yourself even if it means giving away your pocket money. You can be shy, but you're learning to be more confident and making loads of friends as a result.

If you said mostly c, you're Jordan! Sometimes you have a bit of a barrier up against other people but that's because you've had to look after yourself. You should be proud of how independent you are and know that you're allowed to open up because you've got amazing friends around you!

CHECK OUT JACQUELINE WILSON'S BRILLIANT WEBSITE!

Did you know there's a whole Jacqueline Wilson town to explore? There's lots of fun stuff, including games, amazing competitions and exclusive news. You can generate a special username, customize your online bedroom, test your knowledge of Jacqueline's books with exciting quizzes and upload book reviews! And if you like writing, make sure you visit the special storytelling area!

Plus, you can find out about the latest news from Jacqueline in her monthly diary, chat to other fans on the message boards and find out whether she's doing an event near you!

Join in today at
www.jacquelinewilson.co.uk

HAVE YOU READ THEM ALL?

LAUGH OUT LOUD
THE STORY OF TRACY BEAKER
I DARE YOU, TRACY BEAKER
STARRING TRACY BEAKER
MY MUM TRACY BEAKER
THE WORST THING ABOUT MY SISTER
DOUBLE ACT
FOUR CHILDREN AND IT
THE BED AND BREAKFAST STAR

HISTORICAL HEROES
HETTY FEATHER
HETTY FEATHER'S CHRISTMAS
SAPPHIRE BATTERSEA
EMERALD STAR
DIAMOND
LITTLE STARS
CLOVER MOON
ROSE RIVERS
WAVE ME GOODBYE
OPAL PLUMSTEAD
QUEENIE
DANCING THE CHARLESTON

LIFE LESSONS
THE BUTTERFLY CLUB
THE SUITCASE KID
KATY
BAD GIRLS
LITTLE DARLINGS
CLEAN BREAK
RENT A BRIDESMAID
CANDYFLOSS

THE LOTTIE PROJECT
THE LONGEST WHALE SONG
COOKIE
JACKY DAYDREAM
PAWS & WHISKERS

FAMILY DRAMAS
THE ILLUSTRATED MUM
MY SISTER JODIE
DIAMOND GIRLS
DUSTBIN BABY
VICKY ANGEL
SECRETS
MIDNIGHT
LOLA ROSE
LILY ALONE
MY SECRET DIARY

PLENTY OF MISCHIEF
SLEEPOVERS
THE WORRY WEBSITE
BEST FRIENDS
GLUBBSLYME
THE CAT MUMMY
LIZZIE ZIPMOUTH
THE MUM-MINDER
CLIFFHANGER
BURIED ALIVE!

FOR OLDER READERS
GIRLS IN LOVE
GIRLS UNDER PRESSURE
GIRLS OUT LATE
GIRLS IN TEARS
KISS
LOVE LESSONS